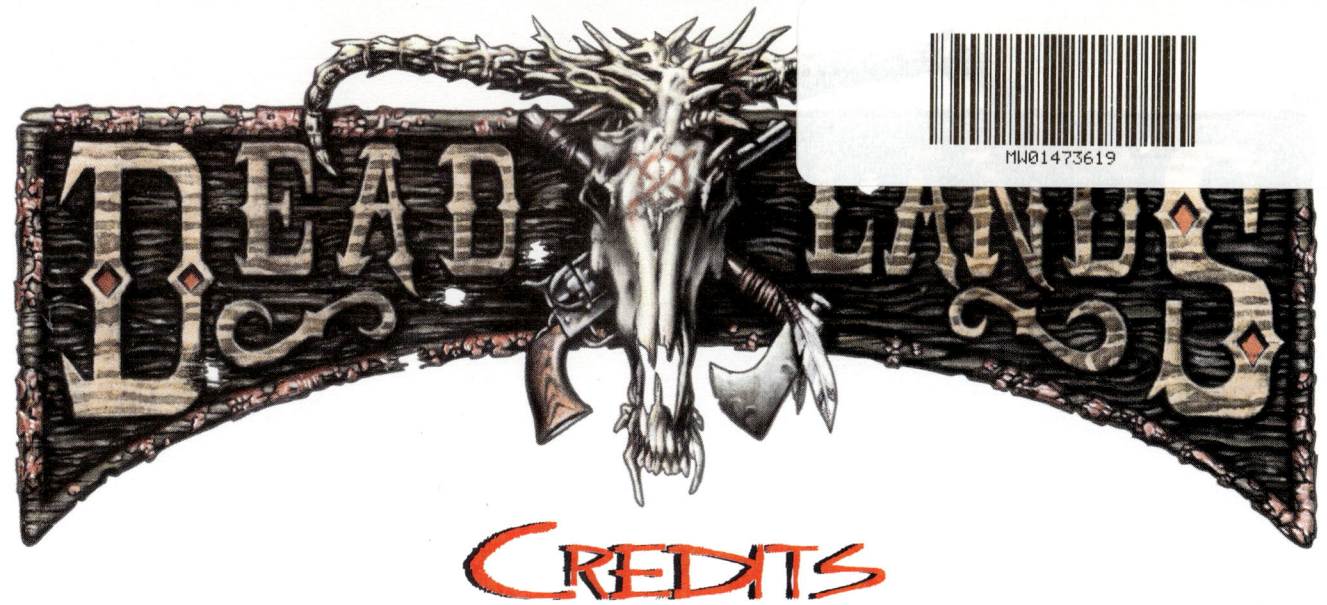

Credits

Written and designed by: Shane Lacy Hensley

Additional Development by: Michelle Hensley, John Hopler, Matt Forbeck, Greg Gorden

Editing: Matt Forbeck, Michelle Hensley, Jason Nichols, Hal Mangold

Layout: Matt Forbeck, Shane Hensley, Tim Link

Cover Art: Brom

Interior Art: Susan M. Bowen, Steve Bryant, Paul Daly, Jay Lloyd Neal, Allen Nunis, Ron Spencer, Loston Wallace

Graphic Design: Tim Link, Jay Lloyd Neal, Charles Ryan

Special Thanks To: All our families and friends, especially our parents.

Playtesting and Advice: Parris Crenshaw III, Christy Hopler, Matt & Tammy Kurtin, Angel McCoy, Jason Nichols, Nate Perkins, Charles Ryan, Dave Sisson, Chris Shively, Dave Wilson

Pinnacle Entertainment Group, Inc.
P.O. Box 10908
Blacksburg, VA 24062-0908
Dedicated To: Game Masters everywhere. You buy the books, order the pizza, and get everyone together to keep our industry alive.

Deadlands is a Trademark of
Pinnacle Entertainment Group, Inc.
© 1996 Pinnacle Entertainment Group, Inc.
All Rights Reserved.

Printed in Canada.

PINNACLE ENTERTAINMENT GROUP, Inc.

Table O' Contents

Credits 1
One: Prospector's Story 5
The Walkin' Dead 5
The Reckoning 6
A History Lesson 7
The Great Quake 9
The Indians 11
The West 12
Posse Territory 13

Two: The Basics 15
How to Use This Book 16
Tools o' the Trade 17
Traits & Aptitudes 18
Coordination 18
Mixing Aptitudes 18
Readin' the Bones 18
Unskilled Checks 18
Aces 19
Target Numbers 20
The Big Round Down! 20
Raising the Pot 21
All About Bones 21
Opposed Rolls 21
Going Bust 22
The Deadlands Lexicon 22

Three: Heroes 25

One: Concept 25
The Fairer Sex 29
Two: Traits 31
More than Human 32
Wind 32

Three: Aptitudes 33
Deftness 33
Basic Skills 33
Nimbleness 35
Quickness 37
Strength 37
Vigor 37
Cognition 37
Knowledge 38
Mien 42
Smarts 44
Spirit 45
Four: Hindrances 46
Five: Edges 53
Six: Background 57
Seven: Gear 57

Four: Gear 63
El Cheapo Gear 63
Notes 66
Everyday Gear 67

Archetypes 69-80

Five: Combat 83
The Action Deck 83
Surprise 83
Actions 84
Speed 84
Cheatin' 85
Skedaddlin' 86
Running 86
Pickin' Up the Pace 86
Gitalong Li'l Doggie 87
Carrying a Load 87
Test of Wills 88
Shootin' Things 89
Rate of Fire 89
The Attack 89
Range 89
Modifiers 90
Shotguns 90
Automatic Weapons 91
Special Maneuvers 92
Reloading 94
Throwin' Things 94

Innocent Bystanders 94
Fightin' 95
Vamoosin' 96
Hit Location 96
Cover 98
Damage Steps 99

Armor 99
Concealment 99
Bleedin' & Squealin' 100
Noggins & Gizzards 100
Size Matters 100
Wounds 101
Stun 102
Wind 103
More Pain and Sufferin' 104
Healin' 107
Six: Fate & Bounties 109
Calling on Fate 110
Trading Chips 111
Bounty Points 111
No Man's Land 121

Seven: Hucksters 123
Hoyle's Book of Games 123
A Huckster's Lexicon 125
The Life of a Huckster 125
Gettin' Caught 125
Casting the Hex 126
Witch Hunters 126
Manitous 127

Table O' Contents

Hexes 127	Fearmongers 173	Bounty Points 204
Poker Hands 127	Legend Chips 174	Coup 204
Eight: Mad Scientists 135	Grit 174	**Seventeen: Adventures** 205
Dementia 136	**Marshal's Handbook** 175	The Story Thus Far 205
Life of a Mad Scientist .. 136		The Setup 205
Creating Weird Gizmos .. 136		Chapters 206
Gizmo Construction Table 138		The Bounty 206
Rushing the Job 139		**Eighteen: Fear** 207
Reliability 139		Fearmongers 207
Marshal Law 139		Tale-Tellin' 209
	Thirteen: Reckoning 176	Terror 209
	The Order of Things 176	No Guts, No Glory 210
	The Old Ones 177	**Scart** 211
	The Great	**Nineteen: Harrowed** 212
	Spirit War 177	Nightmares 212
Weird Gizmos 140-143	A Tale of Vengeance 177	The Nightmare Scenario 213
Nine: The Blessed 145	Raven Reborn 178	Milestones 213
The Life of the Blessed .. 145	The Hunt 178	
Invoking Miracles 147	The Reckoners Awake 178	
Miracles 147	The World Today 179	
Ten: Shamans 151		
The Life of a Shaman 151		
Calling on the Spirits 152		Losing Dominion 214
The Favor 152		Manitous 214
The Ritual 152		**Twenty: Arcana** 215
Approval 152		Mysterious Past 215
Angering the Spirits 152		Draw 215
The Old Ways 153		Madness and Malfunction 218
Ordeals 153	**Fourteen: Shortcuts** 180	Madness 218
Manitous 153	Marshal's Shortcuts 180	**Dementia** 219
Non-Shaman Favors 153	Traits & Aptitudes 180	Malfunction Results 220
Rituals 154	Combat 181	Backlash 221
Favors 156	Actions 181	**Boot Hill** 222
Eleven: The Harrowed 161	Stun Checks 181	**Character Sheet** 223-224
Dominion 162	Quick Hits 182	
The Eternal Struggle 162	Boot Hill 182	
Unlife of the Harrowed . 163	Bloody Ones 182	
Undeath 164	Use the Posse 182	
Powers of the Harrowed . 166	**Fifteen: Abominations** ... 183	
Twelve: Fear 171	Animal Intelligence 183	
Fear Levels 171	Bitin' and Clawin' 183	
Tale-Tellin' 172	**Sixteen: Fate Awards** 203	
	Fate Chips 203	

THE PROSPECTOR

Chapter One: The Prospector's Story

Howdy, Marshal. Thought ya might be gettin' up soon. Those tinhorns that planted ya didn't realize you wuz already dead. Reckon they'da done a lot worse to yer sorry carcass if they'd known better. Course, ya ain't gonna be half as ornery as ya were yesterday—now that I've poured a draught of this here elixir down yer gullet.

Name's Jenkins, Coot Jenkins. Ya don't hafta shake my hand—I can see yers are still busted up from that ambush. Most people just call me "the Prospector," but it ain't gold I dig up these days. Uh-huh—it's leathery hombres like you, friend. I'd tell ya all about it, but I got a feelin' yer more interested in why yer crawlin' up out of a grave than why some 60-year-old geezer's standin' over ya with a scattergun.

So pull yerself on up outta that hole and I'll tell ya what I can. Get comfortable, friend. You've got a lotta catchin' up to do.

And pull that worm outta yer ear. It's makin' me queasy.

The Walkin' Dead

The only job I've ever been good at is diggin' things up out of the earth. I can't say I like diggin' up the dead better'n strikin' gold, but the thrill of the hunt is just as excitin'. See, I skulk around the frontier lookin' for people just like you, Marshal. Good folks that have come back from the grave all twisted inside. They ain't hard to spot if ya know what yer lookin' for.

In yer case, I knew ya had a good reputation as a lawman 'til ya got cut up in '67. Most folks think ya went bad after that, but that's only half the truth. Ya went dead. Walkin' dead. When ya came back, the critter inside ya wuz in charge and has prob'ly been runnin' the show ever since. Made ya start killin' folks and doin' things that woulda made yer momma cut ya out of her belly if she coulda known.

Prospector

The elixir ought to help ya fight back, but there's no guarantee. And don't go gettin' a taste for it 'cause this here's the only bottle I got. An Injun friend of mine whipped it up for me, and I ain't seen him since '72. In case ya ain't figured it out from those fresh tombstones over there, it's 1876, partner.

Yer gonna' have to fight yer demon all by yer lonesome. And if ya can't lick 'em, I'm gonna have to put ya down. That's the reason I got this scattergun—in case I ain't talkin' to the man I think I am. But I reckon we'll find out directly. See, I'm gonna spin you a yarn, and by the end of my tale, I'll know who's listenin'. And if it's that twisted critter 'steada you, I'm gonna have to yank both these triggers and turn ya into a little ol' greasy spot.

It's the only way to be sure.

The Reckoning

I wuz prospectin' for scraps in a tapped-out mine in Colorado when I found an old Injun sittin' deep inside, his hands stained black as sin. He wuz bad off, so I gave him some grub and snow water. When he finally started talkin', he told me his name wuz Runnin' Wolf, an Arapaho, and that he wuz the last of his tribe.

I thought he wuz loco, but I talked with him awhile, and the story he told me made some things I'd already seen make sense.

Wolf said he and some others got into some mischief back in '63. Seems he wuz livin' with some Sioux when this creepy shaman called Raven came lookin' for him. Raven had already gathered up some young bucks lookin' for revenge—Wolf wuz the last.

This Raven feller promised 'em all a "Reckoning." He said he had a plan that would send the white man back across the waters. What he didn't tell 'em wuz that what he wuz gonna do would kill just as many Injuns as palefaces.

Raven called his band the "Last Sons" and took 'em on a long trip—all the way from

the Dakotas to some old Micmac burial ground in the hills o' New England. Runnin' Wolf tried to explain what happened when they got there, but I'm still not real clear on 'xactly what happened. Seems they walked through some kinda door. Wolf said the door led to the Huntin' Grounds, but I think me and you might call it Hell.

Wolf said they went on some kinda' hunt. He wouldn't tell me much more—I guess he wuzn't too proud of what he done there.

Now don't go lookin' at me like I'm loco. Yer the one that oughta be snoozin' in a pine box, Marshal.

Anyway, whatever it wuz, it brought about Raven's "Reckoning." It wuz supposed to punish us white folks for all the things we done to the Injuns over the years. Can't say I blame the Last Sons for that—we ain't been

the most hospitable neighbors after all.

But Raven tricked 'em—else he wuz a danged fool—cause all kinds of nasty spirits came flyin' out, and now they're plaguin' everybody—red, white, black, and yellow. Wolf calls 'em "manitous," but I think that's just a fancy Injun word for "demon."

Now I know that sounds crazier than foxes lovin' hens in a kindly way, but ya can believe it cause ya got one of 'em wrigglin' around inside you right now—like a worm in a rotten apple.

No, ya can't see 'em, ya idjit! I told ya they wuz spirits—so quit pullin' open that hole in yer gizzard. Yer gonna make me chuck up my supper.

A History Lesson

Ya probably don't remember much about the last eight years. Most o' yer kind fight for control every day with their manitou. Judging by yer past, I s'pect ya ain't done nothin' but lose, so let me bring ya up to date.

I ain't much of a teacher, but I reckon ya oughta at least know how the war's goin' and who's in charge these days. You go whistling "Dixie" in the wrong parts, and I'll just have to come dig ya up again. 'Less of course they cut ya up just right—then yer worm food.

The Civil War

The Last Sons pulled their little prank on July 3rd, 1863. That was the same day a little skirmish at a place called Gettysburg was comin' to a clos. You were alive then, so you oughta have heard about. What you prob'ly didn't hear was what happened afterwards. See, most people think Gen'ral Meade didn't pursue Bobby Lee's army 'cause he was skittish. But that ain't quite so.

PROSPECTOR

After the blue-bellies started pilin' up their dead, some of 'em crawled out and started doin' things. Terrible things. I reckon the soldiers eventually got 'em all, but after rumors got out about what happened, the army wasn't in no shape to go chasin' rebs.

Things weren't much better over in the Confederate camp. Some kinda' butcher snuck into one of their hospitals and started carvin' up the survivors of Pickett's Charge. That one got away, but not before it'd taken off General John Bell Hood's arm.

Fear

See, it's all about fear. The manitous feed off of it like flies on honey. Or like those flies on your scalp there—you wantta watch that. They lay eggs. Gets real messy.

Anyway, somehow the manitous take all this fear and make new monsters with it. Runnin' Wolf once told me the manitous were servants somethin' bigger, but I couldn't understand much more 'n that. I call 'em the "Reckoners" since turnin' 'em loose was Raven's "Reckoning."

If you buy into all this, then a battle is like a feeding frenzy to these things. But all that fear isn't just swallowed up—it's used to make more monsters. And I'm not talkin' 'bout more manitous—I mean everything from old legends like the Headless Horseman to brand new critters that nobody'd ever dreamt of. Ya may not believe in vampires, werewolves, haunts, and witches, but ya should. I've seen a lot worse.

I don't know 'xactly where they come from. Some 'pear to have been around since before the Reckoning, but now they're gettin' more powerful. Others just seem to spring up overnight. I got a feelin' the Reckoners somehow take the fear the manitous bring 'em and send back little bits to make somethin' even bigger and badder.

Rangers and Pinkertons

Anyway, some of the generals on both sides started figgerin' things out. All this weirdness wuz spookin' the troops, so the armies detailed smaller groups to take care of the monsters and keep things quiet. Lee put the Texas Rangers in charge of takin' care of the weirdness. In the North, Lincoln replaced Meade with Ulysses S. Grant in early '64. Grant had seen his own share of weirdness when he took Vicksburg the same day as Gettysburg. When he got out East he hired on the Pinkerton Detective Agency to figger out what wuz going on.

Like the Rangers, the Pinkertons prowled the ranks watchin' for anything out of the ordinary so they could deal with it before word got too far. Both sides did their jobs, I reckon, and soon tales of the walkin' dead and other such strangeness fell back into the realm o' rumors rather than that o' debatable fact.

That wuz back in '65. Now the Pinkertons and the Rangers only gather together when they get word of a big battle. Most times they just prowl around in small groups lookin' for trouble. They don't let the rest of us in on what they're doin'—and for good reason. See, when folks hear about this stuff, they just get more scared. And if you've been payin' attention, that just makes more critters for 'em to deal with.

Mostly you'll find the Pinkertons and Rangers creepin' 'round out here in the West. Things are just as violent as you remember—prob'ly worse. Samuel Colt's little Peacemaker has done just the opposite in places like Dodge, Tombstone, and Deadwood. The boomtowns are full of young bucks tryin' to make names for themselves. And like I told ya', where there's violence, the manitous and what they bring with 'em ain't far behind.

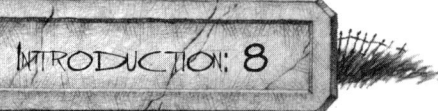

The Great Quake

You remember Raven? The one I told you started this whole mess? Well, Runnin' Wolf said he was still out wreakin' havoc as late as '72. I reckon the nastiest thing that sum'bitch done since the Reckoning was drop California into the sea.

Accordin' to Wolf, Raven went out to the coast and tricked the "earth spirits" into shaking up a storm. They musta been listenin', 'cause a few days later, the biggest earthquake ever known cut through California like a hot knife through butter. When it wuz over, California was a maze of crevices that makes the Grand Canyon look like an oversized post-hole. Worse, the Pacific flooded in and filled the "Great Maze" full o' sea water.

Ghost Rock

No one knows how many died in the quake, but the survivors discovered somethin' that almost made it all worthwhile. Y'see, the sides of the Maze is riddled here 'n there with seams of gold, silver, and somethin' new—ghost rock.

I know you ain't heard o' that, 'cause no one figured out just what it could do 'til just a few years back.

I still don't understand it, but scientists from back East and even overseas started comin' out to the West in droves. Y'see, ghost rock burns better than coal. Put it in a steam engine and you can do incredible things. The only part I don't like about it is that, when it burns, it puts out this creepy white vapor and moans worse'n a dying mule. Kinda eerie.

Prospector

Now, they can do 'most anything with the stuff. There's a gang of thieves in Nevada that uses ghost-rock-powered steam wagons all covered with armor and Gatling guns to chase and rob trains. Course the rail barons hardly took that lyin' down. I've even heard one of 'em has some kinda crazy flyin' machine to watch over their cars.

The Maze

Anyway, it didn't take long for folks to rebuild out of whatever they could salvage and set up camp. Now there's a shantytown on every canyon ledge in the Maze. Folks have rigged platforms to lower 'em up and down the sides so they can get at gold, silver, and now ghost rock. Then they load it up on steamboats and take it to the City of Lost Angels, the biggest boomtown of 'em all, right there on the inland side of the Maze. The city wuz founded right after the quake by a group of survivors led by some preacher named Grimme.

You can imagine the shenanigans that went on when the price of ghost rock hit a hundred bucks a pound. Pirates and Union and Confederate Ironclads popped up anywhere someone found a new strike, ready to pluck those miners like turkeys on Thanksgiving.

The New Mexican Army

When word got out about California, France and the "Napoleon of the West," Santa Anna, struck a deal. Santa Anna—that feller that killed all them folks at the Alamo if ya remember—wants revenge on Texas. I reckon he holds them accountable for secedin' and takin' his leg in '36, then startin' Polk's war in '48.

PROSPECTOR

Anyway, rumor is the Frenchies told Santa Anna they'd give him the Foreign Legion to invade Texas if he can take hold of the Maze. They even outfitted him with a Mexican armada of ghost-rock-burnin' ironclad gunboats under some fancy Spanish pirate from the Barbary Coast.

The Battle of Washington

Then in '69, ol' Jeff Davis got slick and annexed the Maze. He claimed the old Union state of California no longer existed, and if the Union wuzn't going to protect what wuz left from the Mexicans, he would. Then he declared the Maze a Confederate territory.

But what he wuz really after wuz English troops. Davis got money from the Brits after freein' the slaves in '64, but he figured a few divisions of redcoats would finish off the Yanks once and for all. And now he had something they wanted—ghost rock.

But Davis needed a big victory to cinch the deal, and he figured showin' off the power of ghost rock wouldn't hurt none neither. So he got a bunch o' overeducated kooks together and dreamed up a mess of incredible machines, gadgets, and gizmos. Then he gave 'em to Bobby Lee and told him to take Washin'ton.

The Rebels attacked the capital with steam wagons, firechuckers, and cannons firing clear back from Richmond early in '71. Grant and President Johnson got chased halfway to New York before they managed to fight back. They didn't get their capital back 'til the reb's toys finally broke down.

Davis's attack wuz a brilliant plan, but the English bent ol' Davis over their knee and spanked him like a redheaded stepchild. Seems they had their own troubles in India and Africa and all they could spare wuz some East Indian sepoys and a token line regiment. Davis wuz so mad he's left 'em sittin' in Charleston harbor since they landed in '72. Way I hear it, most of the officers done left their posts since then to get into the action out here.

Hoyle's Hucksters

That's the big news, but there's a few utter things you oughtta know. Fer instance, I bet you didn't know we got ourselves some genuine wizards out here in the West, didja?

I got a friend down Abilene way that told me about a book called *Hoyle's Book of Games*. Accordin' to him, this feller Hoyle left secret messages scattered inside. It takes a real clever eye to pick 'em out, but buried among all them fancy games is details on how to cast spells 'n hexes.

I figure Hoyle had to hide what he wuz talkin' about like that 'cause magic and hexes wuzn't so popular back in them witch-burnin' days. Anyway, maybe one feller in a hundred knows about this, and probably less than that believes it. But it's true.

Them fellers that have deciphered Hoyle's book—or been taught by someone who has—can do things ya wouldn't believe. We call 'em "hucksters." Weirder still, when they cast their hexes, playing cards pop up in their hands and then disappear a few seconds later. Most folks think they're just gamblers pullin' some kinda fancy card trick, but if ya see some slick-looking dude with cards in his hands, you'd better leave him alone. Odds are he's a two-bit shyster. But if he's a huckster, he just might turn yer innards wrong side out.

The Indians

All this spooky stuff goin' on wuzn't as much of a shock to the red men as it wuz us "cultured" types. Most civilized folks've seen something weird in their life, but they only believe their own stories while they're laughing at everyone else's. The Indians have a little better grip on this sort of thing.

In '72, a bunch of Sioux in the Dakotas decided they could deal with the situation better than the few buffalo soldiers the Union wuz willing to send 'em. So they

revolted and set up their own country: the Sioux Nations. I guess they call 'emselves "nations" cause they're actually made up of all the Sioux tribes. Some of the tribes are peaceful; others ain't.

Right now, most ain't. Can't say I blame 'em. The government ain't kept most of its promises. The 7th Cavalry claims they're gonna ride into the Nations and teach the redskins a lesson. I can't imagine what kind of trouble that's gonna stir up.

The Confederates had a little more luck down South. The Indian lands next to Oklahoma followed the Sioux's lead and declared themselves the Coyote Confederation. Just like up North, the Rebs couldn't spare the troops to put 'em down, so they came up with a better plan. They hired the Coyote Confederation to work with 'em. It's a secret, but not much o' one. You 'n' me 'n' everyone else in the country knows it. Now the Coyotes raid Union towns and outposts in Kansas, Nebraska and across the Mississippi. And it don't cost the Rebs nothin' but some secondhand muskets, rotten food, and whiskey.

The West

At any rate, it ain't a great time to be alive. Or in yer partic'lar case, not quite dead. The Texas Rangers and the Pinkertons are scourin' the border states lookin' for fellers like you to hire or hang. Shoot it or recruit it is their motto. Of course, they like each other even less than they like fussin' with the dead.

California, Utah, Colorado, Oklahoma and Kansas are disputed territories. US Marshals and Rangers from the Confederate Territories both claim jurisdiction in those areas, but mostly they just fight with each other over who ought to be protectin' the very folks gettin' killed in their crossfire.

Grant's the President of the US. Lincoln got shot in '65, then Johnson took over, but he didn't last long. Jeff Davis has held onto his office in the South, but most are callin' for him to step down. Lee's the man they want, but he seems a might skittish about the whole thing. Both armies are rebuildin' their war machines for one last push, but in the meantime, their raids are makin' a wasteland outta the border states. If ya wanna resume yer career as a lawman, you'll find plenty o' places lookin' for one.

Epilogue

That's the big picture, Marshal. As for yerself, yer wanted throughout US and Confederate territories and most of the lands outside and in between. Murder, arson, rape, rustlin'—I guess you've done just about everything. Or at least that critter inside ya has. But there's one thing about manitous I've learned in the last couple o' years—they got a short attention span.

But since the one in you's been in charge the last 9 years, it already knows everything I just told ya. That's why I had to give ya the long version, y'see.

So I'm gonna' ask ya a question, and if ya get it right, I'll help ya get a fresh start and then we'll see about makin' up for all them things ya did. Maybe me 'n you and some others I've dug up can even find a way to stop the Reckoners.

If ya get it wrong, though, I'm gonna' have to empty both barrels and send ya back to Hell. I sure hope yer momma didn't just raise ya stupid, Marshal.

Everyone knows where they were when they heard about the Great Quake. All ya gotta do is tell me what year it wuz.

"'68," eh? That's right.

But I never told ya that.

And that wuz the last of my elixir.

Damn.

Posse Territory

Chapter Two: The Basics

The world of *Deadlands*™ is a big, evil place. Things don't just go "bump" in the night anymore—they come ripping up out of their graves, screaming and looking for meat. An event called the Reckoning saw to that.

The book you hold in your hands is a roleplaying game set in the towns, deserts and mountains of the Weird West. If you haven't played a game like this before, you're in for a real treat. You and your friends gather around a table or camp out on the floor and play out a macabre little melodrama with chips, cards, dice, and your own overactive imaginations.

Most of you take on the roles of "player characters"—the heroes and heroines of the story. Collectively, you are the "posse." Each of you will try to accomplish your character's goals, defeat nefarious villains, decipher the many mysteries of *Deadlands* and avoid becoming lunch for some unsavory critter.

One of your group becomes the game master, or as we say in *Deadlands*, the "Marshal." He'll set up the adventure and play the parts of all the "extras" (called non-player characters in other games).

The Marshal is your best friend and your worst enemy. He knows most of the secrets of *Deadlands* (we're keeping a few to ourselves for a while), and sometimes he might use them to put your character through Hell—or worse. Survive, and he can be your best friend, rewarding your character with wealth, fame and power. Die, and well...we'll get to that later.

If this is all entirely new to you, think of a roleplaying game as something like a play or a movie. The characters you and your friends roleplay are the stars. The Marshal is the director, and the extras are all the other characters in the film.

Of course, the main differences between a roleplaying game and a movie is that in a game there is no script, and the heroes don't always win. The posse and random chance (that's where the dice and cards come in) determine the outcome of the tale.

With a little imagination and luck, your posse's adventures will become the newest legends of the Weird West.

And that's what it's all about, isn't it?

THE BASICS

How to Use This Book

The first section of this book ("Posse's Territory") teaches you the basic rules of the game and shows you how to blow chunks out of creepy crawlers. Every player, including the Marshal should read through this part.

The "No Man's Land" section features material that only certain players need (or should) know about. When you read about something covered in No Man's Land, the totem symbol will point you to the chapter you need to read. If you're a player, you shouldn't read any portion of No Man's Land without your Marshal's permission.

(Chapter)

(Page)

"The Marshal's Handbook" is for the Marshal's eyes only. Whenever you see the Marshal's badge, like the one here, it means there's some secret tidbit or table hidden in "The Marshal's Handbook." The number underneath tells you what page to look at. If you're a player-type, compadre, don't go there, compadre.

It's your book, so if you're dying to read the rest, go ahead. *Deadlands* is very much a game of discovery, however, so we think you'll enjoy the game a lot more if you read only what you're "supposed" to the first few times you play. Once your posse's been around a while, and the Marshal agrees, feel free to read the rest.

The first time you pick up this book, you should read through Chapter Six. The Marshal should read on through the rest of the book as well.

THE BASICS

Tools o' the Trade

Besides some pencils, paper, and an overactive imagination, there are three things you'll need to play *Deadlands*: dice, cards, and poker chips.

Bones

Because *Deadlands* is a game, we need some way of randomizing certain actions such as determining whether or not your gunslinger hears the varmint creeping up behind him. We pull off this neat little trick with dice—or "bones" as they're sometimes called in the Weird West.

Deadlands uses 4-, 6-, 8-, 10-, 12- and sometimes 20-sided bones. These are abbreviated as d4, d6, d8, d10, d12 and d20. If there's a number in front of the type of die, such as 2d6, it means you should roll that many dice. If you see "5d8," for example, you should roll 5 eight-sided dice.

A d10's a bit special. It's got a "0" in the 10's place, so if you roll a "0," be sure to read that as a "10."

If you need some dice, you should be able to get them where you got this book or in any good game store.

Cards

Deadlands also uses a standard deck of playing cards with the Jokers left in (54 cards total.) You need some way to distinguish between the Jokers. Official *Deadlands* card decks should be available wherever you purchased this book, but if you're using other cards, make sure you designate one Joker red and the other black. The easiest way to do this is to simply mark one of the Jokers with a red marker. That way, you can never forget which is which.

In combat, the cards are used as "Action Decks." You'll need one for the posse and one for all the Marshal. We'll tell you how these work in Chapter Five.

Certain types of characters (like hucksters or mad scientists) need decks of their own, so if you're playing one of these, make sure you've got a spare deck handy. The Marshal should also have an extra deck for when those kinds of characters show up as extras. You should shuffle the deck immediately after casting hexes or building weird gizmos. We'll tell you more about it if you play one of those character types.

The decks used by hucksters and mad scientists are not considered Action Decks, by the way.

Finally, it's good to have decks with different backings if possible. That way you can separate them if they get mixed together. If you don't have different backings, you can take each deck and color the edges with colored markers.

Chips

Deadlands uses standard poker chips to represent the whims of fate. We'll get into how this works later on.

In the meantime, all you need to know is that your group needs 50 white chips, 25 red chips, and 10 blue chips to play. Put all of these into a big cup or "Fate Pot," so that you can draw out of them without looking Once you've set up the posse's Fate Pot, put unused chips away. Only under special circumstances will you ever add chips to the pot.

The Basics

Traits & Aptitudes

Characters, varmints and other critters are mostly made up of Traits and Aptitudes. Traits are things like *Strength*, *Quickness* and *Smarts*. These are always written in *Capitalized Italics* and are expressed as a type of die. A really strong critter might have a d12 *Strength*, while an elderly schoolmarm probably has a d6 or even a d4.

Aptitudes are skills, talents or trades learned during life (or sometimes unlife, but we'll get into that later). These are rated from 1 to 5 initially, and tell you how many Trait dice to roll when using that Aptitude. Their names are always written in *lowercase italics*.

Deadlands uses fairly broad Aptitude descriptions, so you'll often need to choose a "concentration." The *fightin'* Aptitude by itself, for example, is useless. You need to choose a concentration such as *brawling*, *knives*, or *swords*. The same is true for an Aptitude like *science*—you need to specialize in *biology*, *chemistry*, or *engineering*.

Coordination

When you are asked to make a test of one of your character's basic Traits, you roll a number of that Trait's dice equal to its "Coordination." Coordinations function just like Aptitudes—they tell you how many of your Trait dice to roll whenever you need to test that Trait.

Trait tests are usually called for when the Marshal wants to test your character's raw abilities, such as his *Strength* or *Smarts*. *Quickness* is another Trait that you'll use often, especially in combat.

🔫 For instance, Ronan Lynch, a legendary *Deadlands* gunslinger has a *Deftness* of d10 with a Coordination of 4, so he rolls 4d10 to make a *Deftness* test.

Mixing Aptitudes

Aptitudes are normally associated with a particular Trait. The big secret of our nifty system is that they don't have to be. When the Marshal asks for a particular Aptitude test, such as a *climbin'* roll, just use the Trait that *climbin'* is listed under. But sometimes he might ask you for a *climbin'/Cognition* roll. This means he wants to see how much your character knows about *climbin'*, not how well he can actually scale a cliff.

Readin' the Bones

A character's Trait tells you what kind of dice to roll, and the Aptitude or Coordination tells you how many dice to roll. Your result is the highest number you get when you roll all your dice. So if you roll 3d6 and get 2, 3 and 5, your result is a 5.

If there are any modifiers, they are applied to the actual roll. Negative modifiers are penalties of some sort and positive modifiers are bonuses.

🔫 Ronan and his trusty steed are sliding down a hill into the jaws of a nasty varmint. The Marshal wants a *horse ridin'* roll. Ronan's *horse ridin'* is 2d8. He rolls and gets a 3 and a 4. His highest die is a 4. Not too hot. The Marshal decides the horse is kibble and Ronan is in serious sheep-dip.

Unskilled Checks

Sometimes you have to make an Aptitude check, when lo and behold, you discover you don't actually have the Aptitude. In these cases, you can roll your character's Trait dice (using Coordination as its "Aptitude" level), but you have to halve your total.

If your character has a related Aptitude, you can roll that instead, but at a -2 penalty. Concentrations within an Aptitude are always related—such as *shootin'*: *pistols*, *shotguns*, and *rifles*. Other Aptitudes may be

The Basics

related depending on the situation. You and your Marshal have to figure out if an Aptitude might be used in place of another. Traits are never considered "related" to Aptitudes.

Search and *trackin'* are good examples of Aptitudes that are usually related, as are *persuasion* and *bluff*, assuming a few little white lies are involved.

Aces

Trait and Aptitude rolls are open-ended. This means if you roll the maximum number on any of your dice, you can roll that die again and add the next roll to *that* die's current total. The maximum number on a die is called the "Ace." You can keep rolling the die and adding it to the running total as long as you keep getting Aces.

If you should get Aces on several of your dice, you need to keep track of each series separately. When you're done, the series that got the highest total is the number you should give to the Marshal.

🔫 Ronan is hanging on to the hillside for dear life after his horse's unfortunate demise. The Marshal wants a *climbin'* total. Ronan has 2d8 *climbin'* and rolls two 8s. Lucky dog. He rolls both Aces again and gets a 7 and an 8. These dice are hot. Ronan rolls the last 8 again and gets a 3 for a grand total of (8+8+3=) 19. He climbs up the hillside just as the thing below finishes his horse and snaps at his boots.

Posse: 19

THE BASICS

TARGET NUMBERS

Okay, so you've got your total. How do you know how well you've done? Just look on the standard difficulty chart. The difficulty is a rough estimation of how hard a particular task might be. The "TN," or Target Number, is the number you need to meet or beat on your roll to succeed.

DIFFICULTY TABLE

Difficulty	Target Number (TN)
Foolproof	3
Fair	5
Onerous	7
Hard	9
Incredible	11

Ronan finds his good friend, Marshal Dylan, lying in the desert with some gruesome varmints crawling down his gullet. The Marshal tells Ronan he'll have to make a Hard (9) *medicine* roll to get the things out. Ronan doesn't have the *medicine* Aptitude, so he makes a default *Knowledge* roll instead. He rolls 2d6 and gets a 3 and a 4. Since this is a default roll, Ronan has to halve his 4 for a grand total of 2. The Marshal passes on into the great beyond.

THE BIG ROUND DOWN

There's one universal rule in *Deadlands*. Whenever you're told to round something, round down. That's all there is to it. Remember this, and you'll go far in the Weird West.

If you're told you do a wound for every 6 points of damage your character causes, a roll of 13 would cause 2 wounds. If you're told to take half an Aptitude roll and you get an 11, tell the Marshal your total is a 5.

Got it?

Good. That was easy.

The Basics

Raising the Pot

Every time you beat your Target Number by 5 points, you get an extra success level. This is called a "raise." Raises are sometimes used to show your character has done exceedingly well at whatever it was she was trying to accomplish.

> Just as Marshal Dylan dies, he whispers a plea into Ronan's ears. the Marshal wants Ronan to go to Dodge and protect an accused prisoner from a lynch mob. Ronan, being the hero he is, can't turn down a friend's dying wish and sets off for Kansas. The Marshal asks for a Fair (5) *area knowledge* roll to find the trail. Ronan gets a 10, which is 5 points over the TN of 5. He sets off in the right direction and even knows a shortcut with watering holes.

Raises

Successes	Effect
Success	You've barely achieved the desired effect. If this is an opposed roll, the opponent continues to resist normally and you should both roll again next round.
One Raise	You've managed to accomplish your goal with a little room to spare. If this is an opposed roll, your opponent loses or surrenders, at least until he can find another way to recover his loss.
Two Raises	You make it look easy. If this is an opposed roll, your opponent surrenders and will not resist or attempt to recover without a major change in the situation.

Opposed Rolls

Occasionally, someone your character is bamboozling, wrestling or staring down might have the audacity to try and resist. If this is the case, both characters roll against a Fair (5) difficulty. The character who beats the TN and his opponent wins. Raises are always used in opposed rolls, though they are counted from the opponent's total.

> Ronan gets to Dodge just in time. Now he has to convince the mob not to bust through him and the few deputies that have stayed on duty. The Marshal asks for a *persuasion* total. Ronan gets a 7 and the leader of the mob gets a 5. The townsfolk back down, but since Ronan didn't get any raises, they haven't given up just yet.

All About Bones

- The Trait tells you what kind of dice to roll.

- The Aptitude or Coordination tells you how many of those dice to roll.

- The total is the highest die that you rolled, plus or minus any modifiers.

- An Ace lets you roll that die again and add it to the current total.

The Basics

Going Bust

Of course, there's a bad side to all this dice-rolling business. If the majority of your bones come up "1s", you've "gone bust." This means a setback of some sort has occurred. The Marshal determines how bad the catastrophe is based on the situation. Needless to say, you don't want to go bust if you're trying to snuff out a dynamite fuse.

🔫 The lynch mob makes another try for Ronan's prisoner. He makes an *overawe* roll against the mob's leader and gets a 1. Ronan goes bust. The leader of the mob then points out that Kansas is a disputed state and a US Marshal has no authority there. A few minutes later, Ronan finds himself swinging from a rope.

The Deadlands Lexicon

Ace: The maximum number on any particular type of die, such as the "6" on a d6, or the "0" on a d10. Whenever you get an Ace, you can roll the die again and add it to the previous roll.

Aptitudes: Skills, talents, or trades a character has learned or developed.

Traits: Raw physical and mental attributes, such as *Strength* or *Smarts*.

Bones: Sometimes we say bones instead of dice. There are six types in *Deadlands*: 4, 6, 8, 10, 12, and 20 sided.

Bust: You go bust when you roll more than "1s" than anything else. This means your character failed catastrophically.

Extras: These are the non-player characters that populate the world of *Deadlands*. Extras include everything from loyal sidekicks to dastardly villains to strange critters. The Marshal plays the roles of the extras.

Marshal: The game master, or the guy or gal responsible for setting up the adventure and guiding the posse through it.

Posse: The player characters and any extras that happen to be tagging along catching bullets for the real heroes.

Target Number: The difficulty of a particular task. If your dice total is greater than or equal to the Target Number, your character has succeeded at whatever he was attempting.

The Basics

Welcome to the Weird West

Here's an example of one posse's first foray into the Weird West. This should give you a good idea of what roleplaying is all about. Don't worry about rules right now. Just read the story and get an idea for how roleplaying games are played.

There are 3 player characters in this game. Ronan Lynch is a renowned gunfighter played by Matt. Runs with bears is a spiritual Indian brave played by Jason, and Violet is a whip-cracking buffalo gal played by Michelle. Shane is the Marshal.

The posse has been hired by the Pinkerton Detective Agency to find out what the infamous Professor Hellstromme is up to. They've tracked Hellstromme and his thugs to an old mine somewhere in Colorado when the trouble starts . . .

Shane: Okay, you've hitched up your horses nearby and you're standing at the edge of a low, dark cave. What do you do?

Jason: I'll creep up to the entrance and listen.

Marshal: Okay, give me a *sneak* then a *Cognition* roll.

Jason: 8 on the *sneak* and 10 on the *Cognition*—Runs with bears is *keen*.

Marshal: I'm sure he is. You're pretty quiet getting up to the entrance. Inside you hear distant voices and digging. Sounds like the mine's reopened.

Michelle: Hellstromme must have found a vein of ghost rock.

Matt: Hellstromme's always looking for more of that stuff.

Michelle: That would explain the dead prospectors we found in the gully.

Jason: Hmm. But what's he up to this time? Why risk jumping a claim?

Michelle: Yeah, Hellstromme's usually a little more subtle.

Marshal: Suddenly a figure emerges on the sloped tunnel ahead of you.

Marshal: (as Hellstromme): Ah, we meet again, Mr. Lynch. And you've brought your friends.

Matt: We've got you this time, Hellstromme. Murder's a hangin' offense no matter which side of the border you run to.

Hellstromme: Perhaps you're right, Mr. Lynch. For once you seem to have caught me in the act. But I needed the ghost rock for my latest invention. Let me introduce you to . . .the automaton!

Jason: I've got a bad feeling about this. . . .

Chapter Three: The Stuff Heroes Are Made Of

Making a character in *Deadlands* is easy. Just copy the character sheet found in the back of this book and follow along as we explain how to fill it in.

If you're in a hurry or want to try the game out before making your own character from scratch, there are 12 archetypes on pages 69-80. If you want to use one of these, you need to give them a proper name, but other than that, these heroes are ready to hop off of the pages and into the world of *Deadlands*.

One more thing. You might have guessed from our little prologue that death isn't necessarily the end of your character. That's true—but you've got to be careful because it isn't all that easy to come back from the other side.

And even when you do, unlife isn't exactly a bed of roses. For now, let's go ahead and make a living, breathing hero of the Weird West.

To create your own hero, follow these 7 basic steps:
1. Concept
2. Traits
3. Aptitudes
4. Hindrances
5. Edges
6. Background
7. Gear

One: Concept

The first step in making your hero is to have some kind of idea who you want your character to be. There are hundreds of basic types, from gunslingers to explorers to saloon girls to hucksters. If you don't already have a good idea for the type of hero you'd like to play, look at the character sketches on the following pages.

Makin' Heroes

You can even mix them together if you want. There's no reason you can't be a former cavalry officer turned marshal or a saloon girl who occasionally turns in her customers for bounty.

At the end of each sketch you'll see a few Aptitudes, Traits, or Edges these character types usually have. These terms are explained in their appropriate steps, so you can come back and check your character sketch's recommendations again once you've read through the rest of the creation process.

Finally, remember that these sketches are broad generalizations—you can alter a sketch to fit your own ideas any way you choose. Not all United States marshals are brave and honorable, and there's no reason an Indian brave can't make his living as a gambler.

Character Sketches

Bounty Hunters chase down outlaws and turn them in for the reward. This is a dangerous job, so your character needs some decent combat skills like *shootin'* and *fightin'*. A good *trackin'* skill is almost mandatory. Watch out, though. The hunter sometimes becomes the hunted if the prey gets wind someone's on its trail.

Buffalo Hunters saw a strange development in their trade in the last few years. The Sioux Nations have herded most of the larger buffalo herds into their borders. This means that buffalo meat and hides—once fairly cheap because they were so common—are now bringing in good prices at the few surviving and very secret skinning camps. The Sioux have warned off buffalo hunters on several occasions, but now they shoot on sight. Buffalo hunters need to be sneaky sorts with few scruples and steady hands for firing their Sharp's Big Fifty rifles.

Cattle Kings spend most of their time on their ranches raising hundreds of heads of steers. Once a year, they have to drive the herd to a market of some sort, usually a railhead or stockyard. If you play a cattle king, your character needs some knowledge of the land and trail routes. He'll also need the *dinero* or *belongings* Edge for his herd, unless he's recently lost it to rustlers or some kind of critter.

Cavalrymen serve both the USA and CSA. They act as scouts, Indian fighters and occasionally raiders. Officers need good leadership skills such as *overawe*, a high *Mien* to keep their troops in line, and some skill with a saber or pistol. Soldiers need good *horse ridin'* skills, a high *Vigor* to survive long marches, and a decent aim with a rifle or carbine.

Cowpokes spend most of their days out in the open range, tending to steers owned by cattle kings. They need to have good *shootin': rifles* and *horse ridin'* skills, and knowing how to use a lariat can come in

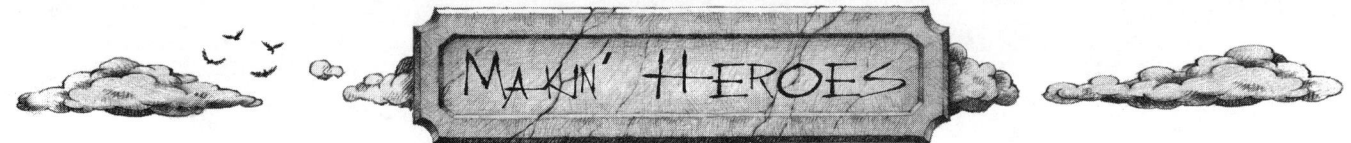

Makin' Heroes

just as handy for roping monsters as it does cattle. Of course, long horns are rarely known to rip a fellow's head off after they're roped. A good *Vigor* also helps a cowpoke tough out those long weeks on cattle drives through the open plains.

Deserters have left their posts for various reasons. Some leave out of cowardice, some because their officers were insane, and others because they've seen their fair share of death and misery and just can't be a party to it any more. Either way, deserters are branded cowards and traitors by the military branch they've left behind. In both the Union and Confederate armies, deserters are usually executed. Your character's skills should fit the branch of service he deserted from, and the *sneak* and *bluff* Aptitudes might also serve him well.

Explorers know there is no longer a true frontier, but many areas have yet to be fully explored. (Maybe there's a reason for that.) They need a good *Knowledge* Trait and several different *area knowledge* concentrations as well as a way to defend themselves when they're hundreds of miles from civilization. The *sense of direction* Edge might also come in handy.

Greenhorns come West to see if all the wild stories they've heard back East are true. As one of these pampered "dudes," your character wouldn't dream of touring the West in anything less than the comfort of 1st class. He has to figure out how he's going to make his way through any troubles that arise. Most do it by fast-talking the "yokels."

Gunslingers are feared killers and revered desperadoes. Some are tinhorn dandies with fancy New York target pistols while others are Texas outlaws looking to escape some past misdeed. A few are noble souls struggling to protect the weak, but others work for crooked rail barons, terrorizing towns and ranches that won't sell them the right-of-way. Regardless, these characters must have a high *Quickness*, a good *Deftness* and be crack shots with a pistol, rifle, or shotgun.

Hucksters are mysterious souls who have learned the secrets of *Hoyle's Book of Games*. Some say that within this cryptic text are hidden messages detailing ancient incantations and rituals of the black arts. Some say they are frauds and fakes, but their hexes are just as deadly as a gunslingers' bullets. Ask your Marshal to let you see Chapter Seven if you think you might want to play a huckster.

Seven

Indian Braves have won new respect in the West. The long Civil War means that neither the USA nor the CSA has the manpower to subjugate the new Sioux Nations or the Coyote Confederation. Some braves now wander outside their homeland to learn the ways of the white man. Others

Makin' Heroes

use their knowledge of the spiritual world to seek and defeat the evils awakened by the Reckoning. Indian braves need high *sneak* and *guts* Aptitudes, as well as some way to handle themselves in combat with horrors beyond imagining.

Indian Shamans are often tragic figures. Their communion with strange spirits costs them dearly, yet they know it is their duty to protect humanity and the earth itself from the ravages of the Reckoning. Shamans need high *Spirit* Traits and *faith* Aptitudes to deal with the nature spirits that grant them favors.

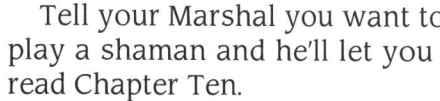

Ten

Tell your Marshal you want to play a shaman and he'll let you read Chapter Ten.

Mad Scientists are inventors and engineers who use ghost rock to create infernal devices of steam and steel. These often deranged individuals need high *Knowledge* and *Smarts* Traits as well as skill in one or more scientific fields and the *tinkerin'* Aptitude. Ask your Marshal if you can read Chapter Eight if you think you might want to play one of these demented tinkerers.

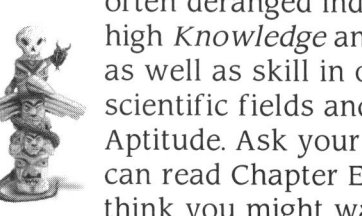

Eight

Marshals chase hardened criminals all over the West. Though they have the authority to assemble posses on occasion, they usually have to work alone. Marshals need a decent *trackin'* Aptitude as well as good combat skills. The *friends in high places* Edge should also help them keep track of fleeing bandits and outlaws.

Muckrakers are journalists who believe in reporting the truth above all else—no matter who it offends. If you play a muckraker, yellow journalism is your character's stock and trade. These fellows are curious beyond belief, and it amazes them that the common folk can't see what's going on right before their very eyes. That's why the "truth" often needs some embellishment to appeal to the skeptical masses. Muckrakers need the *professional: journalism* and *tale-tellin'* Aptitude to get their messages across. Many of them have extensive networks of *friends in high places* as well.

Makin' Heroes

The Fairer Sex

In the world of *Deadlands*, the Civil War has dragged on for more than 16 years—from 1860 to the present date of 1876. Manpower in both the North and the South is at an all-time low. This is good news for women because now many of them are able to fill roles they could only dream about before.

Women in *Deadlands* can play Marshals, gunslingers, gamblers, sheriffs, bank robbers, Indian medicine women and warriors, explorers, politicians (at local levels), and just about any other position you can imagine.

Photographers are rare and often in great demand in the Weird West. Traditional cameras of the day are too slow to capture action, but they can certainly record the aftermath of a gunfight or an encounter with a strange critter. Of course, most people think the latter pictures are staged phonies, but at least the *Tombstone Epitaph* usually buys the plates. Photographers can also make a few bucks off famous outlaws looking to get their portrait made. It's steady work, but occasionally dangerous. Your character needs the *professional: photographer* Aptitude to operate his equipment.

Pirates are most common in the California Maze, a labyrinth of flooded sea canyons left in the aftermath of the Great Quake of '68. These daring rogues might prey on honest miners, or they might fight for their country against Union or Confederate patrols or their common enemy—the Mexican Armada. The *trade: seamanship* Aptitude is their bread and butter, and the time-honored cutlass is what they spread it with.

Preachers, whether they be Pastors, Reverends, Rabbis or leaders of any other denominational flock, are often the most powerful weapons against the Reckoning. They need the *arcane background: blessed* Edge as well as a good *Mien* to deliver sermons of hellfire and brimstone. A high *Spirit* Trait also helps them call upon the power of their chosen religions. Priest characters should also be well-versed in the *professional: theology* Aptitude.

See Chapter Nine should you choose to play one of these pious individuals.

Prospectors know there's a fortune in gold, silver and ghost rock out there—if they can just find it. These characters must be willing to endure many hardships to uncover the mother lode that will set them up for life. Then again, perhaps it's not gold they're digging for. Some prospectors claim to have heard about even more fantastic treasures out there—somewhere. Either way, they'll need the *trade: minin'* Aptitude, as well as high *Strength* and *Vigor* Traits to help them dig for ghost rock or pan for gold for hours on end.

Saloon Gals know everyone—though their clients often claim they don't. Sometimes these hard-working gals stay in a single saloon. Other times they travel from town to town, leaving when the locals get tired of them. But though saloon girls might seem innocent enough, they can be found in the roughest boomtowns in the West, so most have learned to handle themselves. As one of these ladies, your character needs a high *Mien* and *persuasion* to gather the locals' secrets, and the *purty* Edge also helps.

Makin' Heroes

Sheriffs have a tough job in the West. They are often the only thing that stands between a ruthless gang and the common citizens of the towns they've sworn to protect. Worse, their authority stops at the town limits, making it easy for outlaws to escape their grasp. As a sheriff, your character needs a high *Mien* and *overawe* Aptitude to make troublemakers back down before gunplay begins, and a good *shootin'* Aptitude for when all Hell breaks loose anyway.

Snake Oil Salesmen are sometimes called "hucksters," but there's a big difference between these fast-talking hawkers and their hex-slinging counterparts. These fakes are known for their worthless elixirs of flavored water and extracts from dubious roots and herbs. But perhaps your character is different. He knows there are real "miracle cures," out there. If he can just find one, he can retire a wealthy man. Your character needs a high *persuasion* and *bluff* Aptitude, and "*the voice*" Edge might also help sell his wares. But make sure your salesman can protect himself somehow, because sometimes the suckers catch on, and they don't like being snookered.

Teamsters drive wagons, stagecoaches and other cattle-drawn vehicles. They carry valuable loads and passengers through hostile country, often having to outrun warbands, robbers, and critters most folks don't believe in. Most teamsters are well skilled in the aptly named *teamster* Aptitude and with some sort of shooting iron for "riding shotgun."

Makin' Heroes

Two: Traits

In *Deadlands*, characters' physical and mental traits are defined by Traits. Each character has 10 basic Traits—five corporeal (physical) and five mental. These are rated on a scale from 4 to 12, with the average being a 6 as shown on the chart below.

Trait Description Table

Die type	Description
4	Sorry
6	Average
8	Good
10	Amazing
12	Incredible

Corporeal Traits

Deftness: Hand-eye coordination and manual dexterity.
Nimbleness: Agility and overall physical prowess.
Quickness: Reflexes and speed.
Strength: Raw muscle and brawn.
Vigor: Endurance, constitution, and general fortitude.

Mental Traits

Cognition: Perception and alertness.
Knowledge: Education from book-learning and experience.
Mien: Presence and influence, as well as charisma and how the character is regarded by others.
Smarts: Wits and deduction. This is the ability to figure things out or piece together clues.
Spirit: Psyche and spiritual presence.

Luck o' the Draw

To generate your character's Traits, you need a standard *Deadlands* deck (all 54 cards). Now deal yourself 12 cards, and throw away any two except deuces (2s)—you're stuck with those. The 10 cards you have left are then assigned to each of your character's ten Traits. The card you assign determines the type of die you get to roll when making rolls with that Trait.

Trait Die Table

Card	Trait
2	d4
3-8	d6
9-Jack	d8
Queen-King	d10
Ace	d12

Jokers

Jokers are wild cards. You can use them as d12s, but drawing a Joker also means your character has a "mysterious past" of some sort. Tell the Marshal when this happens so he can figure out some secret fortune or long-forgotten calamity once you've finished making your hero.

Coordination

Traits are essentially die types. A character's Coordination is how many of those dice you should roll when the Marshal calls for a Trait check.

The card you assign to each Trait determines it's Coordination as well as its die type, as shown on the chart on the following page:

Makin' Heroes

Coordination Table

Suit	Coordination
Clubs	1
Diamonds	2
Hearts	3
Spades	4

Say you draw a 9 of spades. Checking the Trait Die Table shows that you get a d8 for that trait. Since it's a spade, the Coordination is 4. When using that Trait, you'd roll 4d8.

More Than Human

Sometimes you're going to run into people or creatures that are more than human. If your character is a huckster or a shaman, he might even have "supernatural" Traits himself on occasion.

After reaching a d12 in a Trait, the Trait's value rises in steps of 2. The next highest Trait after d12 is d12+2, then d12+4, and so on.

Wind

Wind is a special Trait that is derived from your character's *Vigor + Spirit*. This represents the amount of shock, fatigue or trauma your character can take before he keels over. Wind is represented only by a number. It has no die type. If your character has a d8 *Vigor* and a d10 *Spirit*, her Wind is 8+10=18.

When her *Wind* is reduced to zero or less, the character is effectively out of the action. The Marshal might rarely allow a winded hero to crawl or conduct very simple actions depending on the circumstances, but in general, they're tuckered out.

Makin' Heroes

Three: Aptitudes

Aptitudes are skills, talents, or trades a character has learned during his life. For most people, these skills range from 1 to 5, as shown on the Aptitude Level Table below.

Aptitude Level Table

Level	Description
1	Beginner
2	Amateur
3	Apprentice
4	Professional
5	Expert

Aptitude Points

The sum of your character's *Knowledge*, *Smarts*, and *Cognition* is the number of points you have to put into Aptitudes. If you've got a d8 *Knowledge*, d6 *Smarts*, and d12 *Cognition*, you have (8+6+12=) 26 points to spend on Aptitudes.

During character creation, each Aptitude level costs one point, so that a 1 point skill costs 1 point, and a 4 point skill costs 4 points. You can't start the game with an Aptitude higher than 5.

The next few pages list the standard Aptitudes available in *Deadlands*, grouped by the Trait they are normally associated with. Feel free to make up new ones if none of the standard Aptitudes fit. We've left space on the character sheet for these extra "specialty" skills.

Concentrations

"Concentrations" are listed in italics below some of these Aptitudes. If Concentrations are listed, then one must be chosen. *Shootin'*, for instance, must be followed by a *pistol*, *rifle* or *shotgun* Concentration.

Deftness

Fannin'

Fanning is the art of using a pistol to put a lot of lead in the air fast.

A character has to have a single-action revolver to fan. When he does, he holds down the gun's trigger and slaps its hammer back repeatedly with his other hand, firing a whole lot of bullets real fast.

Chapter Five tells you how to use *fannin'* to blow holes in deserving varmints.

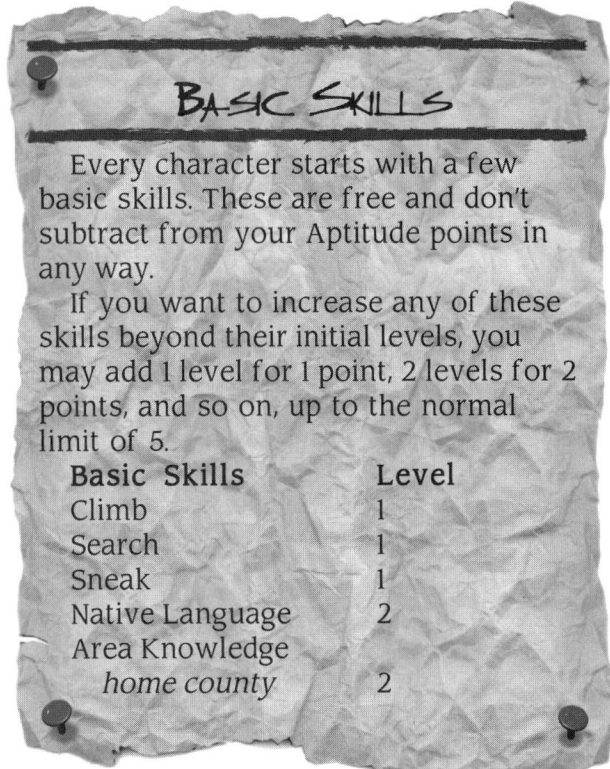

Basic Skills

Every character starts with a few basic skills. These are free and don't subtract from your Aptitude points in any way.

If you want to increase any of these skills beyond their initial levels, you may add 1 level for 1 point, 2 levels for 2 points, and so on, up to the normal limit of 5.

Basic Skills	Level
Climb	1
Search	1
Sneak	1
Native Language	2
Area Knowledge *home county*	2

Filchin'

When most people think of western outlaws, they picture gunslinging badmen and bank-robbing desperadoes. Light-fingered pickpockets, thieves, and scoundrels are actually far more common. This is the skill they use to practice their illicit trade.

Makin' Heroes

Thieves can make an opposed *filchin'* roll versus a target's *Cognition* to lift objects from pockets, purses, or holsters. The Marshal should modify either character's roll based on the size of the object lifted, the situation and whether or not the thief has managed to distract his prey first.

Lockpickin'

Good locks are hard to come by in the West, so if you find one, it's probably protecting something worth getting at.

A character with this skill and a set of lockpicks can attempt to open any door, chest, boudoir, chastity belt, or other valuable compartment. A character can attempt a failed *lockpick* roll multiple times, but each try after the first incurs a cumulative –2 penalty.

The difficulty depends on the lock itself. This skill works on safes too.

Lock Difficulty Table

Type of Lock	TN
Interior household door	3
Desk drawer	5
Front household door	7
Padlock	9
Safe	11
Improvised lock-picks	–2

Shootin'

Automatics, Carbine, Flamethrower, Pistol, Rifle, Shotgun

There's an old saying that says there are only two types of gunslingers: the quick and the dead. In *Deadlands*, some characters are quick *and* dead.

Shootin' is the ability to fire pistols, rifles and shotguns quickly and accurately in stressful situations—such as when someone's shooting back.

The *automatics* concentration is used with machines like Gatling guns. The other concentrations are pretty much self-explanatory.

Sleight of Hand

Cheating at cards can get you plugged in the Weird West. If you're going to do it, you'd better make sure you're good at it.

Sleight of hand allows a character to draw small items out of his sleeve or pockets quickly and without notice.

Sleight of hand can be used like the *quick draw* Aptitude on derringers, small knives, or any other weapons smaller than a pistol.

Speed-Load

Pistol, Rifle, Shotgun

Speed-loading helps serious gunslingers get those empty hoglegs smoking again.

Reloading a single bullet in a pistol, rifle, or shotgun usually takes an entire action. A successful *speed-load* check allows a character to reload up to 3 rounds during a single action. Check the weapon's maximum number of shots to make sure you don't load more rounds than it can hold.

If a pistol has a speed-loading cylinder (a spare cylinder already loaded with bullets), a Fair (5) *speed-load* roll slaps the entire thing in place in a single action. Otherwise, it takes two actions.

If you fail at a regular *speed-load* roll, you still get one bullet into the gun. If you fail with a speed-load cylinder, though, you don't get the cylinder in at all. Try again.

Speed-Load Table

Rounds Loaded	TN
2 rounds	9
3 rounds	11

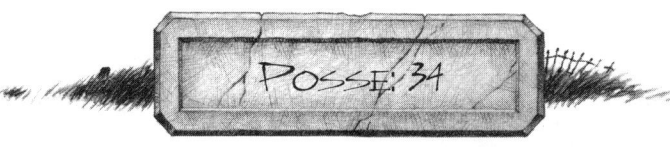

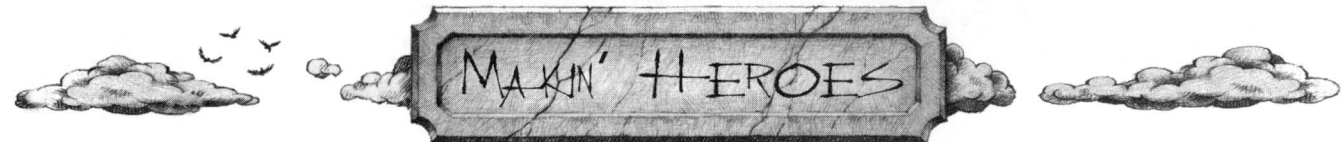

Makin' Heroes

Throwin'

Axes, Knives, Spears

If a cowpoke's relying on throwing things at people to get them to listen, then he's probably already won the fight and just having a little fun.

That said, this skill will cover him if he occasionally needs something a little quieter than a Peacemaker.

Nimbleness

Climbin'

Not too many folks in the Weird West go out of their way to climb sheer rock faces. A few scoundrels have had to scamper down rose trellises on occasion, however.

See the Gitalong Table on page 87 for movement rates for *climbin'*.

Dodge

No, we aren't talking about the town in Kansas (as in "get the Hell out of..."). We're talking about the ability to use cover and be where the bullets aren't.

The *dodge* skill is used as an "active" defense when your character is about to get drilled. We'll tell you more about it in Chapter Five.

Drivin'

Steam Boat, Ornithopter, Steam Wagon, Others

There's a lot of strange gizmos in the Weird West. Horseless carriages and flying gadgets powered by steam require a new set of skills.

This is the skill a character needs to drive a steam wagon, pilot an ornithopter, or steer a steam-powered boat. Driving a wagon pulled by animals uses the *teamster* Aptitude.

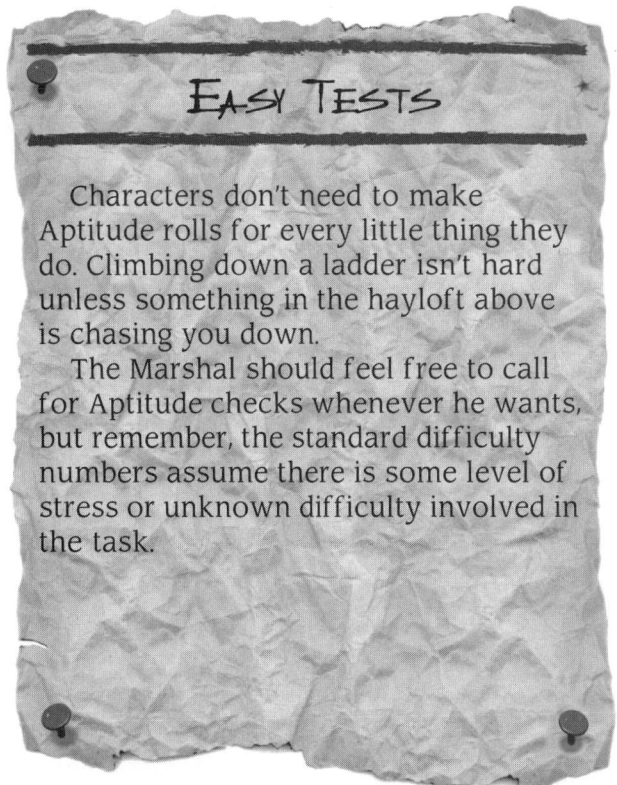

Easy Tests

Characters don't need to make Aptitude rolls for every little thing they do. Climbing down a ladder isn't hard unless something in the hayloft above is chasing you down.

The Marshal should feel free to call for Aptitude checks whenever he wants, but remember, the standard difficulty numbers assume there is some level of stress or unknown difficulty involved in the task.

Makin' Heroes

Fightin'

Boxin', Brawlin', Fencin', Knife, Lariat, Sword, Whip, Wrasslin'

Sometimes you just don't have enough bullets to get the job done. If you find yourself in one of these situations, it's time to whip out your trusty Bowie knife and start carving. Some skill with the thing might help.

A character uses this Aptitude to make hand-to-hand attacks. We'll tell you how in Chapter Five. Promise.

Horse Ridin'

No self-respecting cowpoke admits he can't ride a horse. A tinhorn without this skill often finds his companions leaving him in the dust.

The quality of the animal may also add or subtract from a character's skill roll. See page 64 for more information.

Sneak

Sometimes charging right down into the face of death doesn't make a whole lot of sense. Occasionally subtler tactics are called for.

When your character wants to sneak past someone, she's got to make an opposed *sneak* roll against the *search* Aptitude of anyone that might hear or see her. The Marshal should dole out bonuses and penalties depending on the situation. It's a lot easier to skulk about by the light of the moon than to avoid a murderous outlaw stalking you at high noon.

Swimmin'

Few frontiersman can swim. Those that can't usually sink like stones just trying to take their annual baths.

See your local watering hole or Chapter Five to find out about drowning. The Gitalong Table in the same chapter also tells you how fast a character can move while swimming.

Teamster

This skill lets your character drive wagons, stagecoaches, buggies, and carts and control the ornery animals that pull it.

The basic movement rate for a wagon depends on the animals pulling it. See the Gitalong Table on page 87 for specific movement rates.

Makin' Heroes

Quickness

Quick Draw

Knife, Pistol, Rifle, Shotgun, Sword, Others

When one Peacemaker won't get the job done, you might have to whip out another. You'd better be able to do it fast.

As you'll see in Chapter Five, it usually takes an action to draw a new weapon. If you've got this Aptitude, you can draw a new weapon and use it in the same action. The TN is usually Fair (5). If you fail, you draw the weapon normally and can't use it that action. If you botch, you've dropped it. If you botch and you've got *bad luck,* you might blast or cut off your favorite body part off.

Strength

Strength is not usually tied to particular Aptitude checks. The Marshal might call for certain Aptitudes to use the *Strength* Trait, however. For example, if two characters are wrestling for control of a gun, the Marshal might ask for *Strength/fightin': brawling* checks.

Strength is also used to determine your damage whenever your character hits someone in hand-to-hand combat. You'll see how this works in Chapter Five.

Vigor

Vigor is another Trait that has no particular Aptitudes associated with it. The Marshal might use *Vigor* whenever your character's endurance could determine the success of a particular Aptitude test, however. For example, a long arduous climb up a steep cliff might call for a *Vigor/climbin'* check. Too, a long ride to get help for a wounded comrade might be a *Vigor/horse ridin'* roll.

Cognition

Artillery

Cannons, Gatling Guns, Rockets

When you need to blow sizable holes in critters, you'll need to haul out the heavy artillery. Cannons and rockets pack the biggest whollop. Gatling guns can hose down hordes of lesser varmints.

Sighting and placing any of these weapons in strategic locations is a matter of *Cognition*. For Gatling guns, a character uses the *shootin': automatics* concentration when actually firing the weapon.

Arts

Painting, Sculpting, Sketching

Sketch artists who work for the army, pulp magazines, or the *Tombstone Epitaph* get some measure of respect in the Weird West. Painters and sculptors in particular had best not take themselves too seriously, however, since frontier folk are generally too practical to appreciate artistic pursuits.

An artist should generate an Aptitude total whenever he completes a performance or a work of art. This is the quality of the work, and it does not change unless the work itself is later altered in some way. The Marshal should determine the "value" of the piece based on the material it's made of and the artist's skill.

The *Tombstone Epitaph* generally pays $10 for sketches of "unusual" events. Photos are worth more to the *Epitaph* and other papers, but "news" photos aren't considered art and so are covered under the *professional: photographer* Aptitude.

Scrutinize

Any gambler worth his salt can tell when his opponent is lying through his teeth. Being able to *scrutinize* someone might not tell you everything, but it could give you some idea when the buffalo chips are starting to get thick.

Makin' Heroes

Scrutinize is the ability to judge another's character, penetrate disguises or detect lies. A character with this skill is also good at resisting *bluff* and *persuasion* attempts.

Search

Any fool can find an arrow sticking in his backside, but a character with a good eye for detail can find the proverbial needle in a haystack.

This skill covers a character whenever she's specifically looking for items, clues, or evidence. *Search* is also used to detect movement, or creeping enemies. The latter is an opposed roll versus the opponent's *sneak* Aptitude.

Search rolls can be used to find obvious footprints, but to actually read a trail and follow it requires the *trackin'* Aptitude.

Trackin'

Good trackers usually find whoever or whatever they're looking for. Of course, that's not always a good thing in *Deadlands*.

A successful *trackin'* roll helps a character find a trail, stay on it and maybe even figure out how many critters he's following. The difficulty for following tracks is shown on the chart below.

Tracking Difficulty Table

Trail	Target Number
One person	Incredible (11)
3-4 people	Hard (9)
5-8 people	Onerous (7)
9-15 people	Fair (5)
16+ people	Foolproof (3)
Modifiers	
Snow	+4
Night	-4
Rain since tracks were made	-4
Rain before tracks were made	+4
High traffic area	-4

Knowledge

Academia

Philosophy, History, Occult, Others

Bookworms are rarely appreciated in the Weird West until the conclusion of some epic adventure. That's when their obscure knowledge about what might kill a critter that's already gobbled up half the posse tends to come in handy.

Makin' Heroes

The *academia* skill provides a character with information about his chosen subject. A character might also choose a field within a more narrow subject, such as *military history*. The Marshal should take this into account when asking for any *academia* Aptitude checks and modify the difficulty level accordingly.

Area Knowledge

Town, County, State, Region

You'd better know where to run when the bogeyman comes calling.

Area knowledge is a measure of how much a character knows about a place. Every character in *Deadlands* has detailed knowledge of the town and county they spent most of their life in.

Characters who travel a lot, such as scouts and bounty hunters, might have knowledge of other locales as well. A character always knows the basics of an area he's traveled to or through before, but any kind of specific information requires the *area knowledge* skill.

You can concentrate in any size region, but the bigger the region, the less specific the information.

Demolition

Sometimes you just have to blow the snot out of some giant creepy crawler. It's usually best if you don't catch your posse in the blast.

A character with this skill knows how much explosive material is needed for the job at hand and how far away to stand. Going bust on a *demolition* roll usually has disastrous consequences.

Makin' Heroes

Disguise

Only actors and sneaky Pinkertons are actually trained in the art of *disguise*. Sometimes an outlaw has to learn on the fly, however, and knowing a fake beard from a hairpiece might keep you from looking too silly.

Whenever a character in disguise is spotted by someone who might catch on, the character must make an opposed *disguise* roll vs. the observer's *scrutinize* Aptitude. One success on the part of the observer might make him suspicious, but a success with at least one raise is required to see through the *disguise*.

Languages

Native Tongue, Apache, French, Gaelic, German, Latin, Sign Language (Indian) Sioux, Spanish, Others

Knowledge in foreign languages can often mean the difference between life and death in the Weird West. If you're exploring an old Spanish gold mine called *Casa del Diablo*, you'd better know it means "House of the Devil."

All characters are fluent (have 2 points) in their native language. A character with 1 point in another language can speak and communicate common verbs and nouns with little difficulty. At skill level 2 and higher, the character can read and write the language and has a larger vocabulary.

Indian "sign language" is a very useful concentration. Nearly all tribes can communicate with this common system. Explorers and scouts working for the Army should consider this Aptitude a must.

Medicine

General, Surgery, Veterinary

Some folks think of "sawbones" as butchers, but a good one knows when to cut your leg off and when to let it be.

A *general* concentration in *medicine* means the doc can make herbs and poultices, stop bleeding, set broken bones and perform simple surgery such as lancing boils or digging out a shallow bullet. This concentration lets a character heal up to heavy wounds. He can do nothing for serious and critical wounds other than stop bleeding.

A doc with the *surgery* concentration has had formal training in cutting people open. Surgeons can stop internal bleeding, perform operations and dig bullets out of the deepest wounds. Your character has to have studied somewhere before you can take this Aptitude. Ask your Marshal if you're not sure whether or not you can take it.

Vets take care of wounds and ailments in animals. If pressed, a vet can treat a human as if he had the *general* concentration. Since this is a related skill, he'll have to subtract -2 from the roll. Regular doctors can also treat animals, but the wide variety of critters doubles the usual penalty for a related skill to -4.

Professional

Journalism, Law, Military, Politics, Theology, Others

Gunslingers might rule the streets, but it's the politicians who hire them, the journalists who make their reputations, and the lawyers who get them off the hook when the long arm of the law finally catches up with them.

The *professional* Aptitude is a catch-all category for "social sciences" that require formal education or training of some sort, such as law, journalism, or theology. A character can use this Aptitude whenever he needs to recount a law or battle, write a news story, or write a sermon on the evils of strong drink. Actually performing any of these tasks usually falls under another Trait. A minister who needs to deliver a sermon, for instance, would make a *Mien/ professional: theology* roll.

Concentrations within the professional Aptitude are *never* considered related.

Makin' Heroes

Science

General, Biology, Chemistry, Engineering, Physics

The discovery of ghost rock changed the face of the world forever. Scientists can now make incredible devices of steam and steel they could only dream of before. Even those who don't use the strange new mineral benefit from its research and the inventions it has spawned.

This Aptitude covers book learning, experience and skill in scientific pursuits.

If your character is a mad scientist, you must take at least 3 levels total in any number of scientific concentrations.

Trade

Blacksmithing, Carpentry, Seamanship, Mining, Telegraphy, Undertaking, Others

Somebody's got to actually do all the work. The hard jobs are done by the folks with the practical skills.

Trade is a catch-all skill like the *professional* Aptitude. It covers hands-on jobs like blacksmithing and undertaking. The usual Aptitude used for *trade* checks is *Knowledge*, though this will change depending on the task. A sailor who needs to steer a sailing ship through the Maze, for instance, would need to make a *Deftness/trade: seamanship* roll to avoid disaster.

Like its counterpart the *professional* Aptitude, *trade* concentrations aren't related.

Makin' Heroes

Mien

Animal Wranglin'
Bronco Busting, Dog Training

Life in the Weird West often depends on the obedience of a good horse. Similarly, in the North, a pack of sled dogs might help an explorer escape the wrath of something "man was not meant to know." In either case, this is the skill a character needs to teach an animal how to obey a human master.

Animal wranglin' skill checks are opposed rolls versus the animal's *Mien*. Teaching a horse or a dog a new trick usually takes 4-5 days.

Leadership

In the military, careers are often made on whether or not an officer can get his men to do as he tells them. Lawmen also use this skill to stare down mobs and lead their posses into hostile territory.

Besides using *leadership* to control troops, followers, or lackeys, this Aptitude has two specific uses.

In a combat situation, a *leadership* roll can keep people from being surprised. Whenever a friendly character fails a surprise roll (explained more in Chapter Five), you attempt to make the roll for her as long as your character is not surprised as well. This counts as an action. Every success and raise allows the leader to affect one other individual.

You can also use *leadership* to help trade Action Cards during combat. When it's your turn to take an action, make a Fair (5) *leadership* roll. For every success and raise you get, you can help any two players (possibly even including yourself) trade a single Action Card in their hands. The only catch is that in each trade, both players must agree to make the trade first.

🔸 Hank "One Eye" Ketchum, a stern Texas Ranger, is pinned down alongside Ronan Lynch by a band of desperadoes. On Hank's turn, he decides to use his *leadership* to trade some of his high Action Cards for Ronan's lower ones since Ronan's got some dynamite handy. Hank yells for Ronan to throw the bundle and rolls his *leadership* for a 13, giving him a success and a raise. He can now trade up to two cards with Ronan, as long as Ronan agrees to accept the trade. Ronan does, and the bad guys go boom in a big way.

Overawe

The most successful gunmen can often back down their opponents before anyone slaps leather. An *overawe* attack might come in the form of a surly stare, a deadly threat or even the feel of cold iron in someone's back.

An *overawe* attack is an opposed roll versus a character's *guts*. See Chapter Five for information on tests of will.

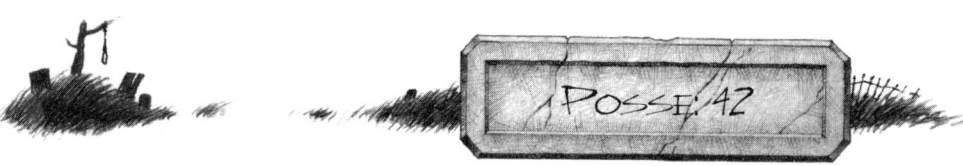

Makin' Heroes

Performin'

Acting, Singing

There isn't a lot of entertainment in the West, so most people appreciate a good actor or a sexy singer. Crowds are rough on the acts they don't like, but they treat a good performer like gold.

A good performance against a Fair (5) TN can net the character 2d6 dollars plus another 1d6 bucks per raise. Better wages can be earned, of course, but this rate works for impromptu performances for good-sized crowds.

Persuasion

Fast-talking snake-oil salesmen, sultry saloon girls and nosy muckrakers often depend on their powers of *persuasion*. Talking someone into providing aid or information in times of need can be as crucial as skill with a six-shooter.

Persuasion attempts are opposed rolls versus the target's *scrutinize* Aptitude.

Tale-Tellin'

How can you become a legend of the Weird West if no one tells your tale?

Tale-tellin' is the talent of capturing an audience's attention with a ripping yarn or exciting story. Preachers use the skill to deliver their fiery sermons and politicians use it to

Twelve Spreading the word of your posse's deeds is very important to becoming a legend of the Weird West. You can find out why once you've adventured a while and your Marshal lets you read Chapter Twelve.

Smarts

Bluff

In poker, a good *bluff* can win a thousand-dollar pot on a pair of deuces. Telling lies, spinning tall tales, and making exaggerations is all part of the game.

Bluffing is a test of wills versus an opponent's *scrutinize*. The more raises the character gets, the more the opponent falls for the tall tale.

Gamblin'

Most folks can hold their own in poker, faro, blackjack, and other games of chance. Professional gamblers can roam the boomtowns and turn a few dollars into a small fortune.

There are two ways to handle gambling in *Deadlands*. The first is for a single hand, the second is a quick way to sum up an hour's worth of gambling.

For a single hand, the gamblers first decide on the stakes. Then each character involved makes a Fair (5) *gamblin'* skill. Every success and raise lets a gambler draw a card from a card deck. When everyone has their cards, each player flips over her highest. The players with the lowest cards put their stake in the pot, and the winner gets the pot. A Red Joker is the highest card and a Black Joker is the lowest.

To sum up a longer period of gambling, use this method instead. The gamblers first decide on the average stakes. One to five bucks per hand is common for serious gambling. Then everyone makes a *gamblin'* Aptitude check. The lowest total pays the highest total the difference times the stake. The next lowest pays the second highest, and so on. If there's an odd man in the middle, he breaks even.

> For instance, "Velvet" Van Helter, a suave huckster and cardshark from New Orleans, "One Eye" Ketchum, and Ronan Lynch play $5 poker for an hour. Velvet gets a 15, One Eye gets 10, and Ronan gets a 2. Ronan pays Velvet ((15-2=) 13x$5=) $65. One Eye breaks even.

Ridicule

There's a fine art to making fun of someone in the Weird West where trigger fingers are itchier than saddle sores. Knowing when and just how far to push your opponent is the real skill.

Using the *ridicule* Aptitude is an opposed roll versus an opponent's *ridicule*. Someone with a good sense of humor can take a joke better than someone without. Using tests of wills in combat is covered in Chapter Five.

Makin' Heroes

Scroungin'

Scroungin' is the ability to find common items in a hurry. Sometimes this means settling for less than what is needed, but a good scrounger can usually come up with something that gets the job done.

The Marshal sets the difficulty of finding a particular object depending on the item, and the amount of time available.

Streetwise

A *streetwise* character knows how to work the streets and get information from the seedier elements of towns and cities.

This Aptitude is most often used to get illegal items or restricted information. The difficulty depends on the prize and the steps the character has taken to secure it.

Survival

Desert, Mountain, Other

A veteran frontiersman can survive with minimal tools and supplies in hostile environments. This might mean eating the stringy meat of prairie dogs while on the high plains, but it beats starving.

A successful *survival* roll feeds a character for one day. Every success and raise provides the bare necessities for one other person. The difficulty of the roll depends on the environment. An area with plentiful game and water has a difficulty of Foolproof (3), while it's an Incredible (11) task to find vittles in deserts like the Mojave.

In any case, you can normally only make one *survival* roll per day.

Tinkerin'

A steam wagon is a fine gadget to get you across the Mojave. If it breaks down in the middle of the desert, you'd better make sure you can fix it, however.

Tinkerin' is the ability to fix contraptions, gizmos, and gadgets. This Aptitude is a must for mad scientists who want to make the infernal devices they devise.

Spirit

Faith

Faith is a strange thing. Most folks seem to have more of it when some nasty critter is about to stuff them in its pie-hole. Then they're full of praise and promises.

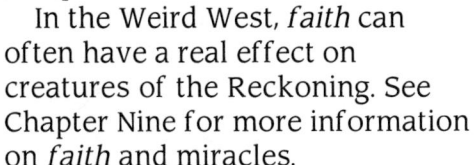

In the Weird West, *faith* can often have a real effect on creatures of the Reckoning. See Chapter Nine for more information on *faith* and miracles.

Guts

There's a lot of strange stuff in the Weird West. When your character stumbles upon a slavering abomination or a gruesome scene, you need to make sure he's got *guts*. It's hard to plug a charging critter when you're wetting your pants.

Once your character has adventured for a while, he'll start to gain "Grit." Grit is added to *guts* checks, meaning your hombre's psyche will eventually become accustomed to the lesser horrors of *Deadlands*.

Failing a *guts* check can have serious consequences. Don't worry about them right now, though. The Marshal's got all the information she needs to inflict sheer terror on your hapless character.

Makin' Heroes

Four: Hindrances

Hindrances are physical or mental handicaps. You can take up to 10 points in Hindrances during character creation. These points can then be used for additional Aptitudes or Edges.

The number of points each Hindrance is worth is listed right next to its title. Ranges of numbers or numbers with slashes indicate that the Hindrance comes in more than one level of severity. The higher the number, the worse the Hindrance affects you.

While you get points for taking Hindrances now, they're far more important in helping you earn Fate Chips. We'll tell you about these later, but for now, you should know that if you choose a Hindrance, you'd best be willing to roleplay it. That's how you earn rewards (Fate Chips) that can be used to save your skin and help improve your character later on.

Ailin' 1/3/5

There's some things the doctors just can't cure. If you get a rash in your crotch from time to time, it's damned embarrassing and inconvenient. If you've got consumption, you'd better start making friends with the local undertaker.

Diseased characters are affected by their ailments depending on the severity and the circumstances of their particular affliction.

Lesser ailments are things like constant allergies or colds, frequent lice, or worms. Some more serious diseases are consumption (tuberculosis), diabetes, leukemia, and cancer. Remember this is the Weird West, so there are likely far worse ailments out there, like the "tummy twister" the fellow in the picture on the left has picked up.

Ailin' Table

Value	Ailment
1	Minor: Your character has a minor but incurable ailment. This might cause him to cough at inconvenient times, make social engagements difficult, give him the shakes, etc. Subtract -2 from any *persuasion* rolls and *sneak* attempts.
3	Chronic: Your hero has a chronic illness that causes constant agony and/or will eventually kill her. She suffers the penalties for a *minor ailment*, and at the start of each game session, she must make a Fair (5) Vigor roll. If she fails, she suffers -4 to all tasks she performs this game. The Marshal might modify your die roll depending on the weather and your particular illness.
5	Fatal: You've got a chronic illness that might kill your character at any time. Roll as above. On a botch, your character must also make an Onerous (7) Vigor test. Should she fail, death's door swings wide.

Makin' Heroes

All Thumbs — 2

You don't like machines and they don't seem to like you much either.

Scientific and mechanical Aptitudes cost twice the normal bounty points to learn or improve. All rolls made to use or repair machinery are made at -2.

Bad Ears — 3/5

The quick and the deaf.

Choose the level of bad hearing your character suffers from the chart below.

Bad Ears Table

Value	Status
3	Mild: Subtract -2 to all Cognition tests based on hearing.
5	Stone deaf: Your character can't hear at all.

Bad Eyes — 3/5

Sometimes it's better not to see what's coming after you.

Bad eyes subtract from any Trait or Aptitude rolls you make to affect or see things at greater than 20 yards. The Marshal might sometimes allow you to use your *bad eyes* as a bonus to *guts* checks made when viewing gruesome horrors at long range.

Bad Eyes Table

Value	Status
3	Mild: Subtract -2 from your character's Trait and Aptitude rolls made to see or affect things at greater than 20 yards. If your character wears spectacles, reduce the value of the Hindrance by 1.
5	Near Blind: As above but the penalty is -4.

Bad Luck — 5

Calamity Jane's got nothing on you. Don't even think about being close friends with dynamite.

Anytime you go bust, whatever your character is doing has the absolute worst effect possible.

Big Britches — 3

It's good to be confident, but only a fool charges 600 cavalrymen into 5,000 Sioux.

Your character is severely overconfident. He believes he can do anything and he never turns down a challenge.

Big 'Un — 1/2

Your horse really hates to see you coming. Fortunately, it's pretty hard to bust up someone your size.

The effects of a character's size depend on whether he is merely husky or truly obese. Increasing your character's Size has an effect on the damage he can take. See Chapter Five for details.

Big 'Un Table

Value	Size
1	Husky: Add +1 to your Size; Reduce your hero's base move by one step to a minimum of 4. Your maximum Nimbleness is a d10.
2	Obese: Add +2 to your size; Reduce your character's base move by two steps to a minimum of 4. Your maximum Nimbleness is a d8.

Bloodthirsty — 2

Some folks are just plain mean. Others don't believe in leaving their enemies alive to come back and haunt them later.

Your character rarely take prisoners, and she enjoys confrontations. If she's forced to take prisoners, they don't tend to live long after they're no longer useful.

Curious — 3

If it killed the cat, it can do the same to you.

Your hero wants to know about everything. Anytime a mystery presents itself, he must do everything in his power to try and solve it.

Posse:47

Makin' Heroes

Enemy — 1-5

Remember that every foe you put down likely has some friends or family that might come looking for you later.

Your character has an enemy or enemies of some sort. You and the Marshal should determine the value of any enemies based on their relative power level and frequency of appearance.

A vengeful but inexperienced youth who is stalking the character, for example, would likely be worth two points, since her appearance would be fairly common but she is relatively weak. A deserter should take an enemy as well, but neither the USA or the CSA have much time or interest, so this is usually only worth 2 points.

Ferner — 3

If they can't understand you, they can't help you.

"Ferners" are outsiders in the culture central to your adventure or campaign. Usually, the outsiders are Mexicans, Indians, and Chinese who have a difficult time adapting to the white man's language and way of life. An Englishman who insists on bad-mouthing the "democracy" or a Chinese railroad worker who speaks little English are likely to be shunned by most folks in the frontier.

Sometimes whites are the "ferners." If your Marshal is running a campaign centered in the Sioux Nations, those who don't know the Sioux's practices and traditions will find themselves the subject of prejudice.

As long as your character can communicate well in the culture he's in and doesn't go out of his way to prove himself an outsider, he will likely suffer little prejudice and you need not take this Hindrance. Foreign characters may sometimes suffer from individual intolerance, of course, but by and large they are usually treated fairly in the Weird West.

Greedy — 2

It's one of the seven deadly sins. But while your mortal soul might be damned to Hell, you'll sure have a good time here on earth rolling in loot.

Money and power mean everything to your scoundrel and she'll do most anything to get more of it.

Habit — 1-3

Folks aren't much on cleanliness in the Weird West, but that doesn't mean they like to watch some tinhorn shove his picker up his nose.

Your character has some sort of habit that others find annoying or revolting. Besides putting off other characters, this Hindrance subtracts a number of points from your character's *persuasion* rolls equal to the value of the Hindrance. The value of the Hindrance depends on the frequency of the habit and just how gross and disgusting it is.

Hankerin' — 2/4

If you just can't think without a stogie in your pie-hole, you've got yourself a habit. If it's alcohol or opium you're craving, welcome to Addiction City, population one.

A mild *hankerin'* means the character is highly addicted to some mildly harmful substance (such as tobacco), or slightly addicted to a more dangerous substance. A severe *hankerin'* means the character is addicted to alcohol, opium, laudanum, peyote, or some other dangerous drug.

Hankerin' Table

Value	Status
1	Mild: Subtract -2 to Mental skills if the substance is not available after 24 hours.
3	Severe: Your character suffers the same as above and also subtracts -4 to Mental and Corporeal skills if the substance is not available every 48 hours.

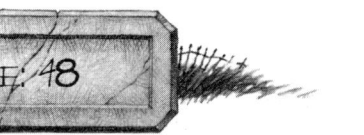

Posse: 48

Makin' Heroes

Heavy Sleeper   1

Logs wake up faster than you.

You must subtract -2 from your hero's *Cognition* rolls made to wake up in an emergency or when some critter is sneaking up on him. He usually oversleeps as well.

Heroic   3

You're a sucker for someone in trouble. Ever hear of nice guys finishing last? Heroes who go chasing down wild critters aren't likely to finish at all.

Your character can't turn down a plea for help. She doesn't have to be cheery about it, but she always helps those in need eventually.

Illiterate   3

It's a terrible thing to come back from the dead and not be able to read the words on your own tombstone.

Illiterates cannot read even the most basic words of their own language or any other language they happen to speak.

Intolerance   1-3

There's some folks you just can't stand. They don't cotton to you, and you'd like to push them off a tall cliff.

Your character does not get along with certain kinds of people (Mexicans, white men, politicians, and so on) and has nothing to with them if possible. If forced to work with them, he insults and provokes them whenever he gets the chance. The value of the Hindrance depends on the frequency of encounters your character has with those he is intolerant toward.

Kid   2

Don't be fooled by a kid with a gun. A bullet fired from little hands will still blow your guts out.

Your character is a kid 12-15 years of age. Most people won't take you seriously, your maximum *Strength* is a d10 and your maximum *Knowledge* is a d8. You must buy off this Hindrance (with bounty points—see Chapter 6) by the time you hit 16.

Lame   3/5

There's an old chestnut that says when something's chasing you, you've only got to outrun one person. Unfortunately, you're usually that one person.

This Hindrance affects a character's move rate and active defense.

Lame Table

Value	Status
3	Limp: You're reduced to 3/4 Move and subtract -2 to active dodge rolls and other tests requiring mobility.
5	Crippled: One leg is missing or disabled entirely. You're reduced to 1/4 move and subtract -4 to active dodge rolls and other tests requiring mobility.

Posse: 49

Makin' Heroes

Loco   1-5

You don't have to be crazy to fight some of the critters of *Deadlands*, but it helps.

Your hero has a mental illness of some sort. This can range from being absent-minded to being a compulsive liar or suffering from phobias, delusions, depression, or schizophrenia. The illness is always present, and it rules your character's actions most of the time. The value of the Hindrance depends on the severity of the illness and its effects on the character. You might want to check out the mad scientist's dementias on page 219 for some ideas.

Loyal   3

You may not be a hero, but your friends know they can count on you when the chips are down.

The character is extremely loyal to his friends or to a specific group, nation, or ideal. He will risk his life to defend it and uphold its traditions.

Miser   3

A miser knows the price of everything and the value of nothing.

Miserly characters must always buy the "cheapest" goods and haggle incessantly. Because of this, you must roll 1d10 whenever your character uses his own mechanical equipment, including firearms. On a 1, the equipment fails to operate and must be repaired.

Mean as a Rattler   2

You think the whole world pissed in your canteen. Maybe it did.

People tend not to like your character. She's hateful and mean-spirited. Besides making it hard for others to like your hombre, subtract -2 from friendly *persuasion* attempts. At the Marshal's discretion, you may occasionally be allowed to add +2 to hostile *persuasion* or *overawe* rolls.

Night Terrors   5

The Indians say nightmares are glimpses into the Hunting Grounds—a mad limbo where evil spirits devour the souls of the newly dead. Your nightmares make you think there might be some truth to this.

Your character's nightmares are far worse than most, something that keeps her from wanting to sleep much. Coffee is her best friend, and she usually only gets about 3-4 hours sleep at night.

Make a Hard (9) *Spirit* check every time your character beds down. If you fail, your character gets no sleep and must subtract -1 from all her Aptitude and Trait rolls the following day. These effects are cumulative to a maximum of -5, so if your character can't sleep for a week, she'll have to subtract -5 from everything she does.

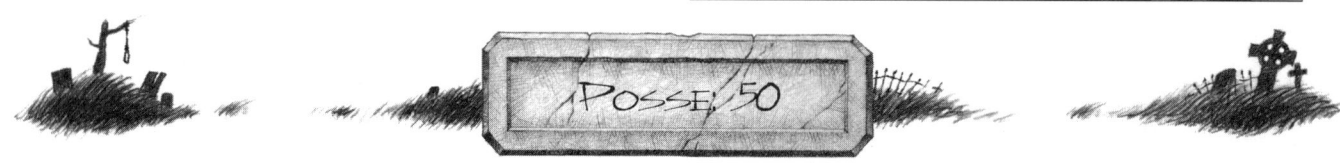

Makin' Heroes

Anytime your character can't sleep, you should roleplay her sluggish delirium the next day. The Marshal will reward you with Fate Chips appropriately.

If you should ever botch the sleep roll, your character's dream self is actually transported into the Hunting Grounds. There she'll experience a horrible nightmare scenario that lends insight into her current predicament but risks her mortal soul.

The Marshal should construct this nightmare as a short solo adventure for your character. In it, she is given vague hints about the local abomination or situation. If she should die in the nightmare, however, her Wind is reduced by -1 permanently.

Oath 1-5

A person is only as good as his word. Go back on it, and you'll find people won't trust you any further than you can run before they gun you down like the lying dog you are.

Your hero has an oath to perform some important task or always react to certain conditions. The value of the *oath* depends on how often it might come into play and the risk it involves.

Obligation 1-5

A man's got to do what a man's got to do. Your character is obligated to his family, his job, the military, a town or a duty of some sort. This should be frequently inconvenient as he has to report to work or go off on assignment from time to time. Note that this is not the same as an *oath*.

Outlaw 1-5

The only authority you abide by is the "law of the West." And even that's subject to exception when it suits your needs.

Outlaws are lawbreakers by nature. They have little respect for the law, and are likely wanted for anything from petty larceny in a single town to being a renowned killer throughout the West.

One-Armed Bandit 3

There's lots of veterans who lost arms and legs in the war. To think this makes them any less dangerous is a big mistake. It only takes one finger to yank a trigger.

Your character has only one hand or arm. You must subtract -4 from any skills that require the use of two hands.

Pacifist 3/5

Being a pacifist doesn't mean a fellow is afraid of a fight. As of 1876, despite years of being a lawman in Dodge and other cattle towns, Wyatt Earp hadn't killed a single man. He was well known for "buffaloing" a cowboy with his pistol butt, but Earp was smart enough to know that killing a man often caused more trouble than it was worth among vengeful friends and kinfolk.

Pacifists range from those who simply don't like to kill until it's absolutely

Posse: 51

Makin' Heroes

unavoidable (3 points) to those who won't kill under any circumstances (5 points).

Poverty — 3

A fool and his money are soon parted.

Your character has a hard time saving, and he spends money like water. Anything he buys with it eventually falls into disuse and is lost or discarded. He starts with only $50 instead of the normal $250.

Scrawny — 5

Beanpoles are thicker than you. At least your horse is happy about it.

Scrawny cowpokes are slight and weak and must subtract -1 from their Size (see Chapter Five.). Their maximum strength is a d10. A character's slight frame might benefit him in certain situations, like crawling through a small cave or window, but usually it just gets him picked on.

Self-Righteous — 3

If you're not always right, then you're at least sure the ignorant masses are always wrong.

Your character believes everything she does serves some greater cause (such as Christianity, the Temperance Movement, the taming of the West, etc). She never backs down from her beliefs. This is a great Hindrance for preachers and nuns.

Squeamish — 3

You can't hold your chow when you see blood and gore. It's a little embarrassing compared to your gunslinger friends who don't flinch even with half their guts hanging out.

Guts checks caused by gory scenes are made at -2.

Stubborn — 2

It's your way or not at all. If the rest of the world is too stupid to realize you're right, they can go hang themselves with an itchy rope.

The hero is pig-headed and as stubborn as a mule. He always wants to do things his way and holds out until everyone agrees or some major concession to his idea has been made.

Superstitious — 2

Owls never hoot "just for the Hell of it" and black cats should be shot before they cross your path.

Your character believes in superstitions and tries to live his life by signs and omens of portent. You should check out a book of superstitions from your local library to help you roleplay this Hindrance.

Tinhorn — 2

Dudes using "two-dollar words" seem like a dime a dozen in the Weird West after gold and ghost rock were discovered in California. Those that lived on the frontier before don't take very kindly to these fast-talking dudes and their New York ways.

Tinhorns are big talkers, usually from back East. They use big words and brag about their families a lot.

Thin-Skinned — 3

You get splinters from your own pistol and won't quit whining about it until you see a sawbones.

Increase your character's wound penalty by 1.

Ugly As Sin — 1

It's too bad the old saying about "stopping a bullet with your face" isn't true. If it was, you'd never have to worry about being shot.

Subtract -2 from friendly *persuasion* rolls made whenever your character's looks might intervene. On the plus side, you can add +2 whenever his looks might actually help, such as when making *overawe* or hostile *persuasion* attempts.

Makin' Heroes

VENGEFUL — 3

The world needs to be taught a lesson, and you're the professor.

Your character must always attempt to right a wrong committed against him. Whether this revenge is violent or not depends on his nature.

YELLER — 3

You usually get shot in the backside.

Cowards don't have the heart for combat and try to avoid it whenever possible. "Real" men don't like them much unless they're female, in which case they might actually be *more* appealing. Subtract -2 from *persuasion* rolls made against those with little respect for your character's cowardly ways.

FIVE: EDGES

Edges are physical or background advantages that you can purchase for your character. You can't use your Aptitude points to buy these, so you must get points for Edges by taking Hindrances. On the following pages are descriptions of each of the Edges and the effects they have on your character.

ARCANE BACKGROUND — 3

Most folks encounter the supernatural and get eaten by it. A rare few have survived the ordeal and come away from it with strange knowledge and sometimes powers beyond mortal ken.

There are four types of *arcane backgrounds* available in *Deadlands*: *hucksters, mad scientists, the blessed,* and *shamans.* Choose one, then ask your Marshal to let you read the chapter that tells you all about your powers and abilities.

Seven Thru Ten

Hucksters are wizards of the Weird West. They use poker hands to help them cast their deadly hexes. Their powers are explained in Chapter Seven.

Mad scientists build incredible devices of steam and steel. Though they don't realize it, their infernal gizmos actually draw on the power of the Hunting Grounds. More information is presented in Chapter Eight.

Blessed characters are nuns, priests, or average folks who have been blessed by a divine entity for one reason or another. When the *blessed* are behaving themselves, they can invoke miracles that help them fight the evils of the Reckoning. Their abilities are explained in Chapter Nine.

Shamans are Indian holy men and women. Their power comes from dealing with demanding nature spirits. Shamans and their favors are detailed in Chapter Ten.

Makin' Heroes

Belongings   1-5

If a cowboy's gun is his best friend, his horse is his mistress. These two commodities satisfy most folks, but a few have something they consider equally valuable.

This Edge covers all the unusual equipment you might want for your character. You need to work out the specific point cost of any given item with the Marshal, but the list on the next page should give you some good ideas.

Belongings Table

Cost	Belongings
1	Some shares in a profitable railroad, a fast horse, a loyal and capable dog, 12 silver bullets.
2	A boat, an object dí art, a silver dagger, an incredibly fast horse.
3	The Colt .45 used by Billy the Kid, a tomahawk blessed by a powerful Indian shaman, a Gatling gun, a riverboat.
4	A ship, a saloon or other profitable business, a relic of specific but limited power.
5	A relic of power, a train, a pardon for all deeds past and present good in a certain region or state.

Big Ears   1

Some folks got "head handles" as big as a donkey's. Those that do usually hear a soft-toed critter creeping over stone at 100 yards.

A character with the *big ears* Edge adds

Brave   2

Most folks aren't really brave—they're just too stupid to know better. Maybe you're different, but it's doubtful.

Characters with this Edge add +2 to their *guts* checks.

Dinero   1-5

Money talks, especially in the Weird West. If you can't take out the bounty hunter that's after you, a little "dinero" might hire someone who can.

Wealthy individuals start with additional funds and can sometimes wire "home" for money. The amount depends on the level of wealth. A character normally starts with $250. A wealthy character can come up with significantly more dinero given enough time, collateral and a good excuse.

Dinero Table

Level	Init. Funds	Extra Dinero
1	$250	$100
2	$500	$500
3	$1000	$2000
4	$2000	$5000
5	$5000	$10000

Friends in High Places   1-3

It's not who you know—it's who knows you.

Your character has friends who occasionally help him out. The value of the friend(s) depends on how powerful they are and how often they show up. A Texas Ranger who shows up with the cavalry every other game or so is worth 3 points, or

Posse 54

Makin' Heroes

1 if he usually shows up alone. A newspaper editor who bails your character out of jail most of the time might be worth 2. There are many ways to use this Edge, so work out the details with your Marshal before you determine the final point cost.

Gift of Gab   1

There are a lot of languages spoken in the Weird West. It helps to understand a few. If some strange German-speaking hermit asks you and your posse to dinner, you'd best make sure he wants to feed you instead of eat you.

This Edge allows your character to learn languages in half the normal time (see "Bounty Points" on page 111). During character creation, you may purchase any additional languages at half cost as well.

Keen   3

Veterans of the frontier learn to expect the unexpected. Other folks are just jumpy and twitch at every little sound or movement. The only thing they've got in common is that they can both sense a mountain lion creeping up on them from 50 yards away.

A character with the *keen* Edge notices little details, sounds, and movements that others often ignore. The character may add +2 to any *Cognition* rolls made under these circumstances.

Law Man   1/3/5

A badge carries a lot of weight in the Weird West. It also means great responsibility. The common folk depend on you to fight off marauders, bandits, and sometimes stranger things.

While this Edge grants your character a great amount of authority, jurisdiction is always limited. Sheriffs operate only within the limits of their town, County Sheriffs patrol counties, and US Marshals' authorities extend to their entire country.

Law Man Table

Cost	Authority
1	Deputized for a specific but long-term purpose (the capture of Jesse James or Geronimo). Pinkerton Detectives typically have no law enforcement powers on their own, but are often given authority in specific regions or situations. This costs 1 point.
3	Sheriff of a small town. Because this Edge is really only appropriate for a saga that will take place in a specific geographic area, it should only be bought with the permission of the Marshal.
5	Federal Marshal or Texas Ranger. You have jurisdiction within the USA or CSA respectively.

Light Sleeper   1

Sleep doesn't always come easy in *Deadlands*. While it might make you grouchy before your morning coffee, being a light sleeper can be fairly handy when some critter tries to slither into your bedroll.

A character with this Edge may add +2 to *Cognition* rolls made when he needs to wake up quickly.

Luck of the Irish   3

A cowpoke with luck like this might catch an incoming bullet on the new pocket watch he just bought a few hours earlier. That's the way it works for these folks—some minor bad luck winds up saving their keister in some genuinely freaky but ultimately fortunate way.

Whenever you spend a red or blue Fate Chip (more about this on page 110) on a die roll, you may reroll any 1s.

Mechanically Inclined   1

Mechanical devices aren't common on the frontier, so neither are those who know how to fix them.

A character with this Edge adds +2 to rolls involving fixing or understanding machinery.

Posse 55

Makin' Heroes

Purty 1

They say an ugly fellow can stop a bullet with his face. A good-looking one might not get shot at in the first place.

A *purty* character may add +2 to most *persuasion* rolls or other situations where his physique might come into play.

Rank 1/2/3

Soldiers are found all over the frontier. Most women like a man in uniform, and a little rank demands a certain amount of authority. The downside is that soldiers are the first people the folks come running to when something strange happens.

Individuals who belong to a military outfit spend most of their time in the service of their country and so aren't normally part of a *Deadlands* posse. Occasionally, however, military personnel are detailed to special assignments and given weeks or even months to conduct their investigations.

If this is the case, a character can buy military rank as an Edge. These characters are usually "operatives" for the military and so should only rarely reveal their rank. Even then, they should use their power sparingly—hence the low cost.

Rank Table

Rank	Cost
1	Enlisted man (Private, Corporal, Sergeant)
2	Officer (Lieutenant, Captain, Major)
3	High ranking officer (Colonel, General)

Renown 1/3/5

A reputation's a funny thing. The bigger it gets, the more most folks stay out of your way. But the fellows that don't get out of the way are most likely gunning for you.

Recognizing a famous character by looks alone is a Fair task for most; a Foolproof task for those within the character's field, home town, etc.

Renown Table

Cost	Reputation
1	Well-known among a small group of people (town, US Marshals, sportsmen).
3	Well-known among a large group of people (county, minor celebrity).
5	Known everywhere (major celebrity, war hero).

Sense of Direction 1

You can usually tell which direction is North—or South if you're a Reb.

To use this Edge, the character must make a Fair (5) *Cognition* roll. With a Hard (9) *Smarts* roll, your character will also know about what time it is.

Posse 56

Makin' Heroes

"The Stare" 1

There's something in your stare that makes others nervous. When your eye starts twitching, someone's about to get carried to Boot Hill.

A character with *"the stare"* may add +2 to his *overawe* attacks, as long as the intended victim is close enough to look into his steely gaze.

Thick-Skinned 3

Whether he's tough-as-nails or just plain dumb, a cowboy who can handle a little pain is a hombre that's hard to beat. Tinhorns cry over a splinter. Thick-skinned gunslingers blaze away with both guns even when they taste their own blood.

Thick-skinned characters may ignore one level of penalty modifiers per wounded area. Thus a character with light wounds in both arms would have no negative modifiers (see Chapter Five).

Tough as Nails 1-5

Some folks keel over in a stiff wind, but you chew razor blades for breakfast. When you're *tough as nails*, you've got some serious raw guts, force of will, and determination. A real hero's got to persevere no matter how hard things get.

Every level of *tough as nails* adds +2 to your character's Wind. This means she can tough out losing blood and getting banged around when others are curling up in a like babies with their thumbs in their mouths.

Two-Fisted 3

A rare few are just as good with their left hand as they are their right. These folks make deadly gunfighters and better cheats.

A *two-fisted* character ignores the –4 penalty for using his off hand.

"The Voice" 1

You've got *"the voice."* Whether it's the seductive lilt of a singing stage girl or the gravely drawl of the gunslinger, whatever comes out of your mouth commands attention.

You can choose what kind of *voice* your character has. A *soothing voice* adds +2 to persuasion rolls made in calm, seductive or otherwise peaceful situations. A *threatening voice* adds +2 to *overawe* rolls. A *grating voice* adds +2 to *ridicule* rolls. You can buy multiple *voices* as well.

Six: Background

Now it's time to add the "meat" to your hero's skeleton. You need to answer some basic questions about where he's been, where he's going, and what he wants out of life. There's room for the answers to these questions on the back of your character sheet in the "Background" box. Take some time to fill it in now.

If you can't think of all the answers right away, go ahead and play a session or two. Once you've gotten a feel for your hero's style, you can come back and fill in whatever you've left out.

Seven: Gear

Characters start with $250 and the clothes on their back. Everything else needs to be purchased. A complete list of guns, horses, and other gear can be found in Chapter 4,

Makin' Heroes

Ronan Lynch

So let's make a character together. The first thing we need is a concept. Let's try the "good bad-man" character.

Step One

Our hombre's name is Ronan Lynch. He was a Lieutenant in the War, during which time he learned he had nerves of steel. Lesser men ran while he stood his ground, firing his six-guns until the barrels grew hot.

After his discharge, Ronan headed west. He's looking for something better than killing, but it seems his reputation always precedes him. Every cowtown he visits wants him to be their sheriff or clean up the local trouble.

Step Two

Now we need to draw 12 cards for Ronan's Traits. Here are the cards we draw and the dice they give us:

Ronan's Cards

Card	Coordination/Trait
Joker	
King of Hearts	3d10
Queen of Spades	4d10
Jack of Spades	4d8
Ten of Hearts	3d8
Ten of Diamonds	2d8
Eight of Hearts	2d6
Seven of Clubs	1d6
Six of Hearts	2d6
Five of Diamonds	3d6
Four of Clubs	1d6
Three of Clubs	1d4

We ditch the Three and Four of Clubs, since they only give us 1d6 each. For our Joker, we draw another card for Coordination and get a Diamond, for a final total of 2d12.

Now we need to assign Ronan's Traits. The most important Traits for a gunfighter are *Quickness* and *Deftness*. The former gets the 2d12 and the latter gets 4d10. Look on the character sheet to see where we put the rest of his Traits.

A Mysterious Past

The Marshal, looking eagerly over our shoulder, sees us draw the Joker, meaning Ronan has a "mysterious past." He consults his secret, don't-look-under-pain-of-death, classified table in his section. He wouldn't normally tell us what our mysterious past is, but since this is an example character, he grins and reveals that Ronan is *haunted* by a friendly spirit.

The Marshal comes up with a neat idea and asks us if it fits our character concept. The idea is that one of Ronan's old buddies got in a fight with him over a girl a few years back. One night, the two were drinking and Ronan's friend, Tom McCullen, drew his gun. Ronan put him down before he could even think about it.

Now Tom's ghost appears every now and then to warn Ronan of danger. Tom knows his death was his own fault. His spirit is just trying to make up for pulling a gun on his best friend and causing him such grief.

Ronan was unnerved by the spirit at first, but now he just thinks he's gone loco since no one else can see or hear it. Still, the spirit has saved his life on several occasions.

We think the Marshal's idea is way cool. Like we're going to argue about something that might warn us of danger!

Makin' Heroes

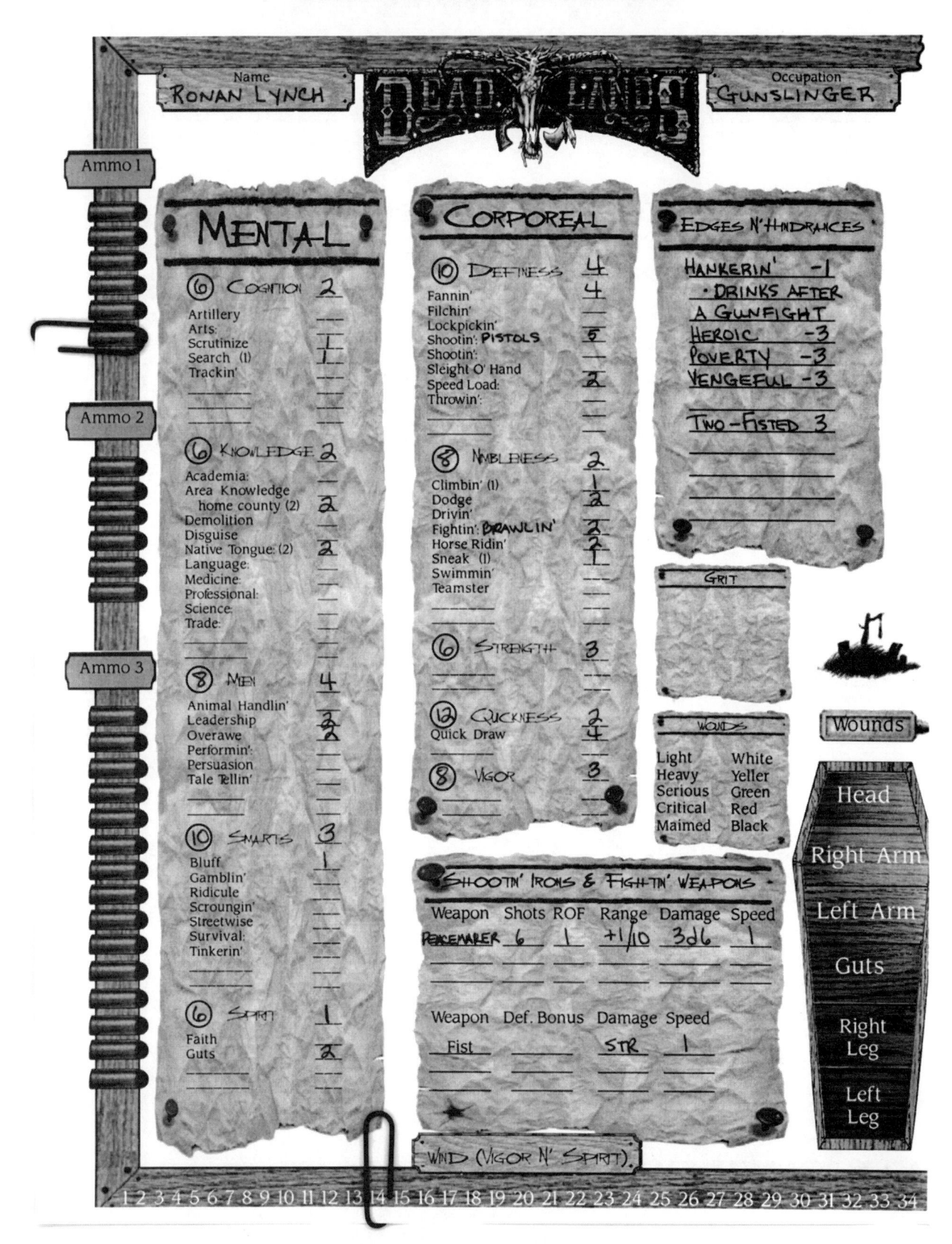

Name: Ronan Lynch
Occupation: Gunslinger

DEAD LANDS

MENTAL

(6) Cognition 2
- Artillery: ___
- Arts: ___
- Scrutinize: ___
- Search (1): 1
- Trackin': ___

(6) Knowledge 2
- Academia: ___
- Area Knowledge home county (2): 2
- Demolition: ___
- Disguise: ___
- Native Tongue: (2) 2
- Language: ___
- Medicine: ___
- Professional: ___
- Science: ___
- Trade: ___

(8) Mien 4
- Animal Handlin': ___
- Leadership: 3
- Overawe: 2
- Performin': ___
- Persuasion: ___
- Tale Tellin': ___

(10) Smarts 3
- Bluff: 1
- Gamblin': ___
- Ridicule: ___
- Scroungin': ___
- Streetwise: ___
- Survival: ___
- Tinkerin': ___

(6) Spirit 1
- Faith: ___
- Guts: 2

CORPOREAL

(10) Deftness 4
- Fannin': 4
- Filchin': ___
- Lockpickin': ___
- Shootin': Pistols 5
- Shootin': ___
- Sleight O' Hand: ___
- Speed Load: 2
- Throwin': ___

(8) Nimbleness 2
- Climbin' (1): 2
- Dodge: 2
- Drivin': ___
- Fightin': Brawlin' 2
- Horse Ridin': 2
- Sneak (1): 1
- Swimmin': ___
- Teamster: ___

(6) Strength 3

(12) Quickness 2
- Quick Draw: 4

(8) Vigor 3

EDGES N' HINDRANCES

- Hankerin' -1
  - Drinks after a gunfight
- Heroic -3
- Poverty -3
- Vengeful -3

- Two-Fisted 3

GRIT

WOUNDS

Light — White
Heavy — Yeller
Serious — Green
Critical — Red
Maimed — Black

SHOOTIN' IRONS & FIGHTIN' WEAPONS

Weapon	Shots	ROF	Range	Damage	Speed
Peacemaker	6	1	+1/10	3d6	1

Weapon	Def. Bonus	Damage	Speed
Fist		STR	1

Wounds: Head, Right Arm, Left Arm, Guts, Right Leg, Left Leg

WIND (VIGOR N' SPIRIT)
1 2 3 4 5 6 7 8 9 10 11 12 13 14 15 16 17 18 19 20 21 22 23 24 25 26 27 28 29 30 31 32 33 34

Posse: 59

Makin' Heroes

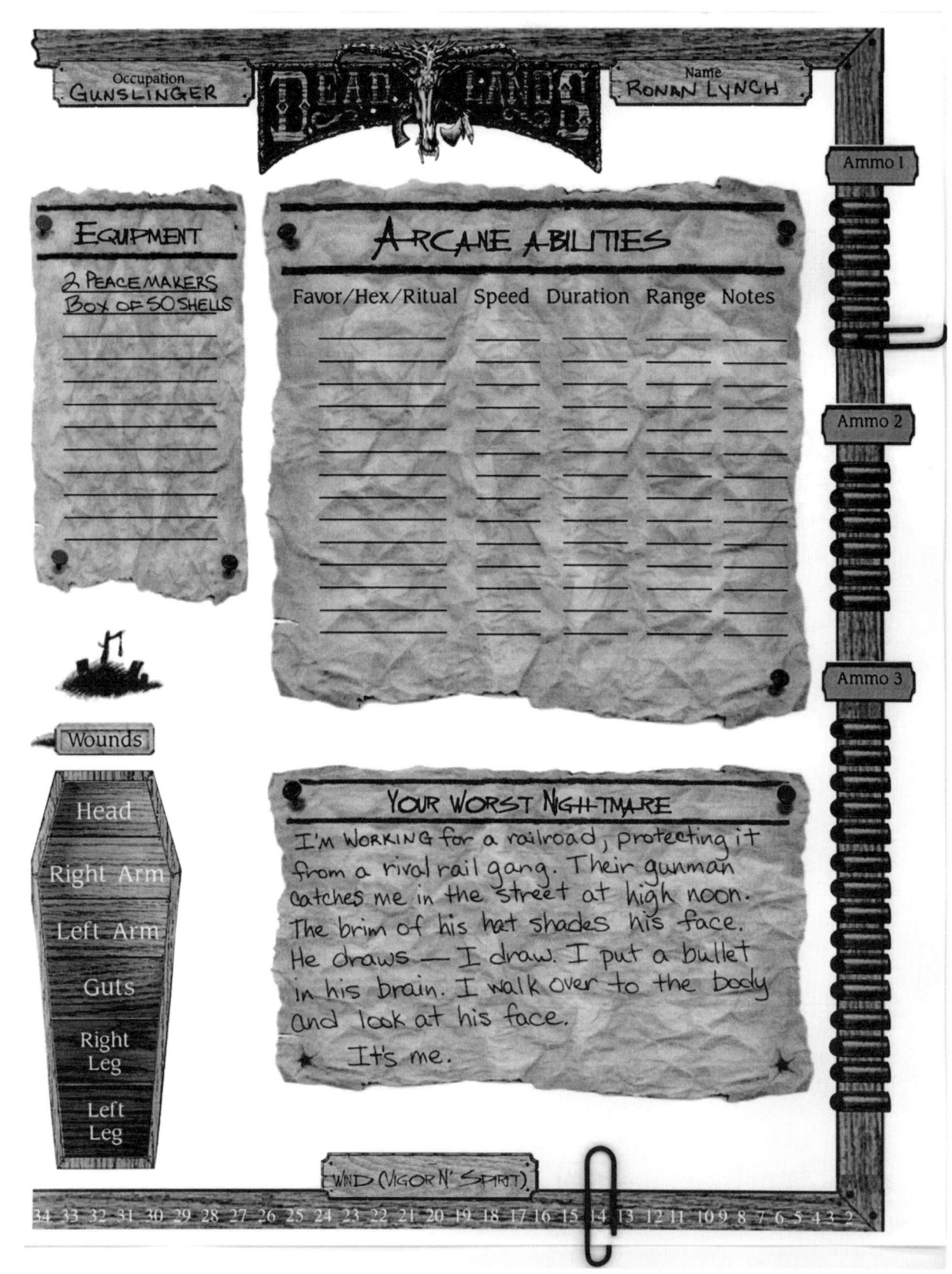

DEADLANDS

Occupation: Gunslinger
Name: Ronan Lynch

Equipment
- 2 Peacemakers
- Box of 50 shells

Arcane Abilities

Favor/Hex/Ritual	Speed	Duration	Range	Notes

Ammo 1

Ammo 2

Ammo 3

Wounds
- Head
- Right Arm
- Left Arm
- Guts
- Right Leg
- Left Leg

Your Worst Nightmare

I'm working for a railroad, protecting it from a rival rail gang. Their gunman catches me in the street at high noon. The brim of his hat shades his face. He draws — I draw. I put a bullet in his brain. I walk over to the body and look at his face.

  It's me.

Wind (Vigor n' Spirit): 34 33 32 31 30 29 28 27 26 25 24 23 22 21 20 19 18 17 16 15 14 13 12 11 10 9 8 7 6 5 4 3 2

Posse: 60

Makin' Heroes

Step Three

A character gets his *Cognition, Knowledge,* and *Smarts* in Aptitude points. For Ronan, this is 22.

He gets 1 level in *climbin', search,* and *sneak* for free. He gets 2 levels in his native tongue and area knowledge as well. Ronan speaks English, and he spent most of his life somewhere in Kansas before the war. We don't have to know the county. We should just have some rough idea of where Ronan grew up.

Ronan has to pay for the rest of his Aptitudes. His first concern as a gunfighter is his *shootin': pistol* Aptitude. We use 5 of our Aptitude points to bring this up to the starting maximum of 5. Ronan also wants a good *quick draw* skill, and raises it to level 4.

The rest of Ronan's points are spent as you see on the character sheet.

Step Four

Now it's time for Hindrances. We need the points since Ronan has already spent 7 more points than he had. Plus, the Marshal awards Fate Chips for roleplaying, and Hindrances are a great way of helping us flesh out Ronan's personality.

Let's start with *heroic* for -3 points. Ronan isn't a goody two-shoes, but he can't turn down a damsel in distress. He won't walk too far away from a town in need before he reluctantly comes back either.

Ronan has a hard time hanging on to his cash. He spends it like water whenever he comes into a bounty or cash from a job. This gives us 2 more Hindrances, -3 point for *poverty* and a -1 point *hankerin'* for a good stiff drink after a gunfight.

We can take up to -3 more points in Hindrances. Looking over the list, we see one that fits Ronan perfectly—*vengeful.* No one crosses this gunslinger and gets away with it.

Step Five

Ronan was 7 points over his allotted points before we took -10 points in Hindrances. Now we've got 3 points to buy some Edges if we'd like.

We'd like. Ronan uses 2 Peacemakers. He needs the 3-point *two-fisted* Edge to avoid off-hand penalties in combat.

Step Six

We're out of points and our character is almost complete. We just need to fill in a few details to round out Ronan's past. Look on the back of his sheet if you're curious. His nightmare says it all.

Step Seven

Our last task is to buy Ronan's gear. Unfortunately, because Ronan has the *poverty* Hindrance, we only have $50 to spend on equipment. Ronan uses 2 Peacemakers. These costs $15 each, and we have to spend another $3 on a box of 50 shells. $33 of our $50 is already gone.

With only $17 in his pocket, Ronan sets out into the Weird West.

Wish him luck. He's going to need it.

GEAR

Chapter Four: Gear

As was mentioned in the last chapter, each character has $250 to start out with to purchase gear with. If you took the *dinero* Edge, you've got a whole lot more than that to play with.

There's all sorts of other things for sale in the Weird West than could possibly be listed in this book, but what follows below should be enough to get you started. If a character wants to buy something not on the list, it's up to the Marshal to set a reasonable price.

Some of the lists below have all sorts of statistics for weapons. If this is your first time through the book, you may not understand them all right now. All becomes clear in Chapter Five.

El Cheapo Gear

Most anything in the equipment tables can be bought at cheaper than normal prices. Common items such as clothes are ratty and torn, hats are crumpled, and playing cards are bent and can't be used anywhere except by the campfire. The effects of these kinds of items are usually social and situational.

Cheap guns, saddles, and the like can cause more life-threatening problems. These items have a malfunction number just like Gatling guns and mad scientist's gizmos. For 75% of the normal price, these items have a malfunction number of 19. If your character buys his gear half off, the malfunction number is 18.

Whenever your character makes a Trait or Aptitude roll that somehow relies on the equipment (like a *horse ridin'* roll if your cowpoke has a cheap saddle), roll a d20 as well. If the d20 is higher than the malfunction number, something's gone wrong. The Marshal will let you know the consequences of your extreme thriftiness.

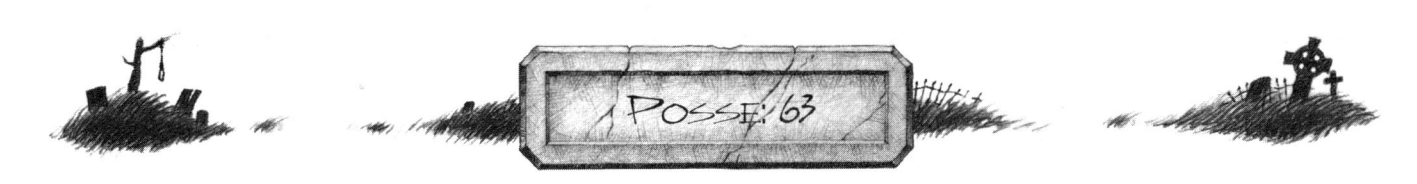

Gear

Horses

Horses come in all colors and qualities. The prices for them vary on the time of year, the location, and the demand, but an average horse sells for $150.

Animal Traits are relative, so don't worry about your mount outsmarting your gunslinger. A horse with a 1d6 *Knowledge* knows a few commands and can figure out a new rider's instructions. Average horses have the following statistics:

Traits and Aptitudes
Deftness 1d4
Nimbleness 2d12
Fightin': brawlin' 1
Swimmin' 4
Quickness 1d8
Strength 2d10
Vigor 2d10
Cognition 2d6
Knowledge 1d6
Mien 1d6
Overawe 1
Smarts 1d6
Spirit 1d4
Guts 2
Size: 10
Pace: 20

Exceptional Horses

Exceptional horses can be found on occasion. If a cowpoke makes an Onerous (7) *Cognition/horse ridin'* roll, she can tell if a horse has an exceptional quality or not. If the seller knows his horseflesh, he usually charges an extra $150 for such an unusual animal. Below are a few qualities that might be found among common stock:

Brave: The horse has a *Spirit* of 2d8 and a 4 in *guts*.

Fast: The horse has a pace of 24.

Smart: The animal responds exceptionally well to its master's commands. The horse's owner can add +2 to her *horse ridin'* rolls.

Strong: The horse has 3d12 *Strength*.

Surly: The horse is ill-tempered to those he isn't used to. He kicks and bites with only a little provocation.

Tough: The horse has 2d12 *Vigor*.

GEAR

Shootin' Irons

Weapon	Shots	Speed	ROF	Range Inc.	Damage	Price
Single-Action Pistols						
.44 Army Pistol	6	2	1	5	3d6	$12
.36 Navy Pistol	6	2	1	5	2d6	$10
Derringer .44	2	1	1	3	3d6	$8
Double-Action Pistols						
Peacemaker	6	1	1	5	3d6	$15
Rifles						
.45 Winchester '73	6	2	1	20	4d8	$25
Buffalo Gun (Sharp's Big 50)	1	2	1	20	4d10	$20
Muzzle loading Springfield .58	1	2	1	20	5d8	$8
Carbines						
Spencer Carbine	7	2	1	10	4d8	$15
Shotguns						
Single barrel	1	2	1	10	2d6+4d6	$25
Double barrel	2	2	1	10	2d6+4d6	$35
Scattergun	2	1	1	5	2d6+4d6	$35
Other Weapons						
Bow & arrow	1	2	1	10	STR+1d6	$3
Thrown knife	1	1	1	3	STR+1d	$3

Weapon	Speed	Burst Increment	Damage
Dynamite	2	10	3d20
Nitro	1	10	3d20

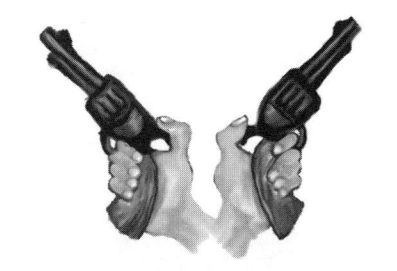

Weapon	Speed	ROF	Range Increment	Reliabillity	Damage
Gatling Gun	1	3	20	19	3d8

Posse: 65

GEAR

NOTES

Below are a few notes on some of the items your hombre might want to carry into the Weird West.

Explosives

Anytime a character carrying dynamite is hit by a bullet, hand-to-hand weapon, or other physical force in an area where he is carrying dynamite, roll a d6. On a 1, the dynamite is hit and detonates. Boom.

Nitro is a very unstable liquid. The slightest impact might set it off. Nitro can be set off by stray hits just like dynamite. In addition, any time a character carrying nitro tumbles or takes a jolt of some sort, roll a 1d6. On a 1-3, it detonates. Kaboom! If a character ever takes a big fall, the nitro automatically explodes.

Fast-Draw Holsters

Fast-draw holsters add +2 to *quick draw* rolls. No gunfighter would be caught dead without one. Unless, of course, she's already been on the wrong side of a headstone.

Gatling Guns

Gatling guns are normally not available for direct sale to civilians. Unless your character has some special arrangement with the local authorities, you'll have to bribe someone for a Gatling at double the normal price of $1500.

Ammunition

Ammo	Price
.36 pistol ammo (box of 50)	$2
.44 pistol ammo (box of 50)	$3
.45 pistol ammo (box of 50)	$3
.45 rifle ammo (box of 50)	$4
.50 rifle ammo (box of 50)	$5
Powder and .58 shot (20)	$1
Shotgun shells (box of 20)	$2
Arrows (20)	$2

Hand to Hand Weapons

Weapon	Defensive Bonus	Speed	Damage	Cost
Fist	-	1	STR	-
Brass Knuckles	-	1	STR+1d4	$1
Small club (pistol butt, bottle, chair)	-	1	STR+1d4	-
Large club (rifle butt)	+1	2	STR+1d6	-
Knife	+1	1	STR+1d4	$2
Bowie Knife	+1	1	STR+1d6	$4
Tomahawk	-	1	STR+2d6	$3
Rapier	+2	1	STR+2d6	$10
Saber	+2	1	STR+2d8	$15
Whip	+1	2	STR	$10
Lariat	-	2	-	$4

Gear

Everyday Gear

Item	Cost	Item	Cost	Item	Cost
Clothes		*Good stuff*		Tobacco, smoking	$0.50
Dress Shirt/blouse	$3	Shot	$0.25	*Watch*	
Work Shirt/blouse	$1	Bottle	$5	Standard	$2.50
Suit/fancy dress	$15	Beer (glass)	$0.05	Gold	$10
Chaps	$4	**General Equipment**		**Services**	
Boots	$8	Ax	$2	Bath	$1
Shoes	$2	Backpack	$2	Burial	$5
Trousers/skirt	$2	Barbed wire (per yard)	$0.05	Photo	$2
Long johns	$2	Bed roll	$4	*Doctor visit*	
Silk stockings	$1	Camera	$3	Office	$3
Duster	$10	Photo plate	$1	House Call	$5
Winter coat	$15	Canteen	$1	*Room (per day)*	
Spectacles	$5	Cigar	$.05	Boarding house	$1.50
Hats		Detonator, plunger	$10	Low class hotel	$1
Derby	$1.50	Wire (50')	$2.50	High class hotel	$2
Stetson	$5	Drill	$2	Shave and a haircut	$.025
Fedora	$3	File	$0.25	Telegram (per word)	$0.05
Sombrero	$3.50	Guitar	$8	**Explosives**	
Bonnet	$2	Hammer	$0.50	Nitro (per pint)	$2.50
Food & Drink		Handcuffs	$3.50	Dynamite (per stick)	$3
Good Restaurant		Harmonica	$0.50	Blasting cap	$1
Breakfast	$0.50	Hatchet	$1	Fuse (per foot)	$0.05
Lunch	$0.25	Lantern	$2.50	**Transportation**	
Dinner	$1	Lantern oil (per gallon)	$0.10	Horse	$150
Cheap Restaurant		Iron skillet	$0.50	Mule	$50
Any meal	$0.25	Matches (box of 100)	$0.50	Saddle	$25
Trail rations (per day)	$.50	Mess kit	$2	Saddle bags	$5
Coffee (per pound)	$.25	Pick	$2	Conestoga wagon	$200
Bacon (per pound)	$0.15	Pipe	$2	Buckboard	$75
Liquor		Playing cards	$0.25	Buggy/cab	$200
Cheap stuff		Rope (50')	$5	Stagecoach (per mile)	$.10
Shot	$0.10	Shovel	$1.50	Train ticket (per mile)	$.05
Bottle	$2	Tobacco, chewing (tin)	$0.50	Riverboat (per mile)	$.05

Posse 67

Archetypes

Archetypes

Buffalo Girl

Traits and Aptitudes

Deftness 4d10
Shootin': rifle 4
Nimbleness 2d12
Climbin' 1
Fightin': whip 3
Horse ridin' 2
Sneak 1
Quickness 2d10
Strength 2d6
Vigor 4d6
Cognition 1d8
Search 1
Scrutinize 2
Trackin' 3
Knowledge 1d6
Area knowledge 2
Native tongue 2
Language: Indian sign language 2
Mien 3d8
Animal wranglin': bronco bustin' 2
Persuasion 3
Smarts 2d6
Gamblin' 2
Ridicule 2
Survival: plains 1
Spirit 3d6
Guts 2
Edges:
Purty 1
Brave 2
Hindrances:
Big Britches -3
Curious -3
Heroic -3
Intolerance -1: Feminine women.
Gear: Winchester '73, box of 50 shells, whip, horse, $61

Personality

Yee-hah! I'm the wildest thing this side o' the Pecos. I'm a whip-crackin', butt-kickin', pistol-packin' gal o' the plains.

I've seen some ornery lookin' critters out here in the West, and I aim to rope me a few. Maybe I'll catch one and sell it to a rodeo or one o' them newfangled zoos. Or maybe I'll just stuff the durn varmint and mount it on my wall.

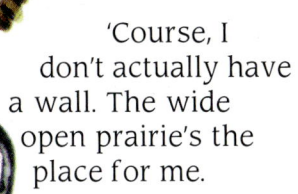

'Course, I don't actually have a wall. The wide open prairie's the place for me.

Quote: "Yee-hah! Outta' my way, boys!"

Posse: 69

Archetypes

Coyote Brave

Traits and Aptitudes

Deftness 1d8
Shootin': rifle 2
Throwin': tomahawk 2
Nimbleness 4d10
Climbin' 1
Fightin': tomahawk 4
Horse ridin': 2
Sneak 3
Swimmin' 1
Quickness 2d10
Strength 2d12
Vigor 3d8
Cognition 4d6
Search 2
Trackin' 4
Knowledge 3d6
Area knowledge 2
Native tongue 2
Language: English 1
Ritual: pledge 1
Mien 2d6
Smarts 1d6
Survival: plains 2
Spirit 3d6
Faith 2
Guts 2
Edges:
Two-fisted 3
Hindrances:
Ferner -3
Poverty -3
Stubborn -2
Superstitious -2
Favor:
Strength of the bear
Gear: 2 tomahawks, Winchester '73, box of 50 shells, horse, $65 in white man's cash

Personality

Yes, the spirits are powerful, but they do not always answer my calls. Bullets always listen. And they answer with thunder.

My brothers and sisters believe your "Civil War" is an opportunity for us to strike back and reclaim our lands. I am not so sure.

My elders say that a greater war rages in the Hunting Grounds. Our true enemies are there. We must unite and fight these evil spirits. Will you join me in my hunt?

Quote: "It's time to bury the hatchet. But let's wait until it looks the other way."

Posse

Archetypes

Gunslinger

Traits and Aptitudes

Deftness 3d10
Shootin': pistol 4
Shootin': rifle 2
Speed load: pistol 2
Nimbleness 1d8
Climbin' 1
Dodge 3
Fightin': brawlin' 2
Horse ridin' 3
Sneak 1
Quickness 2d12
Quick draw 2
Strength 2d6
Vigor 2d6
Cognition 2d8
Search 1
Knowledge 1d6
Area knowledge 2
Native tongue
Mien 1d10
Overawe 3
Smarts 2d6
Spirit 1d8
Guts 2
Edges:
Keen 3
Renown 1
Hindrances:
Enemy -1: Someone's always out to prove they're faster than you.
Heroic -3
Vengeful -3
Gear: Army pistol, Winchester '73, box of 50 pistols shells, box of 50 rifle shells, horse, $56

Personality

I was brought here because I'm the best. You draw that pistol and I'll show you what I mean.

You think you're bad news? I've seen things that would make you wet your pants. Now put that gun away, kid. And do it real slow like. The only live gunslingers are jumpy gunslingers.

Walk away. You don't have to prove anything. And I've got enough notches on my pistol already.

Quote: "Are you going to skin that smokewagon or whistle Dixie?"

Posse! 71

Archetypes

Huckster

Traits and Aptitudes

Deftness 2d8
Filchin' 2
Sleight of hand 2
Nimbleness 2d6
Climbin' 1
Quickness 3d6
Strength 2d6
Vigor 1d6
Cognition 2d8
Scrutinize 2
Search 3
Knowledge 2d10
Academia: occult 2
Area knowledge 2
Native tongue 2
Mien 2d6
Performing 2
Smarts 3d12
Bluff 3
Gamblin' 3
Ridicule 2
Streetwise 2
Spirit 1d8
Guts 2
Edges:
Arcane background 3
Gift of gab 1
Hindrances:
Bad luck -5
Curious -3
Habit -1: You shuffle cards constantly, a habit that annoys most but helps you hide your hexes.
Outlaw -1: Some say you're a shyster, you consider yourself a performer.
Hexes:
Phantom fingers 3
Shadow man 2
Soul blast 4
Gear: .45 Derringer, box of 50 shells, deck of cards, $238.75

Personality

Want to see a trick?
I know a few that will make your head spin. I've dazzled some of the best, from New Orleans to the City of Lost Angels.
You think that gunslinger's fast? He's moving in slow motion compared to me. Well, maybe not. But I can do things that make his Peacemakers look like pop guns.
And I know things, too. Things man was not meant to know. I've looked into the depths of Hell and invited the demons into my very soul. The price is steep, but the power is incredible. It's a gamble, but what's life without a little chance?

Quote: "Take a card. Any card."

Posse: 72

ARCHETYPES

MAD SCIENTIST

Traits and Aptitudes

Deftness 4d6
Shootin': flamethrower 4
Nimbleness 1d6
Climbin' 1
Drivin': steamwagon 4
Sneak 1
Teamster 2
Quickness 3d6
Strength 2d6
Vigor 3d6
Cognition 2d10
Scrutinize 1
Search 4
Knowledge 2d12
Area knowledge 2
Demolition 2
Native tongue 2
Science: engineering
Science: chemistry 3
Mien 1d8
Smarts 4d10
Scroungin' 3
Tinkerin' 4
Spirit 3d8
Guts 2
Edges:
Dinero 1
Mechanically inclined
Hindrances:
Bad eyes -1: You have to wear spectacles to read and see things up close.
Curious -3
Stubborn -2
Tinhorn -2
Gear:
Flamethrower, tool kit, doctor's bag full of strange chemicals, $75

Personality

Just a minute, please. Let me put out this fire. Hair is so combustible, you know?

Now what is it you wanted? A time travel device, perhaps? I've had a few ideas. Or how about a flamethrower? Too unstable? Then how about a Gatling pistol? No, that's too common. Any two bit tinkerer can build one of those.

Let me show you something special I've been working on.

Quote: "Don't touch that!"

Posse: 73

Archetypes

Muckraker

Traits and Aptitudes

Deftness 3d6
Shootin': pistol 2
Lockpickin' 2
Nimbleness 3d6
Climbin' 1
Sneak 2
Quickness 4d6
Strength 2d6
Vigor 1d6
Cognition 2d12
Scrutinize 4
Search 3
Knowledge 2d10
Area knowledge 2
Disguise 2
Native tongue 2
Professional: journalism 4
Mien 3d8
Persuasion 4
Tale tellin' 4
Smarts 4d10
Bluff 3
Streetwise 3
Spirit 1d8
Guts 2
Edges:
Friends in high places 2
More friends in high places 2
Even more friends in high places 2
Luck o' the Irish 3
Gift of gab 1
Hindrances:
Curious -3
Oath -5: It's your vow to tell the truth, no matter what.
Pacifist -3
Gear: Pad and paper, Navy pistol, box of 50 shells, $236

Personality

Tell me everything you can remember, but hurry. I've got to telegraph my story to the *Epitaph* by morning to make the Sunday edition. That pays the best, you know.

Do you mind if I take a picture of the thing you killed? Good. A picture really does say a thousand words, you know.

Now I've just got to get the Sheriff to help us get the rest of these things. Could you come with me? I've been bugging him all week and I'm afraid he's getting a little annoyed. He even threw me in jail last night. Said my yammering was "disturbing the peace."

Hah! Disturbing the peace, indeed. If he'd only wake up and realize what's going on, guys like me and you wouldn't have to do all the dirty work.

Quote: "Let's check it out. I smell a story!"

Archetypes

Pinkerton

Traits and Aptitudes

Deftness 3d8
Lockpickin' 2
Shootin': automatic 3
Nimbleness 2d10
Climbin' 1
Fightin': brawlin' 2
Sneak 3
Quickness 4d6
Strength 1d6
Vigor 2d6
Cognition 2d12
Scrutinize 3
Search 3
Knowledge 1d8
Academia: occult 3
Area knowledge 2
Native tongue 2
Professional: law 2
Mien 4d10
Leadership 2
Overawe 2
Persuasion 2
Smarts 3d6
Bluff 2
Streetwise 3
Spirit 2d6
Guts 2
Edges:
Belongings 3: Gatling pistol
Hindrances:
Enemy: -2: Texas Rangers hate Pinkertons.
Habit -3: You never tell your posse everything unless you absolutely have to.
Obligation -3: You are frequently called on to investigate unnatural phenomenon.
Tinhorn -2
Gear: Gatling pistol, derringer, pad and paper, 2 boxes of 50 shells, $235

Personality

Tell me all about the thing you say you saw. Not too loudly, please, the neighbors might hear.

Were you drinking when you saw the creature? Calm down, I'm just trying to get the facts straight, you understand.

Okay. If that's all you know, I'll round up my posse and take care of it. Sounds like a standard class 3 malevolent specter at work here. I've been classifying them myself, you know. I'm going to publish my findings someday. When this is all over.

Until then, mum's the word, got it? Word about something like this gets out and everyone begins to panic. Then we'd have a *real* situation on our hands.

Quote: "The truth *is* out there. And I'm going to keep it from you."

Posse: 75

Archetypes

Preacher

Traits and Aptitudes

Deftness 1d8
Shootin': pistol 2
Nimbleness 1d6
Climbin' 1
Fightin': club 3
Horse ridin' 2
Sneak 1
Quickness 3d6
Strength 3d6
Vigor 2d6
Cognition 4d6
Scrutinize 3
Search 2
Knowledge 3d8
Area knowledge 2
Native tongue 2
Language: Latin 2
Medicine: general 2
Professional: theology 3
Mien 4d10
Overawe 3
Persuasion 2
Smarts 2d10
Spirit 2d12
Faith 5
Guts 2
Edges:
Arcane background: blessed 3
Hindrances:
Heroic -3
Obligation -1: You must give a sermon to whatever audience you can find every Sunday.
Pacifist -3
Self-righteous -3
Rituals: Protection, Holy Roller, Inspiration, Lay on hands, Smite
Gear: Hickory club (STR+1d6 damage), Peacemaker, 50 shells, bible, cross, $227

Personality

There are devilish abominations loose in the world. We are being punished for our sins.

But fear not. Though we walk through the valley of the shadow of Death, my hickory rod and my Peacemaker will comfort thee. I am a vigilant crusader of the light.

Remember the power of the Good Book in these times of darkness. In it you will prayers and parables of salvation.

Should you encounter the forces of darkness, my child, first try a simple prayer and a stout piece of hickory.

If that doesn't work, try a load of blessed buckshot.

Quote: "Say yer prayers, varmint!"

ARCHETYPES

SALOON GAL

Traits and Aptitudes

Deftness 3d6
Lockpickin' 2
Shootin': pistol 2
Nimbleness 4d6
Climbin' 1
Sneak 4
Quickness 3d6
Strength 1d6
Vigor 2d6
Cognition 4d10
Scrutinize 3
Search 3
Knowledge 1d8
Area knowledge 2
Native tongue 2
Medicine: general 3
Mien 2d12
Persuasion 4
Smarts 4d10
Bluff 3
Gamblin' 3
Ridicule 2
Scroungin' 3
Streetwise 3
Spirit 3d8
Guts 2
Edges:
Light sleeper 1
Purty 1
The Voice 1: sweet & seductive
Hindrances:
Curious -3
Greedy -2
Poverty -3
Vengeful -3
Gear: Derringer .44, box of 50 shells, fancy dress, $24

Personality

Howdy, sugar. You wantta tango? It's a dime a dance. This is a high-class joint, you know.

Oh, so you want information. That'll cost you even more.

Yeah, I've been "out" with the Mayor a few times. Though I'd appreciate it if you didn't tell his wife.

Now that you mention it, he does act a little strange. Always carrying that black bag around. Was he with me the night of the murder? No. Not the whole night anyway. He's got a short fuse—if you know what I mean.

Hey, I've got an idea. Let's set a trap. If he's the culprit I'll get it out of him. I can get anything out of any man, sugar.

Don't worry about my safety. I've got a little something hidden up my garter for just such an emergency.

Quote: "Why don't you come up and see me sometime, big boy?"

POSSE

Archetypes

Sioux Shaman

Traits and Aptitudes

Deftness 2d6
Nimbleness 2d6
Quickness 1d8
Strength 1d6
Vigor 3d6
Climbin' 1
Fightin': spear 2
Sneak 3
Cognition 2d10
Knowledge 3d8
Mien 2d10
Smarts 3d8
Spirit 4d12
Academia: Occult 3
Area knowledge: Dakotas 2
Faith 4
Guts 3
Language: English 1
Medicine: General 3
Scrutinize 2
Search 2
Survival 2
Wind: 18
Rituals:
Dance 2
Fast 2
Paint 2
Pledge 4
Favors:
Wilderness Walk
Medicine
Shapeshift
Soar With Eagles
Edges:
Arcane Background 3
Hindrances:
Curious 3
Lame 3
Oath 4: You must follow the Old Ways.
Gear: Spear (3d6), medicine bag filled with roots and herbs for healing, $240

Personality

I don't speak often, so listen carefully to my words of wisdom. I have looked into the Hunting Grounds and talked with the spirits of nature, and I have made a discovery. The spirits are angry. They say we have forgotten the Old Ways. The simple ways. You young braves believe in bullets made by machines, not arrows made from living hands.

Now I must go into the white man's world and fight the abominations. Only then will you believe that the Old Ways are best.

Quote: "Hmm. That looks painful. I will help you, but only if you promise to remember the Old Ways."

Posse: 78

Archetypes

Soldier

Traits and Aptitudes

Deftness 2d12
Shootin': carbine 4
Speed load: carbine 2
Nimbleness 4d10
Climbin' 1
Dodge 2
Fightin': brawlin' 2
Horse ridin' 2
Sneak 1
Quickness 3d8
Strength 2d10
Vigor 1d8
Cognition 4d6
Artillery 2
Search 1
Trackin' 2
Knowledge 1d6
Area knowledge 2
Native tongue 2
Language: Indian sign 2
Mien 3d6
Leadership 2
Smarts 2d6
Survival: any 2
Spirit 3d6
Guts 2
Edges:
Brave 3
Rank 1
Hindrances:
Intolerance -2: You're not too fond of the soldiers on the other side of the Mason-Dixon line...
Enemy -2: ...and they're not fond of you either.
Loyal -3: You'd never desert the unit or your friends.
Obligation -3: Your duties are lighter than most, but you still have to report for duty for a few hours each day.
Gear: Spencer carbine, 30 rounds of ammunition, horse, $75 (saved pay)

Personality

The Captain told us to ride out and see what was killin' all those folks. Well, we found it. And filled it full of holes, just like we was told.

Only that didn't kill it. Now it's got us trapped here in the fort. No food, no water. We're even runnin' low on bullets, but I guess that don't matter anyway. Bullets didn't kill if the first time.

Don't ask what it looked like. You wouldn't believe me if I told you anyway.

I don't know why I stay here. It sure ain't the pay.

Quote: "What do you mean we *are* the cavalry?"

Posse: 79

Archetypes

Texas Ranger

Traits and Aptitudes

Deftness 2d12
Shootin': pistol 3
Shootin': rifle 2
Nimbleness 2d10
Climbin' 1
Dodge 2
Fightin': knife 3
Horse ridin' 2
Sneak 1
Quickness 4d10
Quick draw 2
Strength 3d8
Vigor 4d6
Cognition 1d8
Search 1
Trackin' 2
Knowledge 1d6
Area knowledge 2
Native tongue 2
Language: Mexican 1
Mien 3d6
Leadership 2
Overawe 2
Smarts 2d6
Survival: any 2
Spirit 3d6
Guts 2
Edges:
Law man 5
Hindrances:
Big britches -3: One riot, one Texas Ranger.
Enemy -2: Northeners don't like you.
Obligation -5: Hunt down the supernatural and shoot it or recruit it.
Gear: 2 Army pistols, box of 50 shells, horse, $73 in Confederate script

Personality

Hush up. That's crazy talk. There's no such thing as "jackalopes." This paw around my neck? It's a rabbit's foot. I don't care if you think it's too long. They grow 'em big in Texas, you know.

That carcass you gave me didn't have horns. It was just some dumb hare that got all tangled up in some old deer antlers. And if you don't quit arguing, I'm gonna let Jim Bowie settle my side o' the discussion for me.

I thought that'd shut you up. Now show me where you *didn't* see Aunt Minnie crawl up outta' her grave. I got some carvin' to do.

Quote: "You shouldn'ta done that, varmint. You're messin' with the pride o' Texas."

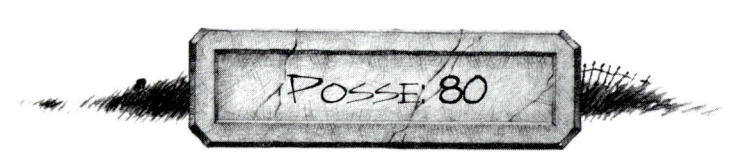

Posse: 80

Archetypes

Using the Archetypes

All of the previous archetypes have been designed for you to photocopy and use right out of the book. Each character has his gear, leftover cash, Edges, and Hindrances all picked out for you.

You may still want to write your character down on a character sheet. That way you can keep track of wounds, Wind, and ammunition a little easier.

You can swap Traits and Aptitudes around if you want, just make sure the numbers add up when you're done. You can also pick out new Edges and Hindrances that better suit your play style.

All of the archetypes are balanced with the same numbers and types of dice. You might do a little better if you make your own character from scratch. Use the archetypes for your first foray into the Weird West, or if you want to run a quick "pickup" game.

If you plan on playing a campaign—we call them "sagas"—you'll probably want to make your own character from scratch.

If your local copy center gives you grief over copying out of your book, show them this: we give you permission to photocopy the archetypes, character sheets, and "mad scientist's blueprint."

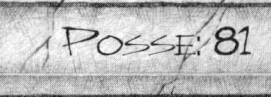

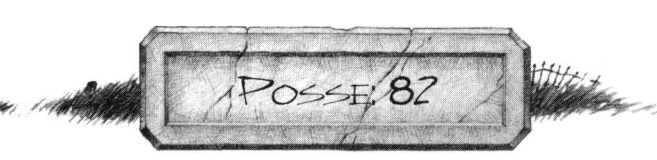

COMBAT

Chapter Five: Blowin' Things All to Hell

Now you've got your character and you know how to make Trait and Aptitude checks. If you're like most gamers, you're wondering how to blow things all to Hell and back. Okay, we'll show you.

When a firefight or a brawl erupts, the Marshal breaks the game down into "rounds" of about 5 seconds each. Now each side (the players and the Marshal) needs an Action Deck. Using the Action Deck lets us have all the action and tension of a gunfight in the Weird West without getting bogged down with lots of complicated rules. Read on and we'll show you how.

The Action Deck

You've heard the expression "the quick and the dead" before. There's a lot of truth to it. It doesn't really matter how good a shot you are if you're slower than a three-legged tortoise on a cold day.

Once the Marshal says the game is in rounds, you need to make a *Quickness* roll and compare it to a TN of Fair (5). You get to draw 1 card from the Action Deck plus 1 for every success and raise. On a botch you get no cards this round, though you might still use a card from up your sleeve (see page 85.)

If your character has taken any wounds, subtract the penalty from your *Quickness* total.

If an Action Deck runs out, reshuffle it immediately. If someone draws a Black Joker, finish the round, then reshuffle.

Surprise

Most folks don't just whip out their pistols and start firing when some blood-simple varmint comes jumping out of the bushes at them. They usually just stand there with their mouths open until their brain kicks in and tells them they're in deep caa-caa.

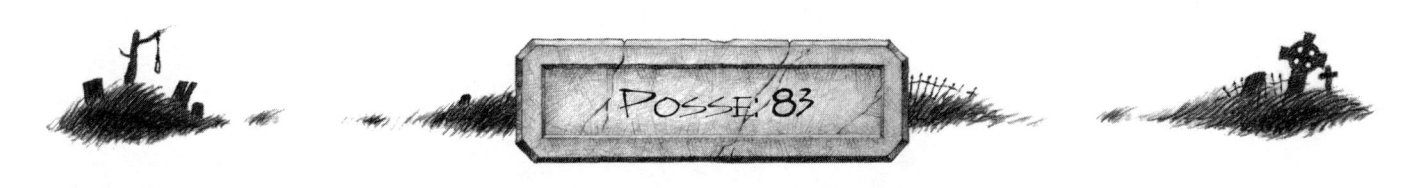

Combat

Anytime there's a good chance your character might be surprised, the Marshal is going to ask you to make a *Cognition* check. The difficulty is Fair (5) if your character's expecting some sort of danger and Incredible (11) if she's not.

If you don't make the roll, you don't get any cards, and your character can't act that round. She can act normally in the next round as long as she makes a Fair (5) *guts* check.

Actions

Once everyone has their cards, the Marshal starts counting down from an Ace. If you have an Ace, you can take one action. If not, you have to wait until one of your cards is called to take an action. When one of your cards is called, flip it over and tell the Marshal what your character is trying to do.

Suits

Compare suits to break ties with other characters who have the same cards. The ranking of suits is:

Suit Rank Table

Suit	Rank
Spades	First
Hearts	Second
Diamonds	Third
Clubs	Fourth

Since the Marshal has his own Action Deck, it's possible for each side to have an action on the same card and suit. If so, these actions are simultaneous.

Speed

Your hombre can only do so much during a single action. How much he can do depends on how fast his weapon or action is. Normal actions such as moving, drawing a weapon, or performing a test of wills have a "speed" score of 1. The speed score tells you the number of cards it takes to resolve an action. How many cards you have depends on your *Quickness* roll (see the previous page.)

Each action is roughly 5 seconds long. An action represents not only a character's raw *Quickness*, but also the chance and ability to find an opportunity for an attack.

Weapons, hexes, rituals, and favors also have a speed score. If the speed score is 1 and the character is using a weapon, he can fire up to its "rate of fire" once per card.

A pistol, for example, has a speed of 1, while rifles have a speed of 2. Hexes, rituals, and favors with a speed of 1 can also be resolved on a single Action Card.

A speed score of 2 or higher for weapons, hexes, rituals, or favors means that the character's action is a little slower. He needs to spend and hold Action Cards to prepare,

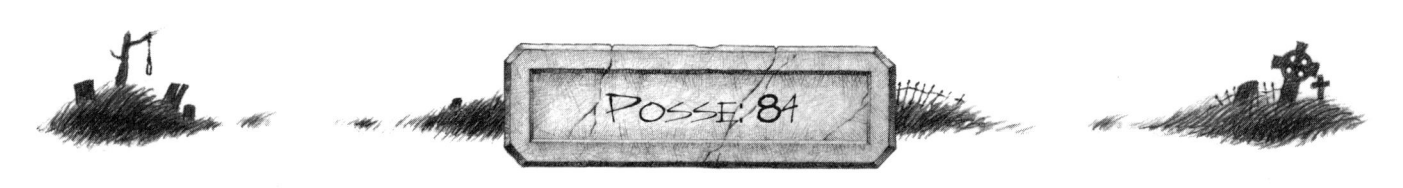

Combat

aim, or otherwise get ready for his attack. Lay these cards aside to help you keep count. They're spent whenever they come up and can't be reused. Once you've spent enough of these to prepare your character's action, you can use any remaining card to resolve it.

If the deck gets shuffled while you're preparing an action, make sure any cards you're holding to prepare an action get shuffled back in the Action Deck. Just make sure to keep count of how many actions you've already spent preparing. A good way to do this is with a d6 or any other easy-to-read die.

Simple & Complex Actions

A character can perform a simple action in coordination with any rolled actions. A simple action is one that doesn't require much concentration such as talking, resisting a test of wills, or moving. A more complex action such as drawing a weapon or starting a test of wills requires an Action Card.

Below are a few examples of what are considered simple and complex actions:

Action Complexity Table

Type	Actions
Simple	Talking, moving, making a stun check, resisting a hex, ritual, favor or test of wills
Complex	Drawing a new weapon, initiating a test of wills, reloading a single pistol, rifle, or shotgun round, any kind of movement that requires an Aptitude roll

Cheatin'

Sometimes you might want to wait until some hombre does something before you take your action. Say you know some slavering beastie is about to come through a door, and you want to wait and blast a hole in it when it comes crashing through.

The way to do this is by "cheating" and keeping a single card "up your sleeve." When the card you want to put up your sleeve would normally be played, tell the Marshal you're going to put it up your sleeve instead and place it face down under your Fate Chips. You can only ever have one card up your sleeve.

Anytime you want to play the "cheat" card afterward, including earlier than normal in the next round, whip it out, show it to the Marshal, take your action, and discard it.

If you want to interrupt someone else's action with a cheat card, like when the beastie comes crashing through the door, you have to beat it in an opposed *Quickness* match. The winner gets to resolve his action first. This way you're never guaranteed to beat someone just because you've got a cheat card.

You can hold your cheat card over several rounds if you like. The only time you have to ditch it is when the fight is over, you draw a Black Joker (see below), or an opponent forces you to discard through a test of wills.

Jokers

Jokers can never be hidden up your sleeve., and as you might have guessed, drawing one also has special effects.

The Red Joker allows your character to go at any time during the round without having to make a second *Quickness* check to interrupt another character's action. In a nutshell, you can always go first.

The Black Joker is bad news. It means your character hesitates for some reason. Maybe he's starting to feel his wounds or he's distracted by the bad guys. Whatever the reason, the Joker doesn't count as an action and you have to discard your highest other action card. If you have a card up your sleeve, it's considered the highest and is discarded.

There's another side effect to drawing a Black Joker. Your side's Action Deck must be reshuffled at the end of the current round.

Combat

Skedaddlin'

You often need to know how far your character can move in a standard combat round. Well, we've got it all figured out for you. The number of yards a character, critter, or vehicle can move each round is called its "pace."

The pace of characters and most critters is its *Nimbleness*. A vehicle's pace is listed in its statistics.

Both creatures and vehicles move a proportion of their pace every action. You'll have to divide the total pace by the number of actions to figure out what the maximum movement is per action.

Don't try to figure fractions, just break up the movement as evenly as possible. If a character can move 20 yards in a round and draws 3 cards, he can move 7 yards on one action, 7 on the next, and 6 on the last, or any other order he chooses.

You can't get extra movement by playing a cheat card. If you have actions left in the round when you play a cheat card, just split the move of your remaining actions with the one from your cheat card. If you have no actions left when you play a cheat card, your character can't move during that action.

Running

A character, critter, or vehicle can double its move during an action by running. Running incurs a -4 penalty to a character or creature's actions. Riders in "running" vehicles or on animals suffer the penalty as well. The faster you go, the bumpier the ride.

Pickin' Up the Pace

If you really need to skedaddle, your character can "pick up the pace." Picking up the pace means your character goes all out and runs, swims, climbs, or rides as fast as she possibly can. The cost is a little extra fatigue.

Whenever you want your character to pick up the pace, check the Gitalong Table and roll the die type listed under the "Pick Up Rate." Add that many yards to the character's running movement for the action. The number listed under "Wind" is the amount of Wind the cowpoke takes for pushing himself so hard.

A rider can make horses or other mounts pick up the pace by making a Fair (5) *horse ridin'* or *teamster* roll. In this case, the animals take the Wind.

Picking up the pace on a vehicle requires a Fair (5) *drivin'* roll. Horseless vehicles and their drivers don't take Wind for this, but they do run the risk of a malfunction (as explained in Chapter Eight).

You can't "run" (double your movement) when swimming or climbing, by the way, and no matter what your *climbin'* or *swimmin'* is, you can't normally move faster than the maximum listed on the Gitalong Table. You can still pick up the pace, however.

Combat

Gitalong Li'l Doggie

The Gitalong Table below tells you how to figure pace when a character is running, climbing, or swimming.

Gitalong Table

Action	Pace	Pickup	Wind	Max
Walkin'	Nimbleness	d4	1	-
Climbin'	2 + *climbin'*	d2	1	8
Swimmin'	*Swimmin'*	d2	1	5
Ridin'	Varies by animal	d10	1	-

Pace is the base movement rate for the entire round. You'll need to split this proportionately among your actions when it's important. For swimming and climbing, use your character's Aptitude levels in *swimmin'* and *climbin'* as the base number.

Pickup is the type of die you roll to get extra movement by "picking up the pace." Unlike most rolls in *Deadlands,* don't roll again on Aces.

Wind is the amount of Wind your character takes when he picks up the pace.

Max is the absolute maximum your character can move for certain types of actions, such as climbing and swimming.

> Ronan's running from a Mojave rattler. His *Nimbleness* is 8. Since he's running, he'll move 16 yards per round. If he picks up the pace, he can move an extra d4 yards at the cost of 1 Wind.
>
> If Ronan gets 3 actions, he can move 3, 3, and 2 yards

Carrying a Load

No, we don't mean the one in your pants. That's a personal problem. What we're talking about is the fact that outlaws trying to haul a safe out of a bank aren't going to run as fast as the sheriff who's after them.

The load is an estimate of the character, critter, or vehicle versus the weight of the load. If it matters, you and the Marshal need to figure out how heavy a load is. A strong character carrying a fainted schoolmarm probably has a light load. Two horses pulling a stagecoach have an average load. If the wagon is full of gold, it would be heavy for even six horses.

The relative loads below are listed along with how much you need to reduce the character or critters' pace by. If a character with an 8 pace is carrying a heavy load, his pace is effectively reduced to a 2 for the round.

Of course, what's a heavy load to Granny might be a feather's weight to an ornery cuss like your character. The minimum for each class of load is listed under "Weight" in pounds.

> For instance, Ronan's *Strength* is 6. He can carry up to 18 with no problems. From 18 pounds up to 36 pounds is a light load. From 36 pounds up to 60 pounds is a medium load. From 60 pounds on up is a heavy load.

Load Table

Load	Weight	Pace
Light	3x *Strength*	x3/4
Medium	6x *Strength*	x1/2
Heavy	10x *Strength*	x1/4

Combat

Test of Wills

When most folks think of combat, they think of yanking triggers and beating things to a pulp. That's a lot of fun, but sometimes it's just as much fun to stare down some lily-livered tinhorn and send him running for New York City. Or trick a Texas hombre into thinking some critter's sneaking up on him so you can shoot him in the back. Of course, in *Deadlands*, there probably *is* some critter sneaking up behind him, so you might just want to keep your trap shut.

Bluff, *overawe*, and *ridicule* are tests of will that can be used to break an opponent's nerve or concentration. *Persuasion* is also a test of wills, but it isn't used in combat.

A test of wills is an opposed roll versus one of the target's Aptitudes. If the test is being made against a group, use the leader's Aptitude.

Initiating a test of wills is an action. Resisting one is not and is done automatically.

Tests of will can have additional effects besides getting the bad guys to do what you want. The number of successes and raises determines the effect of the test of wills.

All this is summed up on the Test of Wills Table.

Test of Wills Table

Test Aptitude	Opposed Aptitude
Bluff	Scrutinize
Overawe	Guts
Ridicule	Ridicule
Successes	**Effect**
1	Unnerved
2	Distracted
3	Broken

Unnerved

Your character's stern gaze or cruel taunt angers or upsets your opponent. The target suffers -4 to her next action. This includes any "passive" defense Aptitudes like *fightin'* or resisting further tests of wills.

Distracted

The target is totally distracted by your hero's jibe, trick, or surly stare. The target is *unnerved*, and in addition loses his highest Action Card. If she's got a cheat card up her sleeve, she loses that instead.

Broken

You've broken the bad guy's will—for the moment at least. He's *unnerved* and *distracted* and you get to draw a Fate Chip from the pot.

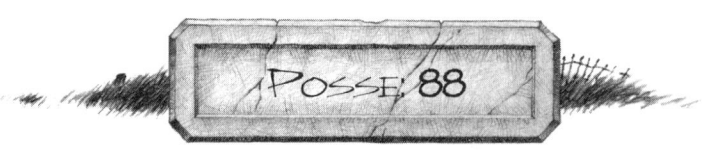

Combat

Shootin' Things

There often comes a point when you need to turn some dastardly villain's head into "high plains pudding."

In simple terms, all you need to do is figure out your Target Number and roll your *shootin'* dice. If one of your bones comes up equal to or higher than the TN, you've hit.

While you're reading this part, remember that you should figure out all the modifiers for the Marshal instead of making her do it all for you. That will free her up to interpret the results in grisly detail and keep all the bad guys and *their* modifiers straight.

The Shootin' Roll

The first thing you need to figure out when you want to blow something to Kingdom Come is what kind of weapon your character is going to fire. There are lots of pea-shooters in the Weird West—from Colt Peacemakers and Winchester repeaters to Gatling guns and flamethrowers powered by ghost rock.

We can classify these into four concentrations: *pistols, rifles, shotguns,* and *automatics*. Flamethrowers and other weird gizmos should fall into one of these categories, depending on the particular device.

Whichever weapon your character uses, that's the kind of *shootin'* concentration he needs. If he doesn't have it, he can use his *Deftness* instead, but since this is a "default" roll, you have to halve the total (round down).

If your character has a related concentration—say she's firing a pistol when she's used to shotguns—you can use the related concentration but you'll have to subtract -2 from the roll. In case you forgot, this was all covered in Chapter Two, partner.

Rate of Fire

So how many shots can you fire per action? That's easy. A character can fire up to his weapon's "rate of fire" each action. Pistols and rifles have a rate of fire of 1. You need several actions to plug multiple bad guys in the same round. Only Gatling guns and weird gizmos have higher rates of fire.

The Attack

Once you've figured out what kind of dice to roll, it's time to figure out the TN you need to make some dirt-slow loser do some daisy-pushing.

Range

The Target Number you're looking for is Fair (5) plus the range modifier. To figure the modifier, count the number of yards between the shooter and the target and then divide it by the weapon's Range Increment, rounding down as usual. The number you get is added to Fair (5) to get the base TN of the shot.

Below are the range increments for the most common weapons. Weird gizmos such as flamethrowers and artillery pieces have their own specific range increment listed in their descriptions.

Range Modifiers Table

Weapon	Range Modifier
Scattergun	+2/10 yards
Pistol	+1/10 yards
Shotgun	+1/10 yards
Rifle	+1/20 yards
Carbine	+2/20 yards
Gatling gun	+1/20 yards

Combat

Modifiers

Now that you've got your TN, you might have to add or subtract a couple of modifiers to your *shootin'* roll.

Shootin' Modifiers Table

Situation	Modifier
Firer is running	-4
Firer is mounted	-2
Firer is wounded	Variable
Size	Variable
Target is moving	-4

Firer is Moving

It's a lot harder to hit a target when you're on the move. As you might remember from our little discussion on movement, any action in which your character runs (doubles his movement for the action), he suffers a -4 penalty to all his actions.

Target's Size

If a target is half the size of a man, subtract a penalty of -1. If it's one-quarter the size of a man, subtract -2, and so on, to a maximum of -6. The opposite is also true. A target that is twice as big as a man gives the character a +1 bonus, a target three times the size of a man has a +2 modifier, and so on, up to a maximum of +6.

Target is Moving

Of course, it's harder to hit a moving target than one that's standing still.

Any time a target is moving faster than a relative pace of 20, subtract -4 from your roll. "Relative" means you need to take into account how fast the target and the shooter are moving in relation to each other. If a rider is chasing a train, for instance, no penalty applies.

Shotguns

Shotguns and scatterguns work a little differently than most weapons. The benefit of either is that one shell unleashes a half-dozen or so .38 caliber balls. This makes them ideal for unskilled shooters since they can make up for their lack of talent by filling the air with lead. Even better, the closer the shooter is to her target, the more balls are likely to hit and the more damage they can cause.

Anyone firing a shotgun adds 4d6 bonus dice to his *shootin': shotgun* roll. Subtract one of these bonus dice every 10 yards after the first. So at 1-10 yards a shotgun adds 4d6 bonus dice. At 11-20 it adds 3d6, and so on.

Shotguns and scatterguns get bonus

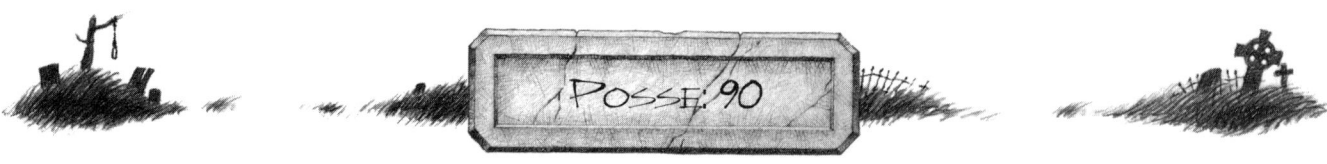

COMBAT

damage dice in much the same way. However many bonus Aptitude dice are left when a character fires is the number of bonus damage dice he can add if he hits. Since a shotgun has a base damage of 2d6, a successful shot at 10 yards or less actually causes 6d6 damage. Ouch!

> Ronan's creeping through a cemetery when a pile of shambling bones rises up just over 20 yards away. Having only a shotgun, Ronan unloads both barrels at the thing. At this range, he'll get 3 bonus dice per shot. He hits with both and adds 3 bonus dice to each damage as well. The undead thing is blown back to the depths of Hell.

Automatic Weapons

Automatic weapons like Gatling guns fire several rounds at once at the expense of accuracy.

When a character fires a Gatling gun, he usually has to fire the weapon's full "rate of fire." For Gatlings and other automatics, the rate of fire is usually 3.

The shooter's *shootin': automatics* roll determines how many of these rounds actually hit. Every raise above the TN means an additional bullet hits the target. Obviously, a target cannot be hit by more bullets than were fired at it. Determine each round's hit location and effects separately.

If the gunner wants to fire at multiple targets, he needs to decide how many bullets each target gets, and then split his dice among them.

Combat

A gunner can never "draw a bead" or make called shots when firing on automatic (see **Special Maneuvers** on the next page).

Gatling guns aren't perfected technology. They have a reliability of 19. When you fire one, roll a d20 along with the Action Roll. If you roll a 20, the Gatling gun breaks down. Tell your Marshal when this happens and he'll figure out the results using the mad scientist malfunction rules

> Violet finds herself guarding a train running through Nevada when a band of desperadoes on steam-wagons move in for the kill. She opens fire with the Gatling mounted on the roof. Her reliability roll comes up 14, so she's safe there. Her *shootin': automatics* roll is a 12 and the TN is 6. That's a success and a raise, so Violet hits with 2 bullets.

Special Maneuvers

Gunslingers use all kinds of tricks and techniques to make sure they get their man.

Called Shots

Occasionally you'll run across some critter that just doesn't want to die even after you've turned it into Swiss cheese. Hopefully it's got a weak spot somewhere, like an eyeball or the brainpan.

Hitting a specific spot on your target is a "called shot," and of course, it comes with a penalty. The smaller the target, the bigger the penalty. The table below is for targeting people, but it should give you an idea for blasting parts off nasty critters as well.

Called Shot Table

Size	Penalty
Guts	-2
Legs, arms	-4
Heads, hands, feet	-6
Eyeball, heart	-10

Drawing a Bead

A normal shot assumes your cowpoke aims his smokewagon only for a heartbeat before squeezing off a round. If a character spends an entire action "drawing a bead," she can add +2 to her *shootin'* total in the next action. Every action spent drawing a bead adds +2 to the character's next *shootin'* roll, up to a maximum of +6. The modifier carries over to the next round if needed.

Fanning

Veteran gunslingers sometimes "fan" their sidearms. Fanning simply means holding the trigger down on a single-action revolver and slapping the hammer repeatedly with the palm of the other hand. This puts a lot of lead in the air fast, but the individual shots aren't very accurate.

Combat

Fanning requires the *fannin'* Aptitude and uses the automatic fire rules we spelled out for you above. The rate of fire is up to you—up to 6 rounds per action if you've got the ammo. The fanner needs one free hand and a single-action revolver.

Fanning a pistol isn't very accurate, however, so the shooter has to subtract -2 from his *fannin'* roll.

The advantage to fanning is that you get to unload your smokewagon in a single action (even though single-action revolvers normally have a speed of 2 and a rate of fire of 1). You can get off up to 6 shots at once—that's even faster than a Gatling gun. The downside is that you don't get all of your skill dice on each shot. You also can't draw a bead or make a called shot either. Use this maneuver wisely, or you'll find yourself out of bullets with a bunch of angry banditos around you.

> One-Eye Ketchum needs to drop three banditos. He has a *fannin'* skill of 4, and decides to fan 2 bullets at each bad guy. The automatic fire rules say he has to split his dice to fire at more than one target, so One-Eye gives the first bad guy 2 of his *fannin'* dice and the next two get 1 each.
>
> One Eye rolls an incredible 27 on his first roll and needed a 7 to hit. Subtracting the fanning penalty of -2 drops his attack roll to a 25. That means he still got 3 raises. Since he only fired 2 bullets at the first bad guy, however, 1 raise is wasted.
>
> For the 2 rounds that did hit, he rolls hit locations of the leg and the noggin. The first bullet does a pitiful 4 points of damage. The second gets 2 extra dice for hitting the noggin and does a whopping 23. The first bandito goes down as One Eye continues his fan and rolls a die each for his shots at the other two.

Shootin' From The Hip

Sometimes an ornery hombre won't wait for you to pull your Winchester '73 up to your eye and take a well-aimed pop at his innards. If not, you'll have to shoot from the hip.

Single-action revolvers have to be cocked before they can be fired. Double-actions cock themselves when the trigger is pulled. This makes single-actions a tad slower, but offers the advantage of letting the user fan. Rifles are also slow since the shooter usually has to pull the weapon up to his eye and aim before firing.

Single-action revolvers, rifles, and other weapons with a speed of 2 can fire faster (making the speed 1) by sacrificing a little aim. This is called "shooting from the hip" and subtracts -2 from the firer's attack roll.

The Two-Gun Kid

Some pistoleros like to fire two pistols at once. They usually don't hit as much, but they sure make a lot of noise.

Any action taken with a character's off-hand is made at -4. A cowpoke can fire with each hand up to the weapons' usual rate of fire. Each shot is a separate roll.

The Rifle Spin

Generally speaking, you need two hands to operate a rifle, but if you're good you can do it with only one. Subtract -2 from any one-handed rifle attack.

A gonzo rifleman could even use two rifles at once, but don't forget about the off-hand penalty we just mentioned above.

The real problem comes from having to cock the rifle between shots. It's hard, but it can be done by spinning the rifle by its lever. If you'd like for your character to do this one-handed too, you need to make an Onerous (7) *Deftness* check for each rifle. This check requires no actions, but can only be made once per action. If you fail, you can try again on your next action.

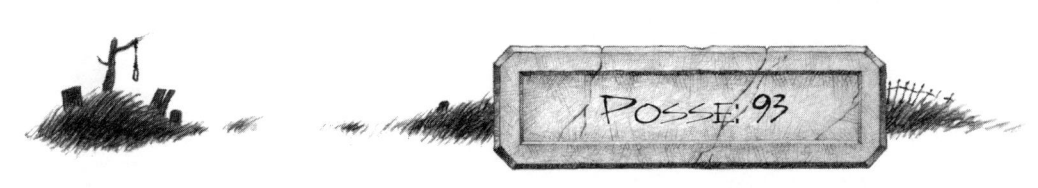

Combat

Reloading

Sooner or later, your sixgun's going to run out of ammo. It takes one action to put a single bullet into a pistol or rifle, or a single shell in a shotgun. Of course, you can always try speed-loading the gun to get more bullets faster. (See *speed-load* in Chapter Three).

Gatling guns fire bursts instead of single bullets. They can fire up to 15 bursts before having to be reloaded. It takes two actions to reload a Gatling gun's feed box. They cannot be speed-loaded.

Black powder muzzle-loading weapons take forever to reload. Five actions, in fact. They can never be speed-loaded.

Throwin' Things

Ever heard of a Mojave rattler? If you cross the Mojave, they'll hear you. When they do, you'd better warm up your throwing arm, because the best way to kill one is to chuck a heap of dynamite down its gullet.

The *throwin'* skill works just like *shootin'* for most weapons. The Range Increment for all thrown weapons is +2/10, so add +2 to the base TN of Fair (5) for every 10 yards distance. A target at 10 yards is TN 7.

The maximum range a character can throw an average size weapon (1-2 pounds) is her *Strength* die type ↔ 5 yards.

Ronan's *Strength* of 3d6 lets him chuck a stick of dynamite 30 yards, with a TN of 11.

Innocent Bystanders

First things first. No one is innocent. Some folks may be more innocent than others, but they stop a stray bullet just the same.

Sometimes you want to know if a missed shot could hit someone near or along the path of the target. This isn't a situation that crops up all of the time, and you shouldn't worry about it if it's not important.

If a bystander is a few feet from the target and directly between it and the shooter—as in the classic hostage pose—you can use the hit location chart. If the bystander was covering up the part of the target that was hit, she gets hit instead. You have to figure out where the bystander gets hit based on the situation or another roll.

If the bystander isn't up close and personal with the target, you can use this simple system.

For single shots that miss their target, a bullet has a 1 in 6 chance of hitting anyone within 1 yard of the bullet's path. Start at the bystander closest to the shooter and roll a d6. If it comes up a 1, he's hit. Roll hit location and damage normally. If the roll is anything but a 1, check any other bystanders in the path until you run out of bystanders or the bullet finds a home.

A spray of bullets fired from a fanned single action revolver, shotgun, or Gatling gun or pistol hits bystanders on a 1-2. Continue to check each target until all the missed rounds have checked each bystander at least once.

Combat

A missed shotgun blast has a bit wider coverage than a single bullet. It can hit bystanders within 2 yards of the blast's path.

If you're using the awesome *Deadlands* miniatures—and we don't know why you wouldn't be—you should have a very clear picture of who's likely to get hit by a stray miss.

Fightin'

It's time to start carving. Whip out your Bowie knife and "stick" with us. We taught you how to shoot, now it's time we taught you how to fight.

Making *fightin'* Aptitude rolls is a lot like making *shootin'* rolls. First figure out the concentration that matches the weapon you're using. Some basic *fightin'* concentrations are *knives, swords, whips,* and *brawlin'*. The last one, *brawlin'*, also covers clubs, hammers, and the like.

The Target Number of the attack is Fair (5) plus the opponent's *fightin'* Aptitude for whatever weapon is currently in his hand. A cowboy gets his *fightin': brawlin'* skill if he is empty-handed or has some sort of "club" in his hand—like a bottle or even a pistol.

As with *shootin'* maneuvers, an attacker can make "called shots" if he wants (see page 92).

Ronan's a rough and tumble kind of guy, but sometimes people like to pick on his wiry self. A drunken cowpoke looking for a fight in the No. 1 Saloon in Deadwood happens to find Ronan Lynch. Ronan obliges the drunkard by punching him square in the face. Since the cowpoke is using his fists, Ronan adds the cowpoke's *fightin': brawlin'* of 2 to the TN of 5, making it 7. Ronan gets a 9 and nails him in the nose.

Weapon Speeds

Most hand-to-hand weapons have a speed of 1, so each action lets the wielder attack one opponent. A few weapons such as lariats are really slow and have a speed of 2. These take an action to ready before they can strike.

If a character has a weapon in each hand, she can make two attacks during one action. Each of these are rolled separately. A penalty of -4 is subtracted from the off-hand attack as usual.

Defensive Bonuses

Certain weapons make it hard for an opponent to get in close. An Indian with a knife will have a hard time burying it in the heart of a cavalryman with a saber. The reach advantage of certain weapons is their "Defensive Bonus."

The Defensive Bonus is applied directly to the attacker's TN when he makes his *fightin'* roll. See Chapter Four for details about each weapon's bonuses.

Whips & Lariats

Instead of doing brawling damage (lariats don't do any), whips and lariats can be used to entangle and trip. Doing either is an opposed roll of the attacker's *fightin': whip* or *fightin': lariat* skill versus the opponent's *Nimbleness*.

A character can break out of an average whip or lariat with an Incredible (11) *Strength* roll. Otherwise, she has to wriggle her way out of it. This is an opposed *Nimbleness* roll versus the attacker's skill with the weapon.

The Marshal should feel free to apply bonuses and penalties according to the situation. Obviously, if your character is being dragged behind a horse, it's going to be a bit tougher to break free.

Combat

Vamoosin'

Before we get into seeing if your hombre actually hit his target, there's one last thing you should know.

If you really don't want your character to get hit, he can make an "active defense." This is called "vamoosin'."

When someone's about to attack your character, you can throw away your highest remaining Action Card to say he's vamoosin'. If you've got a card up your sleeve, that's your highest. Otherwise, this is the only time an Action Card lets you act before it's your turn.

Now you can make a *dodge* or *fightin'* Aptitude roll as appropriate. The TN for the bad guy to hit you is now the greater of his normal TN or your *dodge* or *fightin'* roll. You can't spend any more Fate Chips on your roll once the bad guy starts his attack roll.

To make up for breaking our precious rules, your character actually has to do something to represent the vamoose. If he's dodging, he needs to jump behind cover or throw himself to the ground. In hand-to-hand combat, a vamoosing character has to give ground by backing up 1 yard. Otherwise, subtract -4 from his roll.

Hit Location

Before you can start rolling handfuls of damage dice, you need to see where the attack actually hit and whether or not any cover intervened.

Where you hit a target is often more important than how hard. A good whack on the noggin hurts a lot more than getting your toes stepped on.

Roll 1d20 on the chart below whenever the Marshal tells you you've scored a hit. When arms or legs are hit, roll another d6. A

Combat

roll of 1-3 is the left limb, and 4-6 is the right.

Hits to the gizzards and noggin cause extra damage as you'll see under Bleedin' & Squealin' below.

The hit location chart works best with humans and things that like to think they're human, but it can also be used for critters with a little tinkering. The Marshal may sometimes use a special chart for really weird varmints, but this one will work most of the time.

Gizzards are all the vital parts, by the way, like the all-important groin, the heart, lungs, liver, and all those other messy parts the body needs to keep walking and talking.

Hit Location Table

Die Roll (1d20)	Location
1-4	Legs
5-9	Lower Guts
10	Gizzards
11-14	Arms
15-19	Upper Guts
20	Noggin
Modifiers	
+/-1	Per raise on the attack roll
+2	When fighting
+2	Height advantage when fighting
+2	Point-blank range for firearms

Raises

Every raise on an attack roll lets the shooter adjust his hit location by 1 point up or down. This way a really good shooter is more likely to get a killing blow to the guts or noggin areas. Sometimes you won't want to add the bonus because it will actually make you miss due to cover. Don't worry, you don't have to use the bonus if you don't want to.

Fightin'

The really nifty thing about this chart is that it starts at the legs and works its way up. Adding +2 to the die roll puts most hand-to-hand hits in the guts, head, or arms where they should be.

Height

You can also add +2 to the roll if one character has a height advantage over another in a fight, such as if one fellow is on a horse taking a saber swing at some sodbuster on foot.

Point-Blank Range

Point-blank range is used when one character is holding a gun on another, using him like a shield, holding him hostage, or shooting over a table that they're both sitting at. In general, the gun should almost be only a few feet away to count this modifier. This means that when a hostage tries to break free, his captor is more likely to shoot the victim in the guts or his flailing arms than in the pinky toe. Occasionally you might want to subtract this modifier—such as when someone shoots somebody *under* a table.

Prone Targets

A cowboy laying down is much harder to hit than a tinhorn standing up in the middle of a street.

When you make a successful attack roll against a prone target, roll hit location normally. Unless the attack hits the arms, upper guts, or noggin, it's a miss.

Combat

Cover

Using cover is the most important things a cowpoke can do to save his skin. A gunslinger who stands out in the open might inspire dime novels, but they'll probably be published posthumously.

Once you know where an attack has hit the target, you need to take into account any cover the target might have there. The hit location table is all set up to help you out. If the hit location is a character's left arm and he's leaning around a corner to fire with his right, the bullet is going to hit the corner.

The table is even broken up into lower and upper guts, so if your character is behind a bar and a shot hits his lower guts, you'll know it's probably going into the wood instead.

That's why it's important you tell the Marshal exactly what your character is doing so he can figure out if the hero should get cover or not.

Bustin' Through

Cover does two things to an attack: it deflects it and reduces some of its inertia. When an attack hits cover, you should first roll a d6. On a 1-3, the round is deflected and doesn't hit whatever is behind it. On a 4-6, it goes through the cover and hits the target beyond. This reduces its damage by the "armor" value of the intervening cover, which we'll explain directly.

Combat

Damage Steps

Traits above the human norm go from a d12 to a d12+2, then d12+4, and so on. Damage dice work a bit differently.

After a d12, the next die type is a d20. This lets us assign weapon damages to a general category of die type as shown on the table below.

Damage Steps Table

Die	Weapon Types
d4	Light clubs, Small Knives
d6	Arrows, Heavy Clubs, Pistols, Large Knives
d8	Rifles, Sabers, Axes
d10	Buffalo Rifles
d12	Armor Piercing .50 bullets, Flamethrowers
d20	Dynamite, Cannon Balls

Armor

Now it's time to show you why we cleverly grouped weapon damage values by die types.

A .45 caliber Peacemaker and a .22 caliber derringer are both d6-based weapons, but the Peacemaker's going to roll more d6s than the derringer. If you're talking about penetration, however, both weapons will go through an inch-thick board about the same. The Peacemaker will still do more damage to whatever's on the other side, however.

When bullets, knives, or anything else go through an obstacle, they lose some of their energy. The thicker and tougher the obstacle, the more damage is absorbed.

Obstacles have an "armor" rating. Each level of armor reduces the die type of the damage. An attack that uses d20s (like dynamite) is reduced to d12s by a single level of armor. Two levels of armor would drop the damage to d10s, and so on. If the die type is dropped below a d4, it is stopped entirely.

A 3d6 bullet that goes through something with an armor value of 1, for instance, is reduced to 3d4. A 3d6 bullet that hits something with an armor of 2 is stopped entirely. This means that anything with an armor of 2 is bulletproof to most pistols.

Armor stops *fightin'* attacks as well. Fighting damage uses a character's *Strength* Trait total plus the weapon's damage dice. If the armor stops the weapon's damage dice, it stops the character's *Strength* roll as well. If a character or critter isn't using a weapon, halve its *Strength* die type plus any bonuses and round to the nearest damage step. A critter with a d12+6 has a damage step of d10 (half of 18, rounded up.) Of course the maximum damage step is still d20.

The chart to the right lists some obstacles and their armor levels. We've also listed the type of die each level stops for convenience.

Armor Table

Armor	Material	Stops
1	Wood less than an inch thick	d4
2	1"-3" of solid wood, tin	d6
3	4"-6" of solid wood, very thin metal	d8
4	A small tree, bricks, an iron pan	d10
5	A large tree, armored train walls	d12
6	Inch-thick steel plate	d20

Concealment

If you can see any part of your target, it isn't really concealed. If some cowboy's head is sticking up out of the prairie grass, it doesn't take a genius to figure out where the rest of his body is.

Partial concealment doesn't modify an attack roll. If a target is completely concealed but an attacker knows approximately where the target is (even a general direction), he can attack at -4.

Combat

The penalties for partial lighting apply to targets greater than 10 yards away. Of course, if a target is holding a lantern on a dark night, there's no penalty at any distance.

Concealment Table

Status	Penalty
Total Concealment	-4
Torchlight, twilight	-4
Moonlight	-6
Blind, total darkness	-8

Bleedn' & Squealn'

Once you've hit your target, you need to know just how big a hole you made. Whether you've just put an artillery shell into some ornery critter or sank your cavalry saber up to the hilt in its backside, figuring damage is handled in the same way.

Once you've figured out where an attack hit, it's time to roll the damage dice. Every weapon in *Deadlands* has a listing for "damage." This is the number of dice you roll whenever you score a hit.

Firearms have fixed damage, such as 3d6 for large-caliber pistols. When you've hit your target, roll this many dice, but don't read them like a normal Trait or Aptitude check. Damage dice are always added together. You can still reroll any Aces and add them to the final total, however.

Weapons that rely on muscle—like arrows, spears, or knives—have fixed damage dice plus the character's *Strength* total rolled like a normal Trait check. Roll the weapon's dice and add them to the *Strength* total. This way a character with 4d6 *Strength* will probably do more damage than one with 1d6 *Strength*.

In the middle of a bar fight, Ronan grabs a bottle and smashes it over a cowpoke's head. It connects nicely. Checking for damage, Ronan rolls his *Strength* (3d6) and the weapon's damage die (1d4). He gets 3, 5, and 11 on his *Strength* dice plus 3 for the bottle. The cowpoke takes (11+3=) 15 points of brawling damage. Ouch!

Noggins & Gizzards

A hit to a vital spot causes more trouble than a hit to the little finger. Whenever a character is hit in the gizzards, you can add 1 extra die to the damage roll. A hit to the noggin adds 2 extra dice.

The die type is the same as whatever other dice you're rolling. For hand-to-hand weapons (where you add your character's *Strength* die to the roll), use the weapon's die type.

Size Matters

(Ahem.) Once you have your final damage total, tell the Marshal. For every full multiple of your target's Size you do in damage, your attack causes one wound. In case you're the argumentative type, this is the one time you forget that "round-up" business. Think of it in terms of a full 6 points instead. Okay?

Most humans have a Size of 6, but critters vary considerably. Unless you've taken the *scrawny* or *big 'un* Hindrance,

Combat

your character has a Size of 6 as well.

The target takes the wound(s) in the area rolled on the Hit Location Table.

> Frustrated, the cowpoke draws a knife on Ronan. With lightning speed, Ronan strips the hapless sod of the blade and then turns it on him, stabbing him in the leg. The attack does 14 points of damage and so causes 2 wounds.

Wounds

Everyone—outlaws, critters, and schoolmarms alike—can take the same number of wounds in each body part: five to be exact. Most cowpokes can shrug off a single wound, but more than that starts causing some serious trouble. Check out another of our famous tables to get a better picture of what we're talking about.

Wound Table

Wound Level	Description
1	Light
2	Heavy
3	Serious
4	Critical
5	Maimed

Light wounds are bruises, shallow but irritating cuts, and muscle strains.

Heavy wounds are sprains, deep but nonthreatening cuts, or multiple bruises.

Serious wounds encompass fractured or broken bones or deep and bloody cuts.

Critical wounds are life-threatening cuts across major arteries, compound fractures, or internal bleeding.

Maimed is well. . .maimed. If a character's wounds reach the Maimed mark in his guts or noggin, he's kicking buckets, pushing daisies, buying farms, and the like. You get the idea. If a limb becomes Maimed, it is severed, crushed, burned to a cinder, or otherwise out of action forever.

Wound Effects

Now things get a little trickier. You need to keep track of damage in six different locations—your character's Head, Guts, Right Arm, Left Arm, Left Leg, and Right Leg. Wounds taken to the gizzards add to those in the guts area.

Wounds are only added together when they're taken in the same specific location. For instance, a character who takes a light wound to the right arm in one round and a heavy wound in the same arm later would then have a serious wound in that arm. If a character takes a light wound to the head and then takes a heavy wound to his leg, they aren't added together.

A character can't be killed by wounds to the arms or legs. She can take enough Wind (see below) to put her out of action, but she can't die until she bleeds to death or someone plugs her in the head or guts.

This makes it possible for a hero to get cut and shot to pieces, but one more scratch to the arm can't kill her unless she bleeds to death. Only a hit to the noggin or guts directly plants a fellow in Boot Hill.

Posse 101

Combat

Wound Modifiers

Wounds are not pleasant company. Blood drips in your eyes, broken fingers make it hard to pull triggers, and crunchy ankles make it a real pain to run from angry varmints.

As you might have guessed, wounds subtract from a character's die rolls. The penalties are shown below. Wound penalties are never subtracted from "effect" totals such as damage or hex effects, but they do apply to everything else.

Wound Effects Table

Wound	Modifier
Light	-1
Heavy	-2
Serious	-3
Critical	-4
Maimed (limbs)	-5

The penalty depends on the highest level wound your character has suffered. If he has a light and a serious wound, for instance, you'll have to subtract the penalty for serious wounds (-3) from all your action totals.

Stun

Another word on all this pain and suffering business. Whenever a character takes damage, there's a chance he might miss the next action or two kissing his missing finger or holding in his guts.

When your character takes damage, he has to make a "stun" check. Stun checks are made by rolling *Vigor* against the wound's level, as shown at the bottom of this page. Don't forget to apply the penalty for the worst wound you've taken so far as well.

If you make the roll, nothing happens. If you fail it, your character's stunned and can't do anything besides limp a few yards and cry like a baby until he makes a recovery check.

Your character will need to make a stun check every time he takes a wound unless he's already stunned.

Recovery Checks

You can try to recover from being stunned during any action. This is called a "recovery check," and takes one entire action. A recovery roll is made just like a stun check, except the difficulty is your highest current wound level.

One last thing. Your character will go unconscious if you go bust on a stun check. The amount of time he stays down is 1d6 hours or until someone makes a Fair (5) *medicine* roll to wake him up.

Stun & Recovery Table

Wound Level	TN
Wind	3
Light	5
Heavy	7
Serious	9
Critical	11
Maimed (limbs)	13

Combat

Wind

It just keeps getting better.

Every time your character takes a wound, she also takes Wind. Wind is shock, fatigue, and—in the case of wounds—trauma associated with losing bits and pieces of your favorite anatomy.

For every wound level your character suffers, she also takes 1d6 Wind. If she's hit by an attack but doesn't actually take a wound (because the damage total was less than his size), she still takes at least 1d6 Wind.

Gettin' Winded

When a character is reduce to 0 Wind or lower, he becomes "winded." This doesn't necessarily mean he passes out, but he does feel like crawling into a hole and dying or curling up into a ball and whining like a baby.

Winded characters might lose consciousness for a few minutes, fall to the ground trying to catch their breath, or collapse from sheer fatigue and exhaustion. It really depends on the situation. Most of the time, characters winded from wounds collapse into a corner and vainly try to stop their bleeding and spurting.

Winded characters get no cards and can perform no actions unless the Marshal feels like letting them whisper or crawl a short ways at the end of the round. Fortunately, winded characters generally fall by the wayside and don't get beaten on anymore.

Cowpokes who continue to take Wind even after they've run out might die. This is usually caused by things like bleeding or drowning.

Every time negative Wind is equal to the character's starting Wind level, he takes another wound to the guts. A character with 12 Wind, for example, would take a wound when Wind reached -12.

Combat

Marking Wounds

The character sheet we drew up for you makes it real easy to keep track of wounds and Wind. For wounds, you can use different colored paper clips in each body area to keep track of the levels and modifiers. For Wind, you can slide a single clip down the chart until you've hit 0. If your character goes negative, you can start sliding it back up the other way to keep track.

The same goes for the ammo counters, by the way.

Nifty, eh?

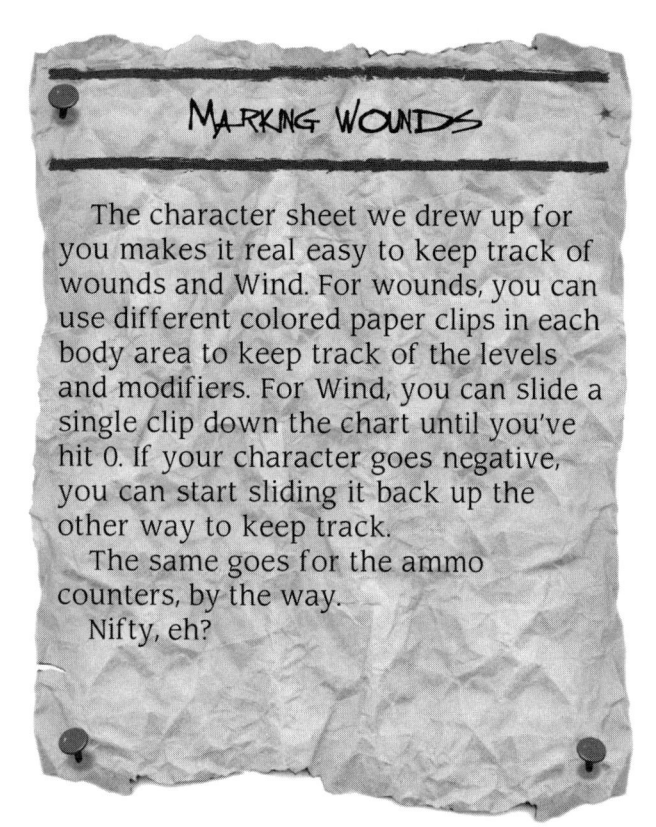

More Pain and Sufferin'

There are lots of ways to buy the farm. Here's a few more ways to maim and dismember the bad guys.

Bleedin'

Serious damage is likely to start a fellow bleeding like a sieve. Whenever a character takes a serious wound, he begins bleeding, losing 1 Wind per round. Critically wounded characters bleed 2 points of Wind per round. Severed (Maimed) limbs bleed 3 points per round.

Boom

Dynamite, nitroglycerin, bombs, and all other explosives cause a certain amount of damage to any fool who happens to be next to them when they detonate. Every 10 yards afterwards, the damage of the explosion drops by a die.

A single stick of dynamite, for instance, does 3d20 damage. Adding extra sticks to a dynamite bundle adds 1d20 to the total damage.

A cowpoke standing up to 10 yards away from a single stick of dynamite would take all 3 dice. The damage at 10-20 yards would be 2 dice, 21-30 yards is a single die, and targets at greater than 30 yards take no damage. Though they might get a little deaf.

Once you've figured how many wounds the characters take and given them the chance to cancel some or all of the wounds with Fate Chips (see Chapter Six), you need to see where the characters take each of the wounds. Roll a hit location for each. Hits to the noggin and gizzards don't do extra damage in this case.

Brawlin'

Certain kinds of attacks, like *fightin': brawlin'*, are generally considered nonlethal. When one fellow hits another with his bare hands or a light club such as a chair leg or a bottle, he rolls his damage dice and causes 3 points of Wind for every wound level he would normally have caused. Every full 2 wound levels causes a real wound.

Heavy clubs like pistol butts, ax handles, or entire chairs allow the attacker to choose whether she would like to cause lethal or nonlethal damage. If she just wants to cause Wind and try to knock her opponent out without causing serious injury, she can do so. Or she can bash the other fellow's brains out to his heart's content.

Hey, it's a harsh world out there.

> Back when Ronan smashed that bottle over the cowpoke's head, he did 15 points of damage. Since the cowpoke has a Size of 6, the attack would have done two wounds if it had been made with a deadly weapon. Since it was just a bottle, the cowpoke suffers 6 Wind and takes a single wound. Lucky stiff.

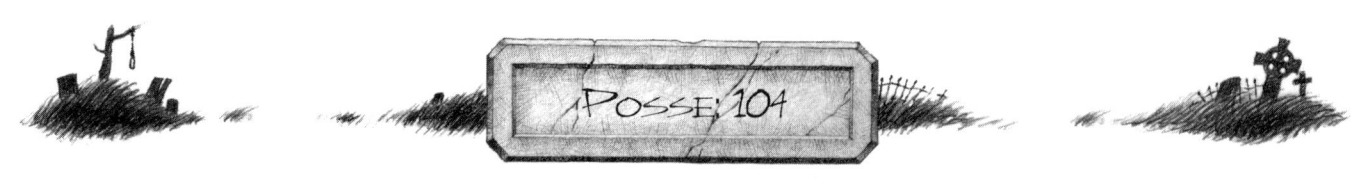

Combat

Drownin'

It's a lousy way to go, but it happens.

Every round a character swims in rough water, his first action must be a *swimmin'* roll. The TN depends on the condition of the water as shown below. If the swimmer doesn't make the TN, he takes the difference in Wind.

A character without the *swimmin'* Aptitude is in big trouble. When he's in *any* kind of water over his noggin, he has to go through the steps above.

Drowning Table

Water	TN
Swift creek	3
Rapid river	5
Rough ocean	7
Stormy sea	9

Fallin'

A fellow might walk away from falling a few yards with no more than a bruise or at worst a broken limb. Take a dive off a cliff in the Grand Canyon and he's smashed flatter than a pancake.

A character takes 1d6+5 damage for every 5 yards fallen, up to a maximum of 20d6+100. Any wounds that result are applied randomly to separate body areas, ignoring noggins and gizzards.

Landing in water reduces the damage by half or cancels it entirely if the character makes a Fair (5) *swimmin'* roll.

Landing on a haystack, awning, or other soft obstacle reduces the damage by half if the character makes an Onerous (7) *Nimbleness* roll.

Fire

Heroes often have to enter burning buildings or the flaming wreckage of a derailed train. Sure makes bad guys seem a lot brighter, doesn't it?

Characters in dense smoke have to make an Onerous (7) *Vigor* check during their first action each round. A wet cloth over the mouth and nose or similar makeshift protection adds +2 to the roll. If the character fails the roll, she takes the difference in Wind. Should this knock her out she continues to lose Wind in this way every round until she dies.

The damage to a character who is actually on fire depends on just how big the flames are. A small fire such as a burning sleeve causes 1d12 damage at the beginning of every turn to whatever area is on fire. A larger fire causes 2d12 to the affected areas. A character totally consumed by flames takes 3d12 damage with the wounds applied to every area.

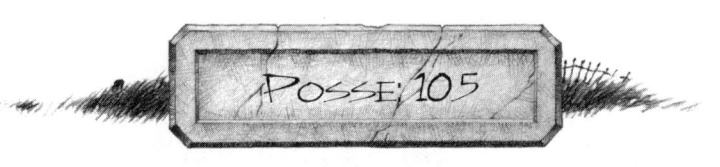

Combat

Hangin'

Deadlands taking place in the Weird West and all, we thought you might occasionally need to know what happens when a characters is fitted with a hemp necktie.

Assuming a character is first dropped a few feet, he needs to make an immediate Hard (9) *Vigor* roll. Subtract -4 from the roll if he's a *big un'*. Failure means the character's neck snaps and he's dead. Fate Chips (see the next chapter) won't stop the wounds, so the hombre better use them to make his *Vigor* check.

A botch on this roll, by the way, does exactly what you think it does. Needless to say, a character without his noggin can't come back from the grave.

Assuming the character's body is still attached to his brain-pan and the rest of his noggin, he'll have to make Hard (9) *Vigor* rolls every round he swings. If he fails, the difference is taken in Wind until he suffocates.

Combat

Healin'

A fellow using his intestines as a belt probably ought to see a sawbones. With a little luck, a good doctor can shove his squirmy insides back in his gut and sew him shut in time for chow.

Wind is easy to get rid of. On a Foolproof (3) *medicine* roll of any kind (including default), a doctor can bandage scrapes or give the sufferer some water to eliminate all Wind. This takes about 5 minutes.

Real wounds are a little trickier to heal. A *medicine* roll can be made up to one hour after wounds have occurred. A character with the *medicine: general* Aptitude can heal light and heavy wounds. Only a sawbones with *medicine: surgery* can heal serious and critical wounds.

The doctor has to roll once for each wounded area (noggin, guts, or individual limbs). If successful, the roll reduces the area's wounds by one level. The TN depends on the level of wounds in the area. Maimed limbs cannot be healed by normal means.

Healing TN Table

Wound Level	TN
Wind	3
Light	5
Heavy	7
Serious	9
Critical	11
Maimed (limbs)	13

After the "golden hour," a wound can only be healed by time (or certain arcane processes which we'll get into later). A character can try to heal a wound every 5 days by making a *Vigor* roll against the same difficulties listed above. If the roll is successful, the wound improves by one level.

Natural healing rolls are made for each area. A character with wounds to an arm and his guts would roll twice, possibly improving the condition of each location by one step.

Fate & Bounty

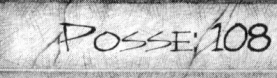

Posse: 108

Chapter Six: Fate Chips & Bounties

Fate is a fickle bitch. Sometimes she smiles on you, and sometimes she spits the biggest, nastiest thing you've ever seen right on your head.

In *Deadlands*, both the good guys and the bad guys store up a little bit of Fate they can use to save their keisters in dire situations. Fate is represented by poker chips and come in three colors (usually blue, red, and white). The Marshal starts the first game session with a pot of 10 blue, 25 red, and 50 white chips. The mix won't change except under very special circumstances which we'll tell you about in Chapter Thirteen.

At the start of each game session, every player gets to draw 3 Fate Chips at random from the pot. The Marshal also gets to draw 3 chips that he can use for extras and bad guys.

If you quit and decide to finish a game later, or the game is part of a campaign, everyone needs to write down the type and number of chips they had so they can pull them out the next time. When you do get your chips back at the beginning of the next game session, make sure everyone gets their old chips before anyone draws their 3 new ones.

Players also get rewarded with specific Fate Chips during play. Fate Chips are awarded for roleplaying your Hindrances. Solving problems and defeating the bad guys gets you extra Fate Chips and adds bounty points to the group's pot (see page 222).

The Marshal's Handbook has more specific information on how to award both Fate Chips and bounty points, but if you aren't the Marshal, keep your nose out of there, compadre.

Fate & Bounty

Calling on Fate

A character can use his Fate Chips in 3 ways: to improve Trait and Aptitude checks, to save his skin by canceling wounds, and to trade them for bounty points.

Trait & Aptitude Checks

White Fate Chips give the character one extra die per chip spent, just as if he had an extra point of Aptitude or Coordination. The player can spend these chips one at a time until he is happy with the result or decides not to spend any more.

Red Fate Chips let you roll a bonus die and add it to your highest current die. This is something like an Ace, except that the first die isn't necessarily the highest it can be. The down side is that using one gives the Marshal a draw from the Fate Pot. Only one red Fate Chip can be spent on a single action.

Blue Fate Chips are just like red chips except they don't give the Marshal any draws. Only one blue chip may ever be spent on a single action.

Savin' Your Skin

Fate Chips can also be used to avoid getting your character's noggin or other important parts of his anatomy blown off. Spending a Fate Chip doesn't make wounds "heal" or stop an attack—it just reduces the effects or makes it so it never happened in the first place.

Whenever your character takes damage, you can spend chips to negate some of it. This applies to damage from a single attack only. If your cowpoke gets shot twice in the same round, you have to reduce each one separately.

These wounds are negated before any Wind is rolled. If you need to negate Wind (after taking a wound or from bleeding, drowning, or brawling), each level of Fate Chip negates 5 points of it.

Fate & Damage Table

Chip	Wounds Negated	Wind Regained
White	1	5
Red	Up to 2	10
Blue	Up to 3	15

Bounties

Fate Chips can be converted into bounty points as well (see the next page). Blue chips are worth 3 bounty points, red chips are worth 2, and white chips are worth 1.

Fate & Bounty

Trading Chips

A player can give another player Fate Chips, but it's expensive. The giver has to give one like-colored chip to the pot for every chip he gives to another player. The giver should also explain exactly how his character helps his companion—whether it's by distracting a bad guy or simply offering a few colorful words of encouragement.

Bounty Points

After a fellow tussles with the creepy inhabitants of the Weird West, he either gets a whole lot smarter or a whole lot dead.

At the end of each night's game session, the Marshal gives you something called a "bounty." Bounties come from defeating bad guys and varmints or getting past major complications in the story.

Every player character in the posse gets a share of the bounty. If there are leftover points, they stay in the pot until the next time the group gets a reward. You can then use your bounty points to raise your character's Traits and Aptitudes if you'd like.

New Aptitude levels cost whatever the new level is. If you want your character's *shootin'* to go from 3 to 4, it costs you 4 bounty points. You can only raise an Aptitude once per game session, and only one level at a time.

Raising your Coordination in a Trait costs two times the new level. So to go from a 4d6 *Strength* to a 5d6 would cost 10 points (2 x 5=10).

Traits can be raised as well. The cost is equal to three times the die type of the new level. To go from a d4 to a d6 would cost 18 bounty points. You'll probably have to save up for a while to pull this off. You don't have to, but it makes for a better story if you say exactly how your character starts getting stronger or smarter. Maybe he spends his off hours lifting calves or reading something besides dime novels.

The Whole Enchilada

Now it's time for us to put everything together. Remember the characters we left to face the infamous Dr. Hellstromme and his "automaton" at the end of Chapter Two? Let's pick up there and see how our heroes, Violet, Runs with Bears, and the indomitable Ronan Lynch, fare.

The Marshal says a creature of iron lumbers forth from the mine. It's time for combat, so game breaks down into rounds. No one has to make surprise checks since they were expecting trouble, so the posse and the Marshal goes right into making *Quickness* totals.

Ronan gets an 11. He gets one card for free and one for a Fair (5) success, plus one more for his raise. He draws the Ace of Diamonds, a ten, and a 2. The Marshal calls for Aces and holds up one of Hellstromme's cards. It's an Ace of Spades.

Hellstromme turns back into the mine and yells "Come and get 'em, boys!"

Ronan's next and he doesn't know how many goons might come pouring out of the mine, so he tucks the Ace up his sleeve, putting it face down under his Fate Chips.

The Marshal calls for Kings and Violet's player, Michelle, holds up a King of Clubs. Violet takes a crack at Hellstromme with her lariat, hoping to tangle him up and drag him away from the fight. Michelle rolls Violet's *fightin': lariat* Aptitude and gets a 6. She needed a base 5 plus Hellstromme's *fightin': brawlin'* of 1, so she just got him.

continued on the next page...

Posse: 111

Fate & Bounty

The Enchlada, Cont.

On Jacks, the automaton strikes. It's right arm looks suspiciously like a Gatling pistol and it points it at Runs with Bears, 23 yards away. The Marshal asks Jason if Runs with Bears would like to vamoose. Jason nods eagerly and makes a *dodge* total of 8. Runs with Bears dives for the cave entrance.

The automaton's pistol has a range increment of +1 every 10 yards, so at 23 yards, its Target Number is (5+2=) 7. Since Runs with Bears *dodge* is higher, the automaton has to use that instead. So it rolls a 9. Go figure.

The Marshal grimaces and rolls a d20 for hit location. He gets a 10, the gizzards. The base damage on the Gatling pistol is 3d6, plus another 2d6 for the hit to the gizzards. The Marshal rolls all 5 dice, gets a couple of 6s, rolls them again, and comes up with a total of 28. Every multiple of Runs with Bears Size is a wound. Since his Size is normal, 6, he takes 4 wounds.

Jason groans and hands the Marshal 1 red chip and 1 white chip, enough to cover 3 of the wounds. He takes a light wound to the guts, then the Marshal tacks on 3 Wind as well.

On ten, two of Hellstromme's goons come into view. The Marshal asks Ronan to make a *Cognition* total, then tells him he can hear several more behind this wave.

Ronan decides it's time to play his cheat card, the Ace he put up his sleeve earlier. Unfortunately, the two goons are on ten as well. All three roll *Quickness*, but Ronan comes out on top. There's only one choice—he fans his single-action. Six bullets race out of the barrel, three at each of the thugs.

Ronan has 4d10 in *fannin'*, so he'll put 2 dice into each goon. The TN is 5 plus 1 for the range of 12 yards for a total of 6. Ronan gets a 13 on his first roll but has to subtract -2 for the fanning penalty. An 11 still gives him 1 raise, so 2 of his rounds strike the first bad guy. He rolls hit location and damage and puts the man down. The second shot is a botch—two 1s. The Marshal says Ronan's pistol goes flying out of his hand and lands behind him. "Damn!" Matt grumbles as the second goon bears down on him.

Fortunately, Violet and Runs with Bears still have actions left...

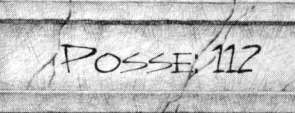

Posse: 112

The Weird West
Disputed land
Union
Confederate
Sioux governed
Scrub or Wasteland
Forested
Plains & Grassland
Swampland
N
Pacific
Atlantic
Lake Superior
L. Michigan
Washington
Seattle
Portland
Oregon
Idaho
Boise
Oregon Trail
Montana
Butte
Wyoming
Cheyenne
Dakotas
Bismarck
Deadwood
Sioux Nation
Nebraska
Minnesota
St. Paul
Wisconsin
Iowa
Des Moines
Chicago
Illinois
Nevada
Virginia City
California
City of Lost Angels
Utah
Salt Lake City
Colorado
Denver
Kansas
Abilene
Dodge
Coffeyville
Kansas City
St. Louis
Missouri
Arkansas
Mississippi
Louisiana
New Orleans
Arizona
Yuma
New Mexico
Santa Fe
Santa Fe Trail
El Paso
Oklahoma
Coyote Confederation
Dallas
Texas
Chisholm Trail
Houston
San Antonio

Huntin' Mojave Rattlers

The Horse Eater

GHOST TOWN

REAL WEREWOLVES IN THE WEIRD WEST

PIRATES OF THE GREAT MAZE

PROFESSOR SPENCER'S BARBECUE

THE GEEZER

No Man's Land

HUCKSTERS

No Man's Land: 122

Chapter Seven: Hucksters

The Reckoning replenished the world's supernatural energy, but that doesn't mean magic and spooks didn't exist beforehand.

A few rare mortals have learned to tap into the power of the supernatural for thousands of years. Some of them used their knowledge for good, and others for evil. Most used it just to help them clean their houses.

But other folks, being the superstitious and jealous bunch they are, usually hung or burned those who could make a broom sweep a kitchen all by itself.

Hoyle's Book of Games

Along about 1740, a fellow named Edmond Hoyle circulated Europe, learning arcane secrets and processes—what most of us would call "sorcery." But Hoyle wasn't fond of being burned on a stake in some backwater village in France, so he came up with a cover story that would help him travel and talk to people about such things as Tarot cards—which, incidentally, were used for games before word got out that some folks used them to tell fortunes.

Hoyle's yarn was that he was compiling a book of games. He was far more successful than he ever dreamed, and soon he had learned more about the world of the supernatural than any mortal alive. Needless to say, he also picked up a thing or two about cards and other games.

What Hoyle learned was that casting spells was a function of communicating with certain mischievous spirits—he called them "Jokers" for obvious reasons. The Jokers were malicious and evil, but if one could best them in a mental duel of sorts, they were forced to carry out some kind of task.

Hoyle eventually refined his mental duels by visualizing them as games of skill. A relatively new game at the time was poker, and this quickly became Hoyle's game of choice whenever he cast his spells—or hexes, as he preferred to call them.

Before he died, Hoyle encoded everything he learned throughout the years in the 1769 edition of *Hoyle's Book of Games*. A person who knows what to look for in the complex bridge diagrams, numeric codes written into card play examples, and sample scores that litter the book can discover secrets beyond their imagination.

Hucksters

Those who knew the secrets of *Hoyle's Book of Games* benefited greatly from the Reckoning. The number of spirits in the world before 1863 was low, and their power was weak. Afterward, a flood of spirits with links to a much stronger supernatural plane made it much easier to make use of Hoyle's formulas.

"Witches" and "warlocks" are still considered evil by common folks, and suspected dabblers are still swung from the gallows poles on occasion. While the Reckoning has given sorcerers more energy to work with, the evil it's caused has made people even more fearful and superstitious. In the civilized world, "sorcerers" are forced to keep their abilities secret lest they be hunted by overzealous priests, the Union's Pinkerton detectives, or the Confederate's Texas Rangers.

The wizards of the Weird West call themselves "hucksters" after the snake-oil salesmen who so successfully pull the wool over the collective public's eyes. Other terms were borrowed from the American Indians, who had a different view of the way things worked. Spirits became "manitous," and the supernatural plane in which they lived became known as the "Hunting Grounds."

Becoming a huckster isn't easy. A person must first learn how to communicate with manitous. Assuming they don't drive him insane, he must then treat with the ornery spirits and learn how to engage them in a

Hucksters

A Huckster's Lexicon

Hex: A spell.
Huckster: A sorcerer, witch, or warlock.
Hunting Grounds: The supernatural plane where manitous and other spirits roam.
Joker: Another term for manitous.
Manitous: The Indian word for malignant spirits.

game of wits. The game takes place in the Hunting Grounds and might seem to take minutes, hours, or even days. But time in the physical world moves much faster, so engaging a manitou usually takes a huckster only a few seconds. A really good huckster can have a manitou licked fast enough in the Hunting Grounds to beat a gunslinger in a fair draw back in the real world.

The Game

The game the huckster plays with a manitou is entirely cerebral, but humans perform much better by visualizing an actual game that is familiar to them. The most common game among hucksters in the Weird West is poker. If the huckster loses his game, nothing happens. Should he win, the manitou is forced to do his bidding.

The drawback is that a manitou cannot normally affect the physical world directly, so the huckster must actually allow the spirit to inhabit his body in order to accomplish its task. Beating the manitou means it is "controlled" and cannot harm the huckster while it enters his body. From there, it can manipulate the energy it needs to do the huckster's bidding.

But a manitou is a sly creature. Sometimes it tricks the huckster into thinking she's won so she allows it into her body uncontrolled. When an out of control manitou cuts loose, it can cause massive damage, insanity, and even death.

The Life of a Huckster

Hucksters are some of the most powerful characters in the Weird West. When things go their way, they can hide in plain sight, summon storms, or squeeze a man's heart so hard it bursts. When a manitou gets its way, the huckster's going to be hip-deep in it.

A character must purchase the *arcane background* Edge and have at least 1 point in *academia: occult* to become a huckster.

Each hex that a huckster learns is considered its own Aptitude. As with normal skills, a huckster may buy up to 5 levels in any hex during character creation.

Gettin' Caught

Casting a hex is a relatively subtle matter. The caster simply seems to concentrate for a few moments as she stares into the Hunting Grounds and makes her deal with the devils that live there. If she wins her mental duel, a number of cards appear in her right hand (or left hand if she's a lefty). The huckster must actually look at the cards to draw the manitou into her body and make the hex take effect.

No Man's Land: 125

Hucksters

Since cards materialize in a huckster's hand when she casts a hex, someone who knows what they're looking for can spot a huckster with relative ease. If a huckster wants to hide what she's doing, she'll usually keep a real deck of cards in her hand and make a *sleight of hand* opposed roll versus anyone who happens to be watching. This fools common folk most of the time, and it's why most hucksters pose as common gamblers.

Casting the Hex

To cast a hex, the huckster must first make an Aptitude check using her level in the particular hex. The type of die is determined by the Trait the hex calls on. If you get at least one Fair (5) success, your huckster has managed to contact a manitou and engaged it in a game of wits.

The next step is to draw 5 cards from a 54-card deck (leave the Jokers in). You also get one extra card for every raise on your hex roll. Your goal is to put together the best poker hand possible with all the cards you drew. (See the sidebar if you aren't familiar with poker hands).

Most hexes require a certain minimum card hand to accomplish. If your hand isn't up to snuff, the hex is unsuccessful.

Witch Hunters

Common folks in the Weird West have never heard of the Reckoning. Most people believe in spooks in general, but anyone who actually claims to have seen something supernatural is considered a raving lunatic. Most of them read the *Tombstone Epitaph* but laugh at the stories within—at least publicly.

Witches and warlocks, on the other hand, are thought to consort with the Devil—which most everyone believes in. For that reason, hucksters know better than to cast their hexes in public. If it becomes known that someone deals in the "black arts," the locals are likely to put together a posse and hang the tainted soul before he or she can cause them harm.

If the locals are too terrified to come after a huckster, word will soon get out to the Pinkertons in the North or the Texas Rangers in the South. Neither of these groups treat "warlocks and witches" kindly.

The Marshal has more specific information on these groups and their methods.

Consider yourself warned.

Hucksters

Manitous

Hexslinging is a dangerous business, since the chaotic denizens of the Hunting Grounds are always looking for ways to get into the huckster uncontrolled.

Whenever your character botches a hex roll or draws a Joker, the manitou has tricked the huckster into letting it in uncontrolled. Jokers count as wild cards, but if your character can't survive the manitou's mischief, it won't really matter.

Tell the Marshal whenever you go bust or draw a Joker while attempting to cast a hex. He then rolls on a special chart tucked away in the Marshal's Handbook to give him some idea of what the manitou is up to.

Hexes

On the next few pages are some of the hexes detailed in *Hoyle's Book of Games.* There are many more, but here are a few to get you started. More hexes (and how to go about creating new ones) are detailed in the *Hucksters 'n' Hexes* book.

Hexes have five entries: Trait, Hand, Speed, Duration, and Range.

Trait is the mental Trait used to cast the hex. Unlike normal Aptitudes, hexes are always tied to a specific Trait.

Hand refers to the minimum poker hand the huckster must draw to empower the hex. Better hands might mean the hex is stronger or lasts longer, depending on the particular hex.

Speed is the number of actions it takes to finish a hex. A few rare hexes might take much longer and aren't really suitable for combat. These hexes have their speeds listed in minutes, hours, or days as appropriate.

Duration is the length of time the hex stays in effect. Concentration means that the huckster must maintain concentration and

Poker Hands

The object of poker is to build a hand consisting of certain card combinations. The more rare the combination, the more valuable the hand is. You can consult a good encyclopedia if you need to know more. You can also read *Hoyle's Book of Games,* but be careful—some say there's strange messages hidden between the lines.

If you aren't familiar with poker hands, here's a handy cheat sheet.

Hand	Cards
Royal flush	10, Jack, Queen, King, Ace of one suit
Straight flush	5 sequential cards all of one suit
4 of a kind	4 cards of the same value and any suit
Full house	3 of one card, 2 of another
Flush	5 cards of one suit
Straight	5 sequential cards
3 of a kind	3 cards of the same value and any suit
2 pairs	2 sets of 2 cards
Jacks	A pair of Jacks or better
Pair	2 cards of the same value and any suit
Ace	A single Ace

Hucksters

can take only take simple actions. Other hexes might require Wind to maintain. A few hexes use a combination of both. This means that as long as a huckster maintains concentration *or* pays a point of Wind, the hex stays in effect.

Range is the distance at which the hex can take effect.

Call O' The Wild

Trait: Knowledge
Hand: Two Pairs
Speed: 2
Duration: Concentration
Range: 1 mile ↔ hex level

This hex lets the huckster talk to critters and varmints. He can't talk to monstrous abominations, only natural animals. The *call* goes out to specific types of creatures, such as bats, rats, wolves, bears, etc.

When the animals show up, they do the caster's bidding as long as he continues to concentrate. The moment he lets go, vermin and lesser varmints vanish. Wolves, bears, and the like either flee or attack the closest target depending on the situation.

Varmints aren't too smart. They do whatever the huckster wants to the best of their abilities, about like a well-trained dog. Don't expect them to figure out how to fire a weapon or start speaking Portuguese.

Varmints also have to make *guts* checks against supernatural opponents, just like anyone else. That's why it's not much use to throw wolves at some shambling creature from the grave. They just run away with their tails between their legs.

The huckster doesn't actually summon the varmints of the wild—he just calls to them. If there's none around, nothing happens, even if he draws a Royal Flush. The Marshal has to determine if the type of creatures the huckster is calling can be found within his range.

The type and number of creatures the huckster wants to call determines the hand he needs.

Hex Table

Hand	Varmint
Two Pairs	3d6 Rats, bats, snakes
Straight	2d6 Wolves, mountain lions
Flush	1-4 Bears

Corporeal Tweak

Trait: Smarts
Hand: Pair
Speed: 1
Duration: Concentration or 1 Wind/round
Range: 5 yards ↔ hex level

This hex alters a target's physical characteristics, making him stronger, faster, nimbler, tougher, or more dexterous. The huckster decides which one of the target's physical Traits he wants to tweak before channeling.

Hex Table

Hand	Die Type
Pair	+1 Step
Two Pair	+2 Steps
Straight	+3 Steps
Flush	+4 Steps
Full House	+5 steps

Corporeal Twist

Trait: Smarts
Hand: Pair
Speed: 1
Duration: Concentration or 1 Wind/round
Range: 5 yards ↔ hex level

Corporeal twist is the opposite of *corporeal tweak*. It actually lowers a target's Traits by one die type for each of the hands listed under *corporeal tweak*. Once the die type has dropped to a d4, the Coordination is dropped by 1 for each level to a total minimum of 1d4.

Hucksters

Earshot

Trait: Cognition
Hand: Pair
Speed: 1
Duration: Concentration or 1 Wind/round
Range: 1 mile ↔ hex level

A huckster can use this hex to hear through a subject's ears.

If the victim makes an Onerous (7) *Spirit* roll when the hex is first activated, he knows something's wrong. At that point he can try to eject the huckster by engaging him in a contest of *Spirit* versus the huckster's *Spirit/earshot* Aptitude level each round.

The huckster can cast this spell on an unseen target if he has an object the subject has touched within the last week.

Helpin' Hand

Trait: Smarts
Hand: Ace
Speed: 10 minutes
Duration: Permanent
Range: 1 yard

Helpin' hand allows a huckster to heal a suffering companion's wounds. Each successful casting reduces the wounds in all areas by 1 level each. During this time, the caster can take no actions other than sitting near the patient and playing hand after hand of solitaire poker.

The hand needed depends on the victim's highest total wound level. Note that *helpin' hand* won't heal more than one level of wounds at a time. The huckster can treat several wound levels by casting the hex

Hucksters

more than once, however. *Helpin' hand* also won't restore maimed limbs. Only the divine favors of shamans and the blessed can do that.

Hex Table

Hand	Wound
Ace	Wind
Jacks	Light
Two Pair	Heavy
Three of a kind	Serious
Straight	Critical

Hunch

Trait: Cognition
Hand: Two Pair
Speed: 10 seconds
Duration: Instant
Range: Touch

A huckster can gain insight into the past with the *hunch* hex. To cast, the huckster places his hand on a person, place, or thing and closes his eyes. If the hex is successful, the magician has a brief vision, feeling, or "hunch" about some event that happened in the target's past. The better the hand, the better the information. The huckster can concentrate on a specific question if he wants, but the target doesn't "know" about events that did not happen in its presence.

Mind Tweak

Trait: Smarts
Hand: Pair
Speed: 1
Duration: Concentration or 1 Wind/round
Range: 5 yards ↔ hex level

Mind tweak is the mental version of *corporeal tweak*. The huckster can affect any mental Trait with this handy ritual.

Mind Twist

Trait: Smarts
Hand: Pair
Speed: 1
Duration: Concentration or 1 Wind/round
Range: 5 yards ↔ hex level

Mind twist is the opposite of *mind tweak*. It actually lowers a target's mental Traits by one die type for each of the hands listed under *corporeal tweak*. Once the die type has dropped to a d4, the Coordination is dropped by 1 level to a minimum of 1d4.

Missed Me!

Trait: Spirit
Hand: Two Pairs
Speed: 1
Duration: Concentration (1)
Range: Self

This hex forces a manitou to deflect bullets and other physical projectile attacks that would otherwise hit the huckster's body. The effect is to add +5 to the TN of anyone trying to shoot the huckster. Explosives, fire from a flamethrower, and other area effect attacks are not deflected, but hexes and other supernatural effects are.

Phantom Fingers

Trait: Spirit
Hand: Ace
Speed: 1
Duration: 1 Wind/round
Range: 5 yards ↔ hex level

Hucksters often use this hex to cheat at cards or pull an enemy's gun from his holster. *Phantom fingers* can perform relatively complex manipulations with an object (such as turning a key or firing a gun), but this taxes the huckster and causes him an additional 1d4 Wind.

Hucksters

Hex Table

Hand	size/weight
Royal flush	Train
Straight flush	Manor House
4 of a kind	Freight Car
Full house	Oak tree
Flush	Wagon
Straight	Iron Safe
3 of a kind	Person
2 pairs	Gatling Gun
Jacks	Rifle
1 pair	Pistol
Ace	Baseball

Private Eye

Trait: Cognition
Hand: Pair
Speed: 1
Duration: Concentration (1)
Range: 1 mile ↔ hex level

Private eyes allows a huckster to see through another's eyes. See the *earshot* hex to see how it works.

Shadow Man

Trait: Smarts
Hand: Pair
Speed: 2
Duration: Concentration
Range: Touch

Shadow Man creates a pocket of shadow around the huckster. It does not make him invisible, but it does add to the shadow man's *sneak* rolls. A pair adds +5 to the *shadow man's sneak* rolls. Better hands add an additional +2 per level.

Shadow Walk

Trait: Smarts
Hand: Pair
Speed: 1
Duration: Instant
Range: Touch

Hucksters with this hex can step into one shadow and emerge from another. The shadow they enter and leave from must be large and dark enough to engulf their entire form. The Marshal gets the final call as to what will work.

The hand needed to *shadow walk* depends on the distance between the two shadows. At any distance, the huckster has to be able to actually see the shadow he wants to emerge from.

Hex Table

Hand	Distance
Jacks	2 yards
Two Pairs	5 yards
3 of a Kind	10 yards
Straight	20 yards
Flush	40 yards
Full House	100 yards
4 of a Kind	500 yards
Straight Flush	1 mile
Royal Flush	Sight

Hucksters

Soul Blast

Trait: Spirit
Hand: Ace
Speed: 1
Duration: Instant
Range: 50 yards ↔ hex level (maximum)

The hexslinger's best friend is the *soul blast* hex. When cast, an almost invisible stream of ghostly white energy races from the huckster's palm toward his target. The stream slams into the victim like a bullet. The caster can roll hit location normally or attempt a called shot.

If the *soul blast* hits, damage depends on the hand drawn, as shown below. Multiple shots use the same hand for determining damage. For some reason, a Dead Man's Hand (2 black Aces, 2 black eights, and a Jack of Diamonds) causes automatic death.

Hex Table

Hand	Damage
Royal Flush	10d20
Straight Flush	10d12
4 of a Kind	9d10
Full House	8d10
Straight	6d8
3 of a Kind	5d8
2 Pairs	4d8
Jacks	3d6
Pair	1d6 Wind

Hucksters

Texas Twister

Trait: Knowledge
Hand: Jacks
Speed: 2
Duration: Concentration
Range: 20 yards ↔ hex level

This hex conjures up a minor whirlwind. In the outdoors, the Texas twister kick up dirt and sand, blinding everyone within a 10-yard radius until they can make a Hard (9) *Vigor* roll or move outside of the Twister's area.

The huckster can move the Texas twister in any direction that she likes for as long as she concentrates and keeps it within sight. It has a pace of 20.

Trinkets

Trait: Knowledge
Hand: Pair
Speed: 2
Duration: 1 round / hex level
Range: Touch

Trinkets allows the huckster to reach into a pocket, pouch, or bag of some sort and pull forth a minor mundane object. The hand required depends on the item the huckster hopes to find. Money can be conjured with this hex, but like anything else created by the hex, it only lasts 1 round for every level the huckster has in the hex.

Hands higher than two pair are required to get very special trinkets—such as a key to open a specific lock. The Marshal will have to set the hand for these items himself.

Hex Table

Hand	Type of Item
Ace	Match, penny
Pair	Scarf, random playing card, nickel
Jacks	Derringer, knife, 2 bit (25 cents)
Two pair	Pistol, 5 dollar coin, specific playing card

MAD SCIENTISTS

NO MAN'S LAND: 134

Chapter Eight: Mad Scientists

Tons of gold and silver were discovered when California fell into the sea in 1868. But those weren't the most valuable minerals exposed by the Great Quake. Short seams of black stone showed up a few hundred feet below the former surface of the new state. Most thought it was coal, but when they tried to burn it, they discovered that it was something else entirely.

The rock burns slowly—so slowly that campfires lit with a fist-sized chunk of the stuff back in 1868 are still burning in 1876. Its dark stain lasts nearly as long. Miners who handle the rock claim it takes months to wash it from their hands. Stranger still—the stone "groans" and emits strange ghostly vapors when burned. For obvious reasons, Californians took to calling the new mineral "ghost rock."

The amazing burning properties of ghost rock drew scientists from all over the world to California and the West. Clever entrepreneurs began mining and selling cartloads of the stuff to the scientists and their backers. Soon, "ghost rock frenzy" took hold of the West, and prospectors began searching for it everywhere. Many found old seams previously thought to be coal in Colorado, Arizona, and scattered throughout the Rockies.

The first breakthroughs occurred in Utah in 1870. Professor Damian Hellstromme, a now-famous English scientist funded by an American philanthropist back East, created and put into use a steam engine fueled by ghost rock that could power a horseless carriage across the Salt Flats. "Steam wagons," as they have come to be called, are still in great use among the Mormons of the region.

Hellstromme's success inspired countless other black-fingered scientists. Soon scores of fantastic devices were making reputations that rivaled that of the great gunslingers, outlaws, and gunmen.

But there is a price to be paid by those who build bizarre gadgets and gizmos.

Mad Scientists

Dementia

Some suggest that creating fantastic devices is actually a form of sorcery. They believe that scientists are consorting with the same spirits as witches, warlocks, and hucksters. If this is true, the scientists seem blissfully unaware of it. They see their new creations as inspired by a great scientific revolution, and they scoff at the idea that they are consorting with demons and devils.

But there seems to be some truth to the matter, for there is a reason these wild academicians are collectively called "mad scientists." Those who create fantastic devices tend to lose their grip on reality. Most eventually become neurotic hermits or raving lunatics, though they leave a legacy of amazing gadgets in their frantic wake.

The Life of a Mad Scientist

Playing a mad scientist can be a lot of fun. Your character gets to create "weird gizmos" and blow things up with them. He might also go a little insane in the process.

Mad scientist characters must take the *arcane background* Edge. They must also have at least 3 total levels in any number of scientific concentrations, such as *science: general, biology, chemistry, engineering,* or *physics.* They should also have the *tinkerin'* Aptitude if they want to actually build the weird gizmos they design.

Creating Weird Gizmos

Making gadgets that defy common sense is easier than some might expect—for a mad scientist at least.

There are four steps that must be taken to create a weird gizmo.
1. Concoct the theory.
2. Devise a blueprint.
3. Gather the components
4. Construct the device.

As you complete each of the steps, fill in any relevant information on a photocopy of the "Weird Gizmo" blueprint we've provided on the next page.

Concoct the Theory

The first thing a mad scientist has to do is decide just what kind of weird gizmo he's trying to make. This means that the scientist's player—that's you—should write down the name of the device followed by a paragraph or two describing the "scientific principles" your character employs to make it work. It's more fun to write the theory from the perspective of the character.

No Man's Land: 136

Mad Scientists

Devise The Blueprint

Now it's time to draft a blueprint. Though the mad scientist doesn't know it, he actually consorts with manitous as he drafts his fantastic creations. Occasionally, contact with these malicious spirits drives him slowly insane.

The mad scientist must now make a *scientific theory* roll with the concentration most applicable to the device. If several concentrations apply he must use the lowest of the bunch.

Compare the total against a Fair (5) TN. If you fail, the inventor is stymied and can't try to build any other devices for the next 8 hours while he clears his head. If you are successful, draw 5 cards from your Action Deck plus 1 for every raise.

> 219
> Jokers count as wild cards, but also mean that a manitou has tricked the mad scientist and driven him mad. Let the Marshal know, so he can tell you what's happened.

Reliability

Every raise on this roll adds +2 to the device's base "reliability" of 10. The reliability is built into the blueprint, so other devices constructed from this blueprint also benefit from a good design. See below for how reliability functions.

The hand you need depends on the device your character is trying to construct and how far above the normal technology curve it is. Should you fail to get the hand you need, your character spends half the time required and must start again from scratch.

My Blueprint

The Theory

Components

Reliability

No Man's Land: 137

Mad Scientists

Gizmo Construction Table

Hand	Description	Item	Construction TN	Base Time
Royal flush	Technology that defies the laws of science	Dimension/time/mind control device	21	1-20 years
Straight flush	New technology that alters the laws of science	Mind control ray	19	1-4 years
4 of a kind	New technology that "flaunts" the laws of science	Heat/freeze ray/sleep gas	17	1-12 months
Full house	Entirely new but "realistic" technology	Ornithopter/submersible	15	1-6 months
Flush	New use of cutting edge technology	Steam wagon/land ship	13	1-4 weeks
Straight	Relatively simple but new use of existing technology	Flamethrower/automatic machine gun	11	1-6 days
3 of a kind	Major improvement on existing technology	Gatling pistol/bullet-proof vest/automatic weapon/25% faster locomotive (total reconfiguration)	9	1-10 hours
2 pairs	Slight improvement on existing technology	Faster printing press/10% faster locomotive ("tune-up")	7	1-5 hours
Jacks	Simple repair of device created by these rules or current top-of-the-line technology	Gatling gun	5	10-60 minutes

Description is a guideline for how far the gizmo is above the normal technology level.

Item is an example of some common weird gizmos in use in the Weird West.

Construction TN is the roll needed to actually create the device.

Base Time is a rough guideline for how long weird gizmos in a particular category *tend* to take. This can change drastically depending on the machine. You and the Marshal should discuss the actual building of the gadget and how long you both think it should take, or simply roll randomly based on the suggested time spans.

Mad Scientists

Gather the Components

Once the scientist has concocted a theory and drawn a blueprint for his weird gizmo, he knows what he needs to actually build the thing. Now it's time for a scavenger hunt.

Write down the major components below the device's theory on the gizmo sheet. Your character then needs to go out and actually buy or find the parts he needs. This is sometimes an adventure in itself.

Construct the Device

Now it's time to actually build the gadget. Your character needs to make a *tinkerin'* roll against the construction TN of the item (see the Gizmo Construction Table, partner).

As long as the builder gets at least one success, the item is built. Every raise on the construction roll raises the reliability by +2.

Rushing the Job

The evils of the Weird West rarely wait patiently while a mad scientist invents something to destroy them. When a weird gizmo is needed in a hurry, the inventor can attempt to rush the job.

Every hand above the one needed for a job halves the construction time. That does mean that a device requiring a Royal Flush can't be rushed.

Reliability

Even the best weird gizmos are forged in the energies of the Hunting Grounds. This means pesky manitous and the limits of the human mind can occasionally cause gadgets to malfunction.

The base chance for a malfunction of any weird gizmo is 10. Each raise rolled when devising the blueprint or constructing the device adds +2 to its reliability as explained above.

Whenever a character has to roll dice to use a device, she also has to roll a d20. It's easiest just to throw the d20 in with whatever other dice you're using. If the d20

Marshal Law

The damage, range, or other specific statistics of an item are determined by the Marshal and the theory the scientist has devised. The flamethrower described at the end of this chapter, for instance, uses methane gas as fuel, and so has a very short range, since it's hard to make clouds of gas travel as far as a bullet.

When figuring the rules for a device, the Marshal should evaluate the mad scientist's theory and fill in the "rules" at the bottom of the blueprint. If a mad scientist is after a specific effect, such as a flamethrower that shoots twice as far as normal, the Marshal should raise the hand required to design it by an appropriate number of levels.

Finally, mad scientists can only build upon the materials and technologies available to them. Galvanized engines powered by ghost rock can do a lot of things. They can't make "guided" bombs or synthetic humans, but they can make trains that go twice as fast as usual or clunky mechanoids of some sort.

Use your head and have fun with these rules. It's your game after all.

Mad Scientists

comes up over the device's reliability, it malfunctions in some way. This means a train powered by a ghost rock engine usually has to roll only when it starts and stops. A Gatling pistol, however, has to check reliability every time it's fired.

If you do roll a malfunction, the Marshal lets you know just how catastrophic the results are. Most times the gizmo just conks out, but you'd better back up a bit in case it malfunctions a little more spectacularly.

Weird Gizmos

A mad scientist can start the game with one of the devices described below or with one of her own creations of similar power (approved by the Marshal). Anyone else who wants one of these devices must purchase it. The cost is that charged by Smith & Robard's, a famous mail-order firm that custom makes weird gizmos and other devices. Since each of these items is unique and cannot be made on an assembly line, the cost is usually quite steep.

Bullet-Proof Vest

It's said a mysterious unnamed gunslinger asked a mad scientist friend to concoct this simple but effective device.

The vest covers the upper and lower guts area with an armor value of 2. This stops any weapon with damage dice of d6s or lower.

Price: $1,800
Reliability: 19

The Epitaph Camera

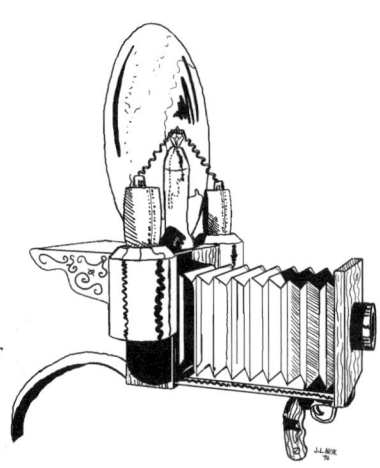

The *Tombstone Epitaph* publishes weekly reports of bizarre creatures and horrible events. Everyone reads them, but few believe them. A picture, however, is worth a thousand words. The problem is that movement of any sort ruins pictures taken by most cameras of the period. So John Clum, the editor of the *Epitaph,* commissioned Smith & Robard's to manufacture a camera that could take pictures of moving subjects. The result is the *Epitaph* camera.

Unfortunately, the very success of these cameras to capture action makes skeptics believe the device somehow manufactures fake images instead.

Price: $1,600
Reliability: 19

Flamethrower

These clever devices were pioneered by Confederate munitions experts. The galvanized tank is filled with methane stored under high pressure. When the trigger of the rifle stock is pressed, the methane shoots out and is lit by a spark of burning ghost rock.

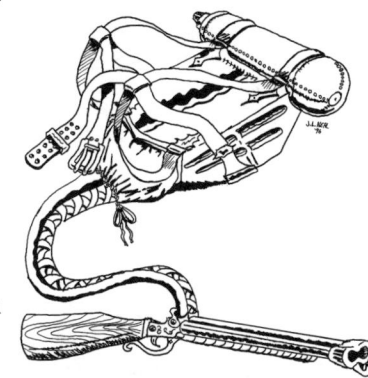

When filled with methane, a flamethrower has 30 "shots." Every time the user depresses the trigger, he fires 1d6 shots. The range of the flame is 20 yards. The flame is shaped like a cone 2 inches wide at the barrel of the flamethrower and 3 yards wide at the other end. The scientist rolls his *shootin': flamethrower* attack against every target in the cone.

The damage caused to everyone hit by the flame is 1d10 times the number of shots. The damage dice are added together, but any wounds caused are applied to separate hit locations. Ignore any bonus damage for hits to the noggin or gizzard.

A major drawback of the flamethrower is the methane tank itself. Bullets that hit the user in the upper guts from the side or behind have a 1 in 6 chance of detonating it. When this happens, the tank explodes causing 1d10 times the number of shots remaining inside. The damage drops by a die every 10 yards after the first. Professors make the most interesting fireworks.

Price: $2,000
Reliability: 18

Weapon	Shots	Speed	ROF	Range	Damage
Flamethrower	30	1	1d6	20 (max)	1d10 shots fired

Professor Fogg is surrounded by prairie ticks. He cuts loose with a gout of fire from his trusty flamethrower. Fogg rolls his *shootin': flamethrower* dice against each tick. The TN is 5 at less than 10 yards. Fogg hits 10 of the ticks. Now he rolls to see how many shots he fired and gets a 6. All of the disgusting critters take 6d10 damage. It's time to break out the toothpicks and hot sauce.

Gatling Pistol

The Pinkertons have long looked for ways to give their agents an edge against the horrors of the Reckoning. The "Gatling pistol," the common name for several brands of multi-barreled rotating pistols, is their most recent solution.

A wind-up gear releases 3 shots every time the trigger is pulled. A Gatling pistol fires on automatic (see Chapter Five), just like a Gatling gun.

Price: $800
Reliability: 18

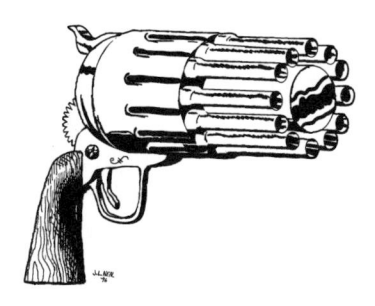

Weapon	Shots	Speed	ROF	Range Inc.	Damage
Gatling Pistol	12	1	3	10	3d6

Mad Scientists

Rocket Pack

The buffalo soldiers stationed at Fort Apache, New Mexico, were always getting ambushed by Apaches firing from high passes. Their commander was browsing through the latest Smith & Robard's catalog when he saw an amazing device. The catalog advertised an experimental "rocket pack" that could lift a man high into the air.

The commander thought this would be a great way to clear the passes of Apaches, and he used his own personal fortune to order five of them. He assigned them to the best platoon of the regiment. These men came to call themselves the "Flying Buffaloes."

The jet pack can lift up to 300 pounds (over the weight of the pack itself) for up to 20 minutes. The stove body is made of iron galvanized in one of Smith & Robard's special kilns. When the fuse atop it is lit, the ghost rock "rod" at the center is ignited and heats the water stored inside the boiler. The steam pushes the wearer suddenly into the air. He can control the amount of thrust by venting extra steam from a large side panel.

The pace of the rocket pack is 20. Vertical movement costs 2 yards of movement for every yard climbed, or 1 yard for every yard dropped in elevation.

Controlling the rocket pack is done by a "fishing rod" handle that changes the angle of the pack's thrusters. This requires a new Aptitude—*flight: jet pack,* which is normally based off *Nimbleness* since the wearer must twist and turn to get the thing to go where he wants. If the wearer ever goes bust on a *flight: jet pack* roll, he heads for the nearest obstacle. If there isn't a vertical obstacle

No Man's Land: 142

Mad Scientists

within range of his current move, he takes a steep dive at the ground instead.

If the device hits an obstacle because of a steering malfunction, the damage is 2d6 if the pack was moving normally or 4d6 if it was moving at double speed. Any resulting wounds are assigned randomly. If it's ambiguous how fast the wearer was going at the time of the crash, base the damage on its last action.

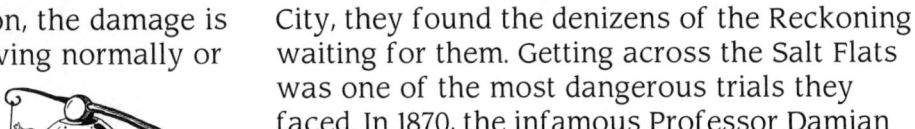

An in-air crash causes the wearer to make a second *flight: rocket pack* roll immediately against a Fair (5) or Hard (9) TN, depending on speed. If the wearer fails this roll, he plummets to the ground, taking falling damage as usual.

Price: $2,100
Reliability: 18

Steam Wagon

When the Mormons first settled Salt Lake City, they found the denizens of the Reckoning waiting for them. Getting across the Salt Flats was one of the most dangerous trials they faced. In 1870, the infamous Professor Damian Hellstromme visited their community and offered them the secret to a new invention: the steam wagon.

This steam-powered horseless carriage could dash across the flats in no time. The devices don't work well in uneven terrain and can't enter rocky areas at all, but in the desert, they can easily outpace a horse over long distances.

Steam wagons gained such fame that bandits in Nevada and other relatively flat areas started using them to rob trains. Some of these bandits even mount Gatling guns on their steam wagons. The Texas Rangers have a particular grudge against these desperadoes, since it often falls upon them to protect the Confederacy's trains.

Steam wagons have a pace of 20.
Price: $1,500
Reliability: 18

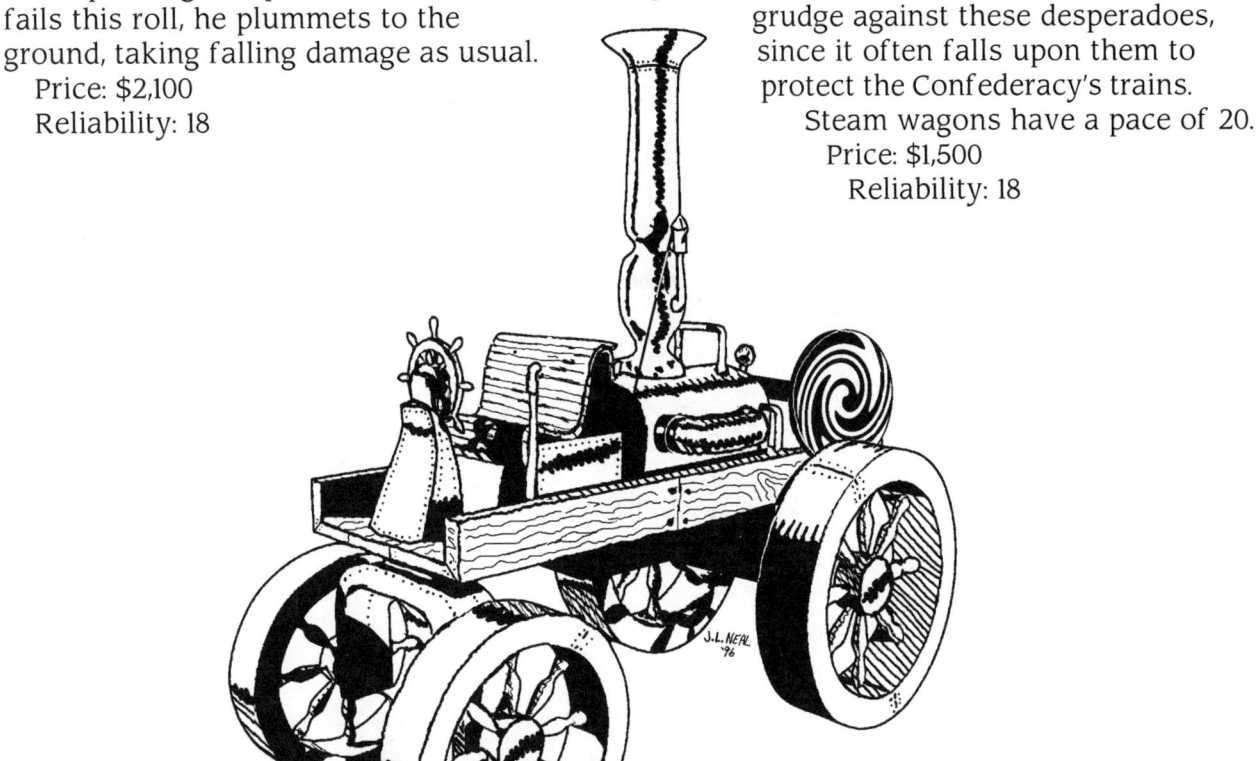

The Blessed

No Man's Land: 144

Chapter Nine: The Blessed

Faith is a funny thing. Most folks seem to have more of it when they're about to get munched on by something with jaws the size of Kansas. If that really worked, most fellows would give themselves to drinking, gambling, and carousing right up to the minute they're about to expire. Then they could say a couple of holy apologies and march right on through the Pearly Gates.

But we all know better. Genuine faith is a rare thing. Most people claim one religion or another as their own, but they don't really stop sinning until they get in trouble.

A few blessed souls are more noble, however. The pure can sometimes call on divine aid for protection against the minions of the Reckoning. Of course, sometimes they're just the first to piss something off and get eaten.

This section deals with western religions. If you want to play an Indian holy person, see Chapter Ten.

The Life of the Blessed

The faithful have certain miracles they can call upon in times of need. Which ones depends on the traditions and teachings of the religion. Regardless of the religion however, invoking a miracle requires at least one level of *faith*, and all but the miracle of *protection* requires the user to have the *blessed* Edge.

Keeping the Faith

Simply taking the *arcane background: blessed* Edge and the *faith* Aptitude and claiming to be a devout follower isn't always enough. True faith requires a little work, even if the religion's practices seem a little strange to others. Baptists lose faith if they don't dunk their "young 'uns," Jews can't get hitched without breaking somebody's best

The Blessed

crystal, and Catholics can't eat meat on certain Fridays without getting dirty looks from on high.

If your character isn't following the tenets of his religion, he starts losing his faith. Divine entities do not share their power easily and are angered when their servants don't uphold their ideals or traditions.

Whenever a *blessed* character commits a sin of some sort, she must make a *Spirit* roll. If she fails, she loses a point of *faith*. If a *blessed* character loses all her *faith*, it costs her 5 bounty points to purchase the first level again. Restoring subsequent levels can be done at normal cost. The Marshal might also make the blessed character fulfill some special goal or go on a quest for atonement.

The Target Number of the *Spirit* roll depends on the sin.

Sinnin' Table

Sin	TN	Example
Minor	5	Taking the Lord's name in vain, refusing to aid those in need
Major	9	Theft, turning away others in dire need
Mortal	11	Adultery, theft of something of great importance from someone, killing other than in self-defense

The Blessed

Invoking Miracles

Calling on a character's savior is easy. Getting him, her, or it to listen is a little more difficult.

Whenever the blessed wants to invoke a miracle, she must make a *faith* total and compare it to the TN of the miracle she's attempting to perform. If she's successful, the miracle goes off as desired.

If she's unsuccessful, the blessed hasn't convinced her deity that she's deserving of aid. This doesn't mean that the blessed individual is necessarily unfaithful. Other circumstances—such as watching one's companions get wrapped up in a thorny tumblebleed—may just have distracted the pious fellow for a few critical moments, or the patron might just be testing its acolyte.

Miracles

Every character with *faith* knows the *protection* miracle. Other miracles take years of study and practice in rituals and meditation to perfect.

A blessed character knows *protection* plus one additional miracle for every level in the higher of her *professional: theology* and *faith* Aptitudes.

Miracles have four elements you need to know before your character tries an invocation:

Target Number: This is the *faith* total the blessed needs to accomplish the miracle.

Speed is the number of actions it takes to complete the invocation.

Duration is the length of time the invocation stays in effect.

Range is the distance at which the miracle can take effect.

Exorcism

TN: Special
Speed: 8 hours
Duration: Permanent
Range: 1 yard

Evicting evil spirits from a mortal host is a slow and painful process. Once the ritual has begun, the spirit is wracked by holy energy and begins an appalling display. It speaks in tongues, vomits all kinds of foulness, and curses the blessed up and down a blue streak.

Attempting to exorcise a manitou (called a demon in western religions) is a test of the blessed's *faith* versus the creature's *Spirit*. At the end of the 8-hour ritual, both sides roll. The manitou's spirit is determined by a draw of the cards—just like during character creation.

If the blessed is successful, the manitou is banished and leaves the host body immediately. If the manitou wins, it gets +2 to resist further *exorcism* attempts by the same exorcist. This will put a Harrowed character to rest, by the way.

Holy Roller

TN: 5
Speed: 1
Duration: Permanent
Range: Self

The blessed know that asking for holy power is normally off-limits. But sometimes the horrors of the Weird West call for desperate measures.

A blessed character can use this miracle to gain a chip from the Fate pot. The chip must be used on the next action. If the character meets the difficulty, she gains a white chip. A raise nets her a red chip, and two raises gets her a blue chip.

The downside is that if the blessed miracle-worker fails the roll, Fate takes her highest chip (put it back in the pot) as penance. It's a gamble—that's why the blessed call this miracle "holy roller."

The Blessed

Inspiration

TN: 5
Speed: 1 minute sermon
Duration: Special
Range: Special

The Reckoners thrive on fear. Only a few folks know this, but it seems the blessed often find out quicker than others. Their good-natured tendencies to help those in need usually bring them face-to-face with things that sometimes don't even have a face.

When the blessed are fortunate enough to survive their adventures, their tales often inspire those around them.

The next part won't make sense until the Marshal lets you read the Chapter Thirteen in No Man's Land. Feel free to take the miracle anyway, and know that you should use it after defeating some major villainous presence and relaying the inspiring story to the masses.

Every success and raise adds +2 to the blessed's *tale-tellin'* roll to reduce the fear level. The blessed has to tell his tale immediately. He can't "save up" an *inspiration* bonus to use later on.

Lay on Hands

TN: Special
Speed: 1 minute
Duration: Permanent
Range: Touch

Holy healers have been around since ancient times. They've just never been in such demand.

The blessed use this miracle to heal the wounds and afflictions of others. The problem is that it can only be used to cure significant ailments. Worse, if the healer is not truly faithful, he takes on the subject's malady as well.

The base TN for healing a subject's wounds is shown on the chart below. The entry for "Maimed" applies to severed limbs, diseases, blindness, and the like. Maimed gizzards and noggins cannot be healed. The blessed can never bring back the truly dead. Or undead, for that matter.

The blessed actually feel the victim's pain, so they must subtract the patient's total wound modifiers from their *faith* roll. They must also add the victim's *faith* if he is of the same basic religion, or subtract it if he is not.

If the healer is successful, the victim is completely healed in all areas. The patient maintains his wound modifiers for the next hour, but he is not otherwise considered wounded.

The bad news is if the healer fails the roll, the patient isn't cured and he takes on the same maladies or wounds. If these are wounds, the priest takes the victim's highest wound level to his own *guts* area.

Healing Difficulty Table

Wound Level	TN
Wind	3
Light	5
Heavy	7
Serious	9
Critical	11
Maimed (limbs)	13

The Blessed

Protection

TN: Opposed
Speed: 1
Duration: 1 round
Range: *Faith* ↔ 10 yards

One miracle used by all major religions is *protection*. This is simply reliance on one's deity or deities to protect the faithful from supernatural evil. Any character with at least one level in the *faith* Aptitude may attempt this miracle by presenting her holy symbol or otherwise declaring the power of her deity.

A supernaturally evil opponent must make a *Spirit* total versus the character's *faith*. Should it lose, the creature cannot touch the character or otherwise cause her *direct* harm. It could still push over a bookshelf the blessed happened to be standing under, but it couldn't fire a weapon, cast a hex, or use its special abilities on her until it wins the spiritual contest.

Faithful characters shouldn't rely on this miracle too often since the winner of the contest is likely to waver back and forth. And any creature affected by *protection* probably doesn't need more than one opening to finish the fight permanently.

Sacrifice

TN: 5
Speed: 1
Duration: Permanent
Range: Sight

A central belief in most religions is that of sacrifice. The blessed can call upon this intervention to give chips to any other character in sight one of his own chips. He doesn't have to pay the usual "two-for-one" cost of trading chips.

The blessed can give chips to nonbelievers as well as members of his own flock unless the recipient's beliefs run counter to his own (such as an evil cultist.)

Failure means no chips are transferred.

Sanctify

TN: 11
Speed: 1 week
Duration: Permanent
Range: Touch

The blessed are able to ask their deity to consecrate hollowed ground, making it painful for evil creatures to walk upon it.

To work this miracle, the blessed must remain in the place to be *sanctified* for an entire week. Once the ritual is completed, a circle with a radius equal to 10 times the blessed's faith is hallowed.

When an evil creature steps upon *sanctified* ground, it must make an Incredible (11) *Spirit* total every round. If it fails, it begins to smoke and steam as if burning and takes the difference in Wind. This damage is spiritual and so can actually affect undead as well as other abominations.

Smite

TN: 5
Speed: 1
Duration: 1 minute
Range: Touch

With this miracle the blessed heroes of the Weird West can smite the evils of the Reckoning back into the last century.

When invoked, the caster's *Strength* rises by one step for every success and raise.

Succor

TN: 5
Speed: 1
Duration: Permanent
Range: Touch

There's one born every minute. Someone who's always getting beat up in a fight—that is.

This is the blessed's quick and dirty version of *lay on hands*. When invoked, it instantly rids the recipient of 1d6 Wind per success. The blessed, being the pious and altruistic individuals they are, can never grant *succor* to themselves.

SHAMANS

No Man's Land: 150

Chapter Ten: Shamans

Indians see the world a little differently than white folks. They've known about spirits for hundreds—maybe even thousands of years. The most spiritual members of a tribe are often called "medicine men," but since some are females, we'll call them "shamans."

Mad scientists deal directly with manitous, though often unwittingly. Hucksters, in a shaman's opinion, are foolish enough to actually contact the demons and attempt to bind them to some supernatural task.

Shamans consider themselves far wiser in the ways of spirits. They never deal with manitous except by accident. They rely instead on asking other denizens of the Hunting Grounds, the nature spirits, for "favors."

These spirits are sometimes seen as good or evil depending on their function, but in truth, nature spirits are ambivalent toward the affairs of man. They sometimes help those who know how to call upon them, but only in exchange for some sort of sacrifice or commitment to the spirit's ways.

The Life of a Shaman

An Indian shaman mast have the *arcane background* Edge. This means that the character had a mystical experience of some sort in his past. Some shamans had near-death experiences. Others gained their status from visions or dreams.

The rituals a shaman uses to ask for favors are described below. Each ritual is its own Aptitude. The highest ritual Aptitude level determines the number of favors the shaman knows. If a ritual Aptitude later rises above this number, the shaman can learn a new favor.

For instance, Little Coyote has 4 levels in the *dance* ritual (his highest-level ritual). This means that he can have up to 4 favors. If he later has 5 levels in a ritual, he can choose another favor.

The life of a shaman is dedicated to the ideals of his particular tribe. Most are spiritual leaders and healers for their people. Some are feared, but all are respected. All

Shamans

must set an example for their people and live a life that pleases the spirits that give them power. Shaman characters who do not uphold these beliefs find the spirits rarely listen to their pleas, as you will see below.

Calling on the Spirits

Obtaining favors from the supernatural inhabitants of the Hunting Grounds requires three steps: selecting a favor, performing a ritual, and appeasing a nature spirit.

The Favor

Favors are based on ancient traditions and relationships with particular spirits. They are not based on the shaman's whims of the moment, so the rituals used to ask for them and the effects they have on the physical world are already determined.

A list of favors commonly asked for by the Plains Indians and the Indians of the Southwest is presented on the following pages. More rituals, favors, and information on specific tribes will appear in future *Deadlands* products.

The Ritual

Once the shaman has selected a favor, he must attract the attention of a nature spirit. This is done by conducting a ritual of some sort, such as a chant or some form of self-sacrifice. The more important or powerful the favor, the greater the ritual must be.

Simple favors usually require only a pledge to the spirit's ideals. Greater favors may require fasting, scarring, or even mutilation. Different rituals require different Aptitudes. The rituals themselves are discussed on the following pages.

Approval

When the ritual required for the favor is complete, the shaman's skill and knowledge is tested by the nature spirit. The shaman should make an Aptitude total immediately on completion of the ritual. The spirit grants the favor only if the shaman has performed the ritual with proper form and respect.

Each ritual generates "appeasement points" based on the number of successes obtained. If the character cannot generate enough appeasement points for the favor he has asked for, the spirit turns its distant attentions back to the chaotic Hunting Grounds.

If the number of appeasement points generated is equal to or greater than the minimum listed to obtain the favor, it is granted by the spirit. The favor can affect either the shaman or some other individual in her presence as she chooses.

Shamans

Angering the Spirits

Although the spirits aid those who show them proper respect, they do so reluctantly. If a shaman continuously disturbs them for the same favor they grow angry. For this reason, the base appeasement cost of a favor is increased by +1 each time after the first that a shaman requests it in a 24-hour period.

The Old Ways

To nature spirits, "natural" clothing, weapons, or other belongings made by and for a particular human being have a history and carry a bit of the maker's soul. This is why they dislike mass-produced items with no past. They're also repulsed by machines that pollute and ravage the earth, such as steam-powered trains and wagons.

Shamans believe the spirit's disapproval of such things has weakened their relationship with the People. Many shamans are attempting to remedy this by urging their tribes to resort to the "old ways."

As for casting rituals, a shaman who carries a gun, metal knife, or any other artifact of "modern" society subtracts -4 from his ritual totals. The spirits won't be fooled by a shaman who quietly sets aside his Peacemaker when he's about to perform a ritual, by the way.

Similarly, any ritual attempted on a train, steam wagon, ship, or other modern conveyance suffers a -4 penalty as well.

Ordeals

A shaman who requests a very powerful favor may need to combine a number of rituals to appease the spirits. The sacrifices made during one of these extended rituals are collectively called an "ordeal."

To begin an ordeal, the shaman must first select which rituals are to be performed. No single ritual type may be used more than once during the trial. Most rituals must be performed consecutively, but some, such as fasting, may be performed simultaneously with other rituals.

Any interruption between rituals causes the ordeal to fail. A botch on any ritual roll also causes the entire ordeal to fail. After all parts of an ordeal have been performed, the appeasement points from each ritual are totaled and applied to the favor.

Manitous

Speaking with the denizens of the Hunting Grounds is a tricky process. The rituals performed by shamans are intended to attract the attention of the nature spirits, but every once in a while they are duped into communicating with a clever manitou. Worse, performing a ritual opens the shaman to spiritual forms of attack. And the manitous have little love for shamans since the Great Spirit War.

If a shaman ever goes bust while making a ritual Aptitude roll, he has been tricked into treating with a manitou instead of a nature spirit. The evil spirit's attack is an opposed *faith* roll. Since manitous come in all shapes and sizes, draw a card from the Action Deck and use the character creation rules (Chapter Three) to determine the number and type of dice it rolls. In this case, the suit determines the Aptitude level, and the card determines the die type.

If the shaman wins, the manitou retreats to the Hunting Grounds in search of easier prey. If the manitou wins, the shaman takes 3d6 points of damage to his guts area, plus an additional 1d6 for every raise the spirit got in the opposed roll.

Non-Shaman Favors

Although only shamans can perform powerful medicine, knowledge of the spirits is an important part of most Indian cultures. Warriors, for example, call on the spirits to help them in battle, while hunters give thanks to the animal spirits for providing food. This means that even non-shaman Indians may ask minor favors of the spirits.

Shamans

The warrior asking the favor must have at least 1 level of *faith* and know an appropriate ritual. Non-shamans may not request favors that have a minimum appeasement greater than 1, but all appeasement points generated by a ritual may be applied to a requested favor.

Rituals

Each type of ritual is learned by shamans as a separate Aptitude. The individual descriptions also list the Trait the ritual is associated with.

Speed is the time it takes to complete the ritual.

TN is the Target Number of the ritual.

Appeasement is the number of appeasement points awarded per success and raise on the shaman's ritual Aptitude.

Trait is the Trait the ritual Aptitude uses.

Dance

Speed: Varies
TN: Varies
Appeasement: 1
Trait: Nimbleness

Few things attract the attention of the spirits like the energy of a rousing dance. Keeping their attention is another matter and depends on the quality of the performance.

Dances may be simple, complex, or elaborate.

Ritual Table

Dance	Speed	TN
Simple	1 hour	9
Complex	2 hours	7
Elaborate	4 hours	5

A *simple* dance is one performed by a solitary dancer with simple repetitive steps and chanting.

In a *complex* dance, the dancer performs complex footwork and athletic maneuvers.

An *elaborate* dance consists of complex steps combined with special costumes and perhaps multiple dancers.

Fast

Speed: Variable
TN: 13-the number of days fasted
Appeasement: 3
Trait: Spirit

Physical discomfort is a sign of great loyalty to the spirits. Going several days without eating (i.e., fasting) is a common way of invoking powerful medicine.

Each day that the shaman fasts, she must make a *Vigor* roll versus a TN of 5 plus the number of days that she has fasted. Failure means that the shaman takes 1d6 Wind. This Wind may only be restored by eating. Even magical healing cannot restore it until she eats—that's part of the sacrifice.

At the end of the fasting, the shaman makes the ritual roll. The TN is 13 minus the number of days fasted. The minimum TN is Foolproof (3). Every success and raise on the roll nets 3 appeasement points.

Maim

Speed: 1
TN: Varies
Appeasement: 3
Trait: Vigor

One of the most frightening Indian rituals—especially to non-Indians—is self-mutilation.

This involves burning, cutting, or even removing certain body parts. While the shaman is hurt, the Marshal should give him penalties or Hindrances to match any major damage or collective minor damage. If he cuts off a finger, for instance, the character should subtract -1 from future *Deftness* totals. If he eventually removes all of his fingers, he gets the *one-armed bandit* Hindrance.

Shamans

Shamans with *blessed* friends can often heal even major "incurable" damage. That's fine. The risks involved for the healer well outweigh the benefits of picking up a couple of quick appeasement points.

Ritual Table

Action	Speed	TN
Minor curable damage	1	11
Minor incurable damage	2	7
Major incurable damage	3	5

Minor curable damage is an injury at least equivalent to a light wound.

Minor incurable damage is removable or disfigurement of a small body part that may apply penalties to certain actions. The immediate effect is a heavy injury to the body area.

Major incurable damage debilitates the shaman in some way. He loses a finger, eye, tongue, or other important body part. Major damage also causes an immediate critical wound to the affected area.

Paint

Speed: Variable
TN: Varies
Appeasement: 2
Trait: Cognition

Sand paintings, cliff paintings, and ceremonial markings on the body are other ways of showing the shaman's commitment to the spirit world. When requesting a favor for another, body painting is applied to the recipient of the favor.

The time required for this ritual depends on the level of Appeasement desired.

Ritual Table

Painting	Time	TN
Simple	10 minutes	11
Complex	30 minutes	9
Elaborate	2 hours	7

Pledge

Speed: 1
TN: 9
Appeasement: 1
Trait: Knowledge

A pledge is a promise to a particular spirit of nature. The promise is to respect and honor the spirit and its "sphere of influence." An eagle spirit, for example, would want the shaman's promise to respect it, the air, and the wind itself. A good-natured shaman likely lives up to these values daily, and so can call upon the spirits without pledging any additional or specific tasks.

Shamans

Scar

Speed: Variable
TN: Varies
Appeasement: 1
Trait: Vigor

Scarring is far less drastic than mutilation. A shaman need only mar his skin, not destroy parts of his anatomy. When requesting a favor for another, the scarring is applied to the recipient instead of the shaman.

An Indian with several large and visible scars (at least three) has the *ugly as sin* Hindrance.

Ritual Table

Painting	Time	TN
Simple	10 minutes	11
Complex	30 minutes	9
Elaborate	2 hours	7

Tattoos

Speed: Varies
TN: Varies
Appeasement: 2
Trait: Deftness

This ritual proves the shaman's dedication to the spirit world by permanently inscribing a tribute directly on human flesh. The greater this tribute is, the more likely the spirits are to honor it with favors.

Tattoos have three basic sizes: small, medium and large. Small tattoos are only a few inches square. Medium tattoos cover a sizable portion of the shaman's body, such as the forearm. Large tattoos cover the majority of a major body part, such as the back or chest.

New tattoos may not be placed over existing tattoos. When requesting the favor for another individual, the tattoo is inscribed on the recipient of the favor.

Ritual Table

Tattoo Size	Speed	TN
Small	1 hour	9
Medium	2 hours	7
Large	8 hours	5

Favors

Below are some common favors that may be granted by the spirits of nature.

A shaman knows 1 favor for every level she has in her combined ritual Aptitudes.

Favors have only 3 elements:

Appeasement is the minimum number of appeasement points it takes to garner the favor.

Duration is how long the favor lasts.

Range is the distance at which the favor takes place or the "reach" of the shaman's effect, depending on the favor. As with hucksters' magic, a shaman must be able to see his target unless a favor says otherwise.

Curse

Appeasement: 3/5/7
Duration: Permanent
Range: 10 yards ↔ appeasement

This favor is powerful medicine that calls down the wrath of the spirit world upon a shaman's enemy. When granted, the character suffers a malady of some sort.

The number of appeasement points determines the power of the curse. The nature of the disease or affliction may vary, but the effects are the same as for the *ailin'* Hindrance. Three appeasement points causes a *minor* ailment, 5 points causes a *chronic* affliction, and 7 appeasement points inflicts a *fatal* condition on the victim.

The curse may be lifted at any time by the shaman who caused it. Other shamans may lift the curse by generating more

Shamans

appeasement points than were used to place the curse and then asking the spirits to check their anger.

Earth Speak

Appeasement: 1
Duration: Concentration
Range: Touch

This favor calls upon the spirits of the earth to guide the shaman along the path of her quarry. Unlike most favors, the shaman does not have to see her quarry to receive this boon.

Each appeasement point applied to the favor gives the recipient an extra level of *trackin'*. A mystical glow surround marks made by the tracker's target, though only the shaman can see them.

Guiding Wind

Appeasement: 1
Duration: 5 rounds
Range: Touch

Using this favor, the shaman calls upon the wind spirits to guide the flight of an arrow, spear, or other "natural" weapon to its target.

Each appeasement point applied to the favor grants the recipient a +1 bonus to hit with a thrown weapon or arrow for the next 5 rounds.

Lightning Strike

Appeasement: 2
Duration: Instant
Range: 50 yards ↔ appeasement

This favor calls upon the spirits of the storm to strike the shaman's enemy with lightning. Though powerful, *lightning strike* may only be used during a thunderstorm.

If the ritual is successful, the target is automatically hits for 3d10 points of damage to the guts area. Every appeasement point beyond the minimum increases the damage by an extra d10.

Medicine

Appeasement: Variable
Duration: Permanent
Range: Touch

This favor calls upon the spirits to accelerate Nature's course and speed a patient's healing.

The number of appeasement points required depends on the highest level wound the character has sustained. If the shaman achieves that many appeasement points, the character is healed completely. If not, he remains wounded. The shaman can try again if he'd like, with the usual penalties.

Favor Table

Wound Level	Appeasement
Light	2
Heavy	3
Serious	4
Critical	5
Maimed	6

Pact

Appeasement: Variable
Duration: Until used
Range: Self

This favor allows the shaman to make a sacred pact with a spirit which it must honor at a later time. In effect, the shaman uses this favor to store another favor in some sort of fetish for later use.

Spirits dislike being bound in this way and require high levels of appeasement for such a service. For this reason, the appeasement needed to forge such a pact is equal to twice the appeasement normally required for the requested favor.

The shaman must use some small token such as a feather or other fetish in the ritual. This fetish serves as a symbol of the spirit's obligation and is needed to redeem it later. When the pact is forged, record the

Shamans

number of appeasement points that were used. Half this number is used to determine the power of the promised favor when the fetish is redeemed.

Anyone possessing an unredeemed fetish may activate it as a simple action by touching it and making a Fair (5) *Spirit* roll. Even favors that can normally be used only by shamans can be granted in this way (including those with a range of "self").

Spirits tend to avoid shamans that habitually bind them in this way. For this reason, a shaman is at -2 per unredeemed promise to all ritual Aptitude rolls.

Shapeshift

Appeasement: 4
Duration: 1 hour per appeasement point
Range: Self

A shaman may use this favor to assume the form of an ordinary animal. The most common animal forms used are the wolf, the eagle, the coyote, and the fish. See page 202 for the statistics of some common varmints.

Only the shaman's body is affected by this transformation. Clothing and equipment carried by the shapeshifter are dropped unless they can be fitted to his new form. This favor may not be used to transform into any form of supernatural creature.

Throughout the experience, the shaman retains his sense of self. He can return to his own form at any time he wishes, but he must then perform another ritual to take on an animal's form once again.

Soar with Eagles

Appeasement: 3/6
Duration: Concentration
Range: Self

The shaman's spirit is guided by the nature spirits into the body of the raptor—a bird of prey—nearest the shaman's location. The shaman may then see through the bird's eyes. If 6 appeasement points are used, the shaman also has full control of the bird's actions.

If the bird takes damage while inhabited by the shaman, the caster must make a *Spirit* roll against the TN of the wound received by the animal. Failure means the shaman takes the same wounds to his own body.

The shaman is in a trancelike state for the entire duration of the favor and may take no actions.

Speed of the Wolf

Appeasement: 1
Duration: 6 rounds
Range: Touch

Speed of the wolf endows the recipient with the graceful speed of a running wolf. He may add an additional 1d4 yards to his pace each round.

Each appeasement point above the minimum increases the movement bonus by one die step.

Spirit Warrior

Appeasement: 1
Duration: 4 hours
Range: Touch

This favor allows a shaman or warrior to call upon the spirits for aid in battle. Unlike other favors, this one is tied to a particular ritual: body painting. The warrior must paint herself conspicuously to show that she is on the warpath prior to engaging in a fight.

The recipient of the favor may add 1 level to her *dodge*, *fightin'*, or *shootin': bow* Aptitude per appeasement point. The one who asks for the favor must select the Aptitude that receives the bonus at the moment the favor is requested.

Shamans

Strength of the Bear

Appeasement: 1
Duration: 6 rounds
Range: Touch

The recipient of this favor is imbued with the powerful strength of a massive bear spirit. Indians with at least one level of *faith* can see the hazy outline of a huge grizzly around the warrior.

The target's *Strength* is increased by 1 level for each appeasement point applied to the favor.

Vision Quest

Appeasement: Variable
Duration: Instant
Range: Self

A *vision quest* is a plea to the spirits for a glimpse into the outcome of a future action or event. Spirits don't like to grant these requests. They are wild and chaotic beings themselves, and they realize the future can change in less than a heartbeat. Still, they can be talked into providing the most likely answer to a particular question if they are sufficiently appeased.

The shaman may ask the spirits a single question. The importance of the question determines the number of appeasement points needed.

Nature spirit's answers are always strange and indecipherable, but they never lie. The Marshal should concoct a story that somehow communicates the answer to the shaman's question without directly giving away the answer.

Favor Table

Wound Level	Appeasement
Light	2
Heavy	3
Serious	4
Critical	5
Maimed	6

Wilderness Walk

Minimum Appeasement: 2
Duration: Concentration
Range: Touch

Wilderness walk allows the shaman to move through the outdoors quietly and without leaving a trace.

The earth spirits quiet the sound of the shaman's footsteps, giving him +8 to *sneak* rolls. They also make it impossible for someone to follow the tracks of the walker.

The nature spirits that perform this service refuse to enter villages, towns, or any other inhabited area. The shaman loses any benefits of the favor if he gets within 50 yards of such a place.

The Harrowed

No Man's Land: 160

Chapter Eleven: Beyond the Pale

There's nothing worse to a gunfighter than having to scratch a notch *off* his pistol. In the world of *Deadlands*, however, it just might happen. You see, death isn't always the last you might hear of a particularly tough hombre.

The Marshal should let you read this chapter whenever your character kicks the bucket and comes back.

The Harrowed

Strong-willed individuals sometimes come back from beyond the grave. As the Pinkertons and Texas Rangers have learned, these individuals are actually possessed by manitous, evil spirits who use the host's mind and body to affect the physical world. These undead are called the "Harrowed," which means "dragged forth from the earth."

Fortunately, a manitou in an undead host is slain if the brain is destroyed, so they only risk their otherwise eternal souls on individuals with exceptional abilities. Weak or infirm mortals are only possessed when it suits some more diabolical purpose.

Whenever a player character dies in the game and their body is mostly intact (especially the head), she draws 1 card from a fresh deck of cards plus 1 for every level she has in Grit.

If the player draws a Joker of either color, her character is coming back from beyond the pale. Otherwise, the manitous were not interested in the character's spirit and it passes unmolested through the Hunting Grounds to the Great Beyond.

Most Harrowed stay in the hole 1d6 days. It takes a few days to fight for the hero's soul and then another 10-12 hours to dig herself out of the hole—assuming she was buried. Some come back quicker, some take longer—especially if the body was mangled worse than usual.

Very few characters come back from the dead, so you shouldn't go catching bullets hoping to come back with all kinds of cool powers. Unless your character has a lot of Grit, odds are you're just worm-food.

If you're really "dying" to play a Harrowed character, *The Book O' the Dead* lets you create an undead from scratch and details all kinds of new powers and abilities.

The Harrowed

Dominion

Manitous need a mortal soul to survive in the physical world. This means they must keep their host's soul around. When they inhabit an undead host, they fight with the soul inside for control.

When the manitou has "dominion," the soul loses all contact with the outside world. It has no memory of anything the manitou does while its in charge. The manitou can still draw on the soul's memories, however. It uses these to pass itself off as the mortal while it causes mischief and mayhem.

Manitous never admit or reveal that their host is possessed in some way. They try to perform their cruel acts while no one is looking, hoping to keep their disguise intact.

Harrowed characters have a number of dominion points equal to their *Spirit*. Whichever entity controls a majority of the character's Dominion points is in charge of the mortal's form. The mortal always wins ties.

The Nightmare

Manitous first battle for dominion moments after snatching mortal souls as they pass through the Hunting Grounds. This spiritual test of wills manifests as a horrible nightmare drawn from your character's past. That's why we had you fill in the "worst nightmare" box on the back of your character sheet.

When your character has his nightmare, the Marshal has two to carry it out. One way is quick and dirty and gets you back in the game quickly. In the other, you actually have to struggle through a solo adventure inspired by your own nightmare. The result determines who's in charge when your character's corpse comes crawling up out of the earth.

The Eternal Struggle

The result of your character's nightmare determines how many dominion points she and the manitou start with. From this point on, you need to keep track track of dominion. The space beneath **Your Worst Nightmare** on the back side of your character sheet is a handy spot. Mark a column with your character's name and another "manitou," then write down the number of dominion each has when you emerge from the grave. Never tell the other players what your current state of dominion is—we want them to worry about you.

After a character's return from the grave, she and the manitou inside struggle for dominion constantly, each trying to gain some advantage and wrest control from the other.

The manitou is best able to steal dominon when the character makes use of its power. The Marshal may occasionally ask you to make a dominion check under special circumstances, but there are two occasions where your hero must always battle for control of her mortal soul. The first is whenever your character uses a power of the Harrowed and botches. The second is whenever you purchase a new power or improve an existing one (see page 162).

The struggle for dominion is an opposed test of *Spirits*. Draw a card from a spare deck (or the Marshal's Action Deck if in combat) to determine the manitou's *Spirit*. The winner takes 1 point of dominion from the loser for every success and raise.

When a manitou gains dominion a point but doesn't control the majority, it controls its host for a short while. This will cause him no end of trouble. The Marshal will take care of things for you when this happens.

No Man's Land: 162

The Harrowed

The Unlife of the Harrowed

So what's it like being undead? It's definitely a mixed blessing. A walking corpse is a tough hombre in a fight, but he doesn't have an easy time making friends.

The first few hours an undead crawls back into the world aren't pleasant. His last memories are of whatever caused his death, and then he usually finds himself waking up in a grave or some other strange place. Whatever wounds the cowpoke died of don't seem as bad as they should, but he bears a scar or some other evidence of his death wound that *never* goes away.

The Harrowed's body doesn't adjust to its new state quickly. At first, rigor mortis causes the character seizures, and his mind is fuzzy as well. For the first 2d6 hours after returning from the dead, the Harrowed's Traits are halved.

Things aren't much better once the fog clears a bit. The character still doesn't know why he thought he died and has now come back. Even more confusing, if he listens for a heartbeat, he hears one, though it sounds more like a pregnant flutter than a heartbeat (that's the manitou wiggling around inside). If he tries to cut himself, he bleeds, but the blood is thick and dark.

After a while, the Harrowed eventually figure out they're undead. When someone blows a hole clean through your gizzard and it's healed up a few days later, it's hard to deny something's up. That's when a fellow starts learning the up side of being a zombie.

The Harrowed

Undeath

The undead can ignore bleeding and Wind caused by physical damage, drowning, or other indirect damage that affects the body's organs. The Harrowed still take Wind caused by magical or mental strain such as failed *guts* checks or miscast hexes, however.

Undead don't suffer greatly from pain, but they still can't shoot as well if half their shooting hand is blown off. This allows them to ignore 2 levels of wound modifiers per area. In other words, serious wounds inflict a -1 penalty per area. Lesser wound modifiers are ignored.

Decay

Undead characters always have pale, sallow skin. They don't rot, since the manitous inside them sustain their bodies with magical energy, but they don't exactly smell like roses either. Anyone dumb enough to put their nose up to a Harrowed character can detect the smell of decay on a Moderate (5) *Cognition* roll.

Animals always react poorly to a piece of rotting meat that has the audacity to walk around on two legs. All *horse ridin'*, *animal wranglin'*, and *teamster* rolls are made at -2.

Regeneration

This same ability to suspend natural decay actually helps the undead regenerate their wounds as well. Harrowed characters may make natural healing rolls once per day instead of once per week.

Grit

Becoming a member of the walking dead hardens the mind. Seeing a werewolf loping across a moonlit plain is still unnerving, but a fellow who can shoot himself in the heart and keep laughing learns to accept these things.

Add +1 to your character's Grit after returning from the grave.

Faith

Manitous can use all the skills and talents of their host except one: *faith*. Should the spirit ever need to make a *faith* roll, the Marshal draws a card from her Action Deck to determine the number and type of dice the manitou rolls. The manitou's *faith* fluctuates because it is channeled directly from the chaos of the Hunting Grounds.

This also means that manitous cannot draw on the spiritual powers of shamans and the *blessed*.

Nature spirits abhor manitous, so a manitou that inhabits the body of a shaman can't perform rituals when it has Dominion. If a shaman is in charge, the risk that the manitou might take over requires him to gather 1 extra appeasement point more than normal for each favor.

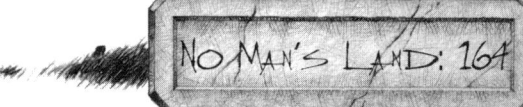

The Harrowed

The *blessed* are treated in much the same way by their holy patrons. As long as they are in charge, they can perform rituals. When the manitou rules, it cannot use the *blessed's* rituals or *faith* totals.

Destroying an Undead

The Harrowed take wounds normally, but they can't be killed except by destroying the brain—the manitou needs that to make the body function.

If the noggin takes a killing blow (is Maimed), the undead and the manitou inside it are destroyed.

Killing blows to the guts area put a Harrowed down until the manitou inside regenerates the damage back down to critical or less.

Powers

Harrowed characters can eventually learn two other types of powers: those they gain from defeating abominations, and those that are extensions of their own personality.

Counting Coup

The greatest abominations are filled with supernatural essences that give them their power. Harrowed characters can steal this energy by standing over the creature as it dies and absorbing its essence. The Harrowed have come to call this "counting coup" after the Indian tradition of touching their enemies.

The particular power gained from an abomination is called its "coup." Any Harrowed characters within a few feet of the

No Man's Land: 165

The Harrowed

creature when it dies absorb its coup automatically.

Only the most powerful abominations—singular "named" creatures such as the Headless Horseman, Dracula, or the like—generally have coup. The Marshal's Handbook has some more specific examples.

Other Powers

The Harrowed first emerge from the grave with only the powers common to all undead. After a while, however, they inevitably find themselves in danger and accidentally tap into the manitou inside them. The manitou eagerly lends its power to the host, since this allows it a chance to steal Dominion.

A Harrowed can buy a new power by spending 10 bounty points. He can choose any power for which he has one of the recommended Edges or Hindrances. With the Marshal's permission, he can also buy a power that fits his particular background or personality. The intent is for the Harrowed's power to be an extension of his character. If the rules don't fit the situation, break 'em. We can call the rules police off just this once.

If the new power has multiple levels, the character starts at level 1. Additional levels may be bought with bounty points. The cost is 2 times the value of the new level. Raising a level 1 power to level 2, for example, would cost 4 points.

The downside is that every time a power is bought or raised, the Harrowed's manitou gets another chance to steal dominion. See **The Eternal Struggle** on page 160 to find out how.

Powers of the Harrowed

The powers available to an undead character are determined by the Marshal. The best guide is the character's own Hindrances, Edges, background, and personality as a whole. The powers that the Harrowed can gain should be natural extensions of these factors. A character with a *nasty disposition,* for example, might be able to raise her *Strength* or grow *claws.*

Improving a power is like raising a Coordination, but the cost is 2 times the new level. Raising *claws* from level 3 to level 4, for example, costs 8 bounty points.

Below are a few powers to get your undead characters moving once they're out of the worm-hole. You can find a bunch more in the *Book O' the Dead,* as well as rules for creating an undead character from scratch.

Each power has three elements: Speed, Duration, and Dispositions.

Speed is the number of actions it takes to activate the power. Some powers, such as *supernatural trait,* are "always on."

Duration is how long the power lasts. Concentration means the Harrowed must maintain concentration and can take no complex actions. A number means the undead takes that many points of Wind each round to maintain the ability.

Dispositions are Edges and Hindrances that fit most easily with a particular power. Remember, these are guidelines, not rules. You should feel free to pick powers you think fit best, regardless of Edges and Hindrances. Aptitudes and background stories are just as important, but we can't list those as easily.

The Harrowed

Cat Eyes

Speed: 2
Duration: Concentration
Hindrances: *Keen, "the stare," bad eyes, curious*

Cat eyes grants an undead character the ability to see things others cannot. When used, the Harrowed's eyes glow slightly, as an animal's does when they catch the moonlight.

The undead does actually have to concentrate to use the ability. It is not considered "always on."

The last ability the power grants is "soul sight." Besides the specific powers it grants (see the table to the right, partner), the Harrowed can also add +4 to his *scrutinize* rolls whenever he concentrates on using the power.

The ability gained at each level is shown on the table:

Harrowed Power Table

Level	Power
1	Distance: The character can see twice as far as anyone else. Add +4 to Cognition checks made to spot distant sights..
2	Heat: The Harrowed can detect heat sources at least as warm as a normal human at 50 yards. Note that background heat might often obscure lesser sources.
3	Night: As long as there is any light source at all, the character can see in otherwise total darkness as if it were twilight.
4	Darkness: The character can see in complete darkness as if it were daylight.
5	Soul Sight: The final stage of cat eyes allows the Harrowed to look directly into another's soul. When activated, he can tell a person's general inclination, if he's lying, or if he's an abomination or Harrowed by making a Hard (9) *Scrutinize* roll.

No Man's Land: 167

The Harrowed

Claws

Speed: 1
Duration: As desired
Dispositions: *Two-fisted, all thumbs, bloodthirsty, nasty disposition, one-armed bandit, ugly as sin, vengeful*

Saloon gals can leave vicious scratches down a fellow's back. These kind of claws can go right through to the spine.

The character's hands turn into cruel claws. The higher the level, the bigger the claws. The damage of the claws is added to the character's *Strength* roll whenever she hits using *fighting': brawlin'*, just like the claws were a hand-held blade.

Harrowed Power Table

Level	Damage
1	+1d4
2	+1d6
3	+1d8
4	+1d10
5	+1d12

Ghost

Speed: 2
Duration: Concentration (Variable)
Dispositions: *Ailin', bad eyes, curious, night terrors, pacifist, thin-skinned*

The character and any objects he wears or carries can become completely insubstantial at will. This allows him to walk through walls and ignore physical attacks. Of course, the character cannot affect the physical world without materializing himself by ending his use of the power. A "ghosted" undead is not invisible, however.

The amount of Wind it requires to remain immaterial depends on the level of the power.

Harrowed Power Table

Level	Wind per Round
1	5
2	4
3	3
4	2
5	1

Soul Eater

Speed: 1
Duration: Concentration (Variable)
Dispositions: *Ailin', greedy, hankerin',*

Soul eater is one of the undead's cruelest weapons. The Harrowed grasps her victim by the throat and squeezes as if trying to choke them. In a heartbeat, the victim's life force is drawn from his body and consumed.

A *soul eating* undead must first get at least one raise on an opposed *fightin': brawlin'* roll. When she does, she has the victim by the throat and can begin to drain out his life force. This is an opposed *Spirit* roll. The difference is the amount of Wind the Harrowed drains if successful.

The Harrowed can use the stolen life-force to revitalize herself in some way. As her skill in the power grows, she has more options to choose from. The amount of Wind the power drains is determined by the level of the power that the Harrowed is using.

Harrowed Power Table

Level	Power
1	Restoration: Stolen Wind restores the undead's Wind on a 1 to 1 basis.
3	Regeneration: Every 5 points of stolen Wind regenerates a wound level from one area.
5	Bolster: Every 5 points of stolen Wind raises the undead's *Strength* by one step. A step is lost every 10 minutes until *Strength* returns to normal.

Fear

Stitchin'

Speed: Special
Duration: Permanent
Dispositions: Thick skinned; big 'un, overconfident

Undead can heal themselves faster than ordinary folks. The manitous inside them draw supernatural energy from the air to stitch up their holes and keep them looking pretty. As pretty as a zombie can get, anyway.

Stitchin' allows undead to regenerate their wounds even faster than normal. The rate at which they do so depends on the level of the power. The time shown on the table is how often the undead can attempt a healing roll.

Harrowed Power Table

Level	Regeneration
1	Every 12 hours
2	Every 6 hours
3	Every 3 hours
4	Every hour
5	Every 10 minutes

Supernatural Trait

Speed: Always on
Duration: Permanent
Hindrances: Any

A gunslinger with supernatural *Quickness* is deadlier than a Gatling gun. A mad scientist with paranormal *Smarts* can make an awful lot of Gatling guns, however.

This power raises any one Trait (chosen at the time the power is awarded or purchased) by one step per level. The power is tied to a particular Trait, though a character can have multiple *supernatural traits*.

The trait raised should somehow reflect the character's personality or past. A gunslinger might gain supernatural *Quickness*, for instance.

FEAR

NO MAN'S LAND: 170

Chapter Twelve: Fear

Soiled pants. Shaky nerves. Stark, raving madness. These are the end results of sheer terror. It is said the mysterious Reckoners feast on the fears of mortals.

Now that you've had some experience with their minions, it's time you learned how to ruin the Reckoners' dinner. The Marshal should let you read this section immediately after your posse has defeated its first major abomination—one of the monsters of *Deadlands*.

Fear Levels

Fear has a real effect on the world. Abominations can draw upon the ambient fear of an area for protection, and those who work against it might find themselves paralyzed with fear.

On a scale of 0-6, the normal state of the world is Fear Level 0. In these areas, folks are mostly afraid of the local bully or getting a bad rash. They might shy away from "haunted" places, but they rarely admit their fears to their neighbors.

In areas with higher Fear Levels, folks begin to get more superstitious and wary. Haunted locales are avoided, and people try not to wander out after dark if they can help it. In these areas, the abominations begin to garner the attention of their faceless masters, the Reckoners.

The Marshal has a chart in her section that tells her what bonuses abominations get at each Fear Level. You don't need to know the details, but in general, your character has to subtract the Fear Level from his *guts* checks, and the abominations get harder and harder to kill.

Fear

Tale-Tellin'

The heroes of *Deadlands* fight the Reckoners and their minions by their very deeds. Banishing the ghost of a haunted shack deep in the backwoods of Missouri might not seem like an earth-shattering event, but every time the heroes defeat evil and spread the tales of their deeds, they chip away at the local's fear—and thus the Reckoners' power.

This makes the *tale-tellin'* Aptitude the greatest weapon the heroes have against the Reckoning. When heroes defeat nefarious evils, they can tell the masses of their victories and attempt to reduce the Fear Level of an area. The world is an average of all the lesser areas beneath it, so one day the actions of the world's heroes might just thwart the Reckoners' mysterious plans.

Some characters may not care. They're more interested in gaining fame and fortune. That's fine. As long as someone tells of their deeds, the world still benefits from their victories.

This means every adventure that takes place in *Deadlands* matters, no matter how insignificant it might seem at first. Better still, your posse isn't forced into saving the world. It just happens naturally as long as your group continues to defeat evil.

Fear

Fearmongers

When your group defeats the main horror of an adventure—the "fearmonger"—you should make sure someone spreads the word. Your character's deeds can have dramatic effects on the local Fear Level, and your posse's exploits may become the subjects of newsrags and dime novels.

Soon after victory against a fearmonger, usually at the climax of the adventure, someone in the posse should tell the tale. Muckrakers and the blessed are the most likely candidates. Low-key gunslingers and mad scientists who tell of their deeds are usually taken for braggarts rather than tale-tellers.

The tale-teller needs to speak to at least half the community that was affected by the fearmonger, or at least some influential portion of it. The largest church congregation in town, the city newspaper, or even the *Tombstone Epitaph* are likely targets for a good yarn.

At the conclusion of the tale, the speaker needs to make a *tale-tellin'* Aptitude roll against the TN of the Fear Level.

Fear Level TN Table

Fear Level	TN
1	3
2	5
3	7
4	9
5	11
6	15

If the speaker is successful, the Fear Level drops by 1 level immediately. Further tales will have no effect on the area until another fearmonger moves in and begins a campaign of terror.

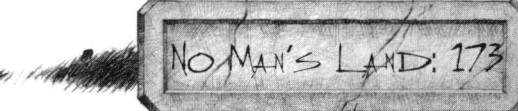

Fear

The down side is that if your character botches a *tale-tellin'* roll, the audience hears only that horrors beyond their wildest imagining exist in their own backyard. They may not publicly acknowledge their fears, but they're not likely to grab their pitchforks and shovels to help you out either.

This raises the Fear Level by 1 point. This is why Texas Rangers and Pinkertons alike don't like big mouths. A few bad speakers can sew enough chaos and confusion to turn the whole Weird West into a Deadland.

Legend Chips

When you successfully lower a Fear Level, the Marshal then places a special chip into your posse's Fate Pot. This is called a "Legend Chip." If you have *The Quick and the Dead* set, you can mark the Legend Chip with the stickers we've provided. Otherwise the Marshal should just mark an extra poker chip with a magic marker and stick it in the pot.

The Legend Chip represents a bit of the legacy your posse leaves in its wake. Fate smiles on those who persevere against the odds, so Legend chips can be used for special purposes above and beyond the norm.

The Legend chip can be played as a blue chip and has a value of 4 when reducing wounds or being converted into bounty points. In addition, the Legend chip can be used to let you completely reroll a Trait, Aptitude, or damage roll from scratch—even if you've already botched or spent other chips.

Grit

There's one last benefit to be gained from defeating a fearmonger.

"Grit" is a measure of your hero's willpower and his exposure to the sinister power of the Reckoners. After he's battled werewolves and walking dead, he gains some resistance to fear and terror.

Every time your character defeats (or takes part in the defeat of) a fearmonger, his Grit goes up by 1 point. Every point of Grit adds +1 to the character's *guts* checks.

No one has to tell the tale or sing your hero's praises for him to gain Grit. As soon as the fearmonger goes down, the character realizes he's fought a creature beyond imagining and won. This gives him the strength to keep fighting the next time his posse encounters the horrors of *Deadlands*.

The Marshal's Handbook

Chapter Thirteen: The Reckoning

The Order of Things

Now that you've read the dirt we fed those gullible player types, it's time to let you Marshals in on the real secrets of the Weird West.

Are you ready?

Do you really want to know?

Do you *really* want to know?

Bet you do. Here's what we can tell you so far.

There have always been monsters in the world. All cultures have their bogeymen, night terrors, haunts, spirits, werewolves, vampires, ghouls, and zombies. Collectively, they are "abominations." And they *are* real—don't let yourself think otherwise.

Abominations dwell in the physical world. In the spirit world—the Indians call them the "Hunting Grounds"—nature spirits and manitous are most common. Nature spirits are generally good or at least neutral towards the affairs of man. Manitous are downright evil.

Manitous drain fear and other negative creations the abominations spawn, and they channel them back to a special place in the Hunting Grounds called the "Deadlands." That's where the ancient and mysterious Reckoners dwell, though even the spirits don't know what these unearthly beings are or why they exist.

What the spirits do know is that the Reckoners horde the energy the manitous bring to the Hunting Grounds. Most of the energy is stored for some strange and unknown purpose, but some small sparks are hurled back into the physical world to bring new abominations to life. These abominations then create new fears to feed the manitous, who carry it back to the Reckoners, and so on.

It's a vicious cycle with teeth, and it's been going on since the dawn of time. As you can imagine, things eventually got out of hand—at least right up until the end of the Middle Ages.

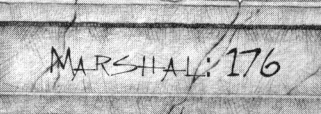

The Reckoning

The Old Ones

That's when the Old Ones—the elder shamans of various Indian tribes in the American East— called a council deep in the mountains of New England. There they discussed the state of the earth and the increasing number of horrors that walked upon it.

The Old Ones knew there was no way to banish all evil from the land at once. The abominations would have to be defeated one at a time. If the manitous were gone, however, they reasoned, far fewer new abominations would be born.

The Great Spirit War

So it was that the Old Ones asked the spirits of nature to war against their evil cousins, the manitous. The spirits agreed, but their price was high. The Old Ones would have to join them in their war.

The Old Ones traveled to an ancient Micmac burial ground and performed a long and arduous ritual. When they were through, a portal to the Hunting Grounds stood open.

The shamans stepped through and began their long fight. The "Great Spirit War" raged for hundreds of years. The Old Ones eventually tracked down and defeated their foes, but the manitous, being spirits, could not truly be destroyed. The best the Old Ones could do was defeat them and hold them to a sacred bond—as long as the Old Ones remained in the Hunting Grounds, the manitous could not meddle in the affairs of man.

The Old Ones were trapped with the malignant spirits they had defeated, but the horrors of our world abated and began to dwindle. The Shamans had won, but the price they paid was dear.

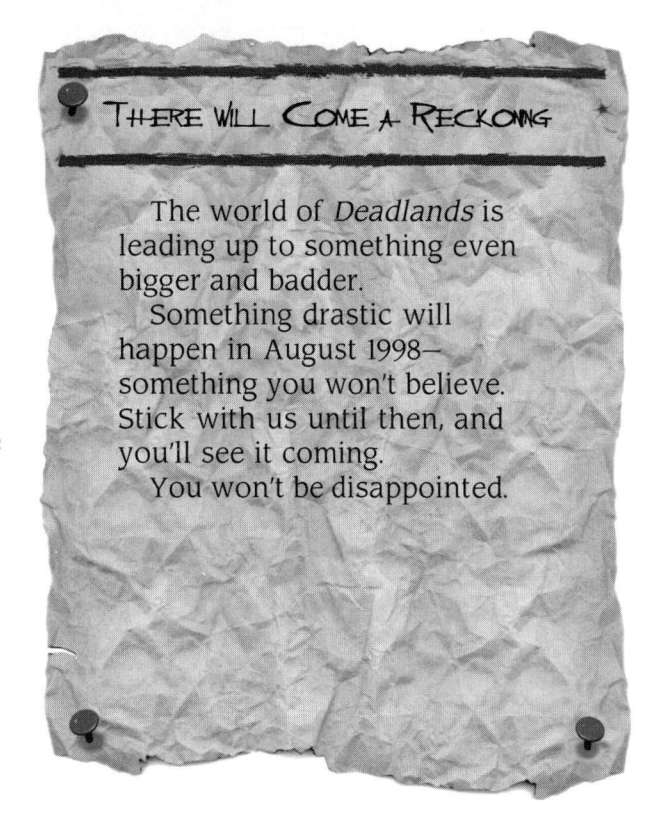

There Will Come a Reckoning

The world of *Deadlands* is leading up to something even bigger and badder.

Something drastic will happen in August 1998—something you won't believe. Stick with us until then, and you'll see it coming.

You won't be disappointed.

A Tale of Vengeance

Centuries later, in 1763, a young Susquehannah shaman named Raven was completing his studies. One summer day, he sat on a high mountain in the new colony the white men called Virginia. As he meditated, the nature spirits told him of the Great Spirit War. But his conversation was cut short by the sounds of musketry near his village far below.

Raven climbed down the mountain as fast as he could, the cruel din of battle mocking his every step. His feet felt as if they were made of stone and the miles seemed like leagues. When he finally arrived, he saw a band of whites butchering his family. They had been the last of the Susquehannah.

Now he was the Last Son.

The Reckoning

Raven Reborn

Raven left the valley and wandered the earth looking for ways to increase his own power and exact vengeance on those who had murdered his people.

The shaman learned many secrets of the world during his travels. The first was that of long life. Though born in 1745, Raven looks no more than 40 years old today.

The most important secret he learned however, was that the Old Ones had left the door to the Hunting Grounds wide open.

Between 1861 and 1863, Raven visited all the other tribes he could find and spoke solemnly of the massacre of his people at the hands of whites. He said that he was the last of his tribe, the "Last Son," and he was searching for other braves who shared his blind anger.

Other shamans often sensed Raven's long quest for vengeance had consumed him with evil. Most banished him. But sometimes a vengeful youth adopted by the tribe would turn his back on them and follow Raven. These young men understood his sorrow and his rage. They were the last of their tribes, families, or villages as well. They were the Last Sons.

Raven told his followers their troubles were caused by the coming of the whites. In some cases, it was the truth. In others, it was yet another gross misunderstanding between two different peoples.

In either case, Raven told the Last Sons that he knew how to defeat their common enemy. He would release the manitous from their old bond.

And there would come a Reckoning.

Raven told the braves that the manitous were the People's protection against the white man's invasion. The Old Ones were fools for their actions. He told the Last Sons it was their sacred duty to travel to the Hunting Grounds and return the spirit world to its natural order.

But there was only way to accomplish their task. The Last Sons would have to enter the Hunting Grounds and destroy the Old Ones.

The Hunt

The Last Sons began their long trek from the southwestern deserts and plains to the wooded mountains of New England in 1863. The group reached the old Micmac burial ground in July. Then and there, the Last Sons stepped through the open gate and into the Hunting Grounds.

They emerged on July 3rd, at the end of America's greatest and bloodiest battle of the Civil War—Gettysburg—and just before America's Day of Independence. Many of the Last Sons had not returned from their battle, but they had been successful in their quest.

The Old Ones were dead, their blackened spirit blood forever on the hands of their slayers.

The manitous were free.

The Reckoners Awake

The Reckoners had turned their attentions to other lands, other dimensions, or perhaps had just begun to slumber when the manitous had ceased bringing them delectable morsels of fear.

Now a flood of energy washed over them, feeding the mysterious beings and waking them from their centuries-old malaise. The Reckoners reveled in the feast and realized the mistakes of their past.

The Reckoning

They would no longer horde their power. They would return bits of it to the world, spawning more abominations and creating even more fear. The mortals below would bleed pure terror. When there was enough fear on the earth to sustain them, when the Earth was fashioned after their own Deadlands, the Reckoners would walk upon it.

The World Today

Now it's 1876. The Reckoners know they cannot flood the world with abominations, or the jaded mortals would stop fearing them and start fighting back. Far more energy is generated by keeping the abominations at the edge of the unknown.

Abominations don't know they are serving darker masters. They know only that their power grows as they cause more terror and mischief. A rare few abominations, such as Vlad Tepes of Rumania, have learned that something greater lurks in the spirit world, but the vast majority of the world's monsters go about their own business never realizing they serve a higher, darker purpose.

Chapter Fourteen: Runnn' the Game

You're the Marshal.

Remember that. You're the fellow who makes all the decisions and keeps things moving. It's your job to make the posse afraid of the dark while still dying to know what's in it. You have to run scenes full of high-action and drama, then turn around and do a little romance and comedy. You need to know enough rules to get you by, and you'll probably wind up paying for more pizza and soda than anyone else in the room.

It's a tough order to fill sometimes. That's why we've made things easier on you. We've designed this game so that you can create extras on the spot. Players need lots of Traits and Aptitudes to round out their heroes. You don't need so much detail when you're running the storekeep, a bandit, or Sally the bar girl.

You also might need a little help keeping with who can do what and when in combat. The Action Deck helps you there. We want you to concentrate on describing the action and the environment to your eager posse instead of worrying about modifiers and numbers.

Marshal's Shortcuts

The sections below tell you all the Marshal's shortcuts. These are ways you can keep up with all the bad guys and extras quickly and easily. This way you can worry about the *game* instead of the *rules*.

Traits & Aptitudes

Player characters have 10 Traits and tons of Aptitudes. They want and need lots of detail because they're the heroes. You, on the other hand, don't need to be so picky. Instead, you can base common extras on averages or the Action Deck.

Average folks have 2d6 in their Traits, 3 levels in Aptitudes relating to their main profession, 2 levels in common Aptitudes like *horse ridin'* and probably one *shootin'* skill, and 1s or nothing in everything else. When you need to know what a shopkeeper's *scrutinize* is, you can figure it's 3d6.

Runnin' the Game

If you want a character to have a few special Traits or Aptitudes, you can write them in afterward.

If you want a little more variety, draw a card from your Action Deck. The value of the card tells you a die type to use, and the suit can tell you the Coordination or Aptitude level, just like in the character creation section in Chapter Three.

Sometimes you might want to prepare ahead of time, especially for extras that are going to appear frequently. Here's a quick and dirty way to write them up:

Ernest McFly, Bartender
Corporeal: 2d6; *Quickness* 1d8
Shotgun 3d6
Mental: 2d6; *Mien* 3d8
Scrutinize 3d8
Gear: Shotgun under bar.
Personality: Doesn't like trouble.

What we've done here is write down the bartender's average Corporeal Trait and any special Traits—in this case, *Quickness*. Below that is his main weapon skill, his average Mental Trait, a higher than average *Mien*, and some exceptional skill in *scrutinizing*. He is a bartender, after all.

You can then add a few notes about his personality, family, or any other details you might find handy in the course of a particular adventure.

You get complete statistics for major extras in published *Deadlands* sourcebooks and adventures, but you should use one of these quick systems for less-important extras who might show up in the adventure on multiple occasions..

Combat

Sometimes there's a lot of bad guys. You don't want to keep track of fifteen banditos' *Quickness* totals, wounds, Wind, and wound modifiers when you're trying to describe the scene and help the posse resolve their actions.

We've got something for you here, too.

Actions

Of all the tricks we give you, the Action Deck is the niftiest. You don't have to roll an "initiative" number for each bad guy and then try to remember it. You can just lay down a few cards and wait until they come up in the round. Then the bad guy can take his action, and you can move on.

You should roll *Quickness* totals for major bad guys' and critters' Action Cards. For numerous extras, deal one and a half cards for each bad guy. If you want to be "fair," assign the cards face down so you don't give one thug all the high cards while some loser gets the deuces.

If you can, keep the cards hidden from the players so they won't know when the bad guys are about to act. *The Quick and the Dead* set contains a handy screen you can use for that very purpose.

Stun Checks

There's one last trick you can play with Action Cards. Whenever a bad guy is stunned, lay a discarded Action Card sideways across any remaining actions so that you remember to check for recovery on her next action. That way you can see at a glance which thug or critter needs to make a recovery check before he takes another action.

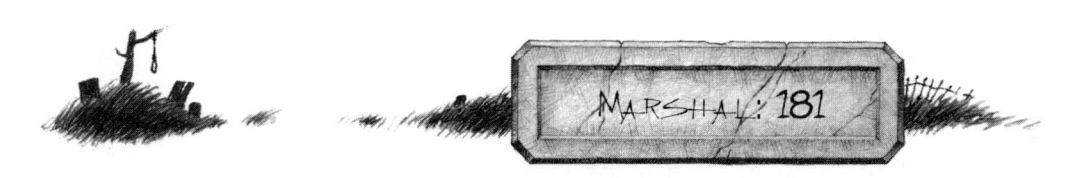

Runnin' the Game

Quick Hits

Instead of keeping track of wounds and modifiers, give "thugs" and other common extras "hits" instead.

An extra or critter has 5 times its Size in hits. This means normal folks have 30 hits. This accounts for accumulated Wind and wounds.

Whenever a player character makes a successful attack, go ahead and let her roll hit location to see if she gets any extra dice for the gizzards or noggin. When she gives you the damage total, simply subtract it from the creature's hits. When the victim runs out of hits, it goes down. You can decide whether it's actually dead or not.

Wind works the same way—just subtract it from the extra's hits.

If you need to know the extra's wound penalties, just divide its damage by 5 and round down. A critter that's taken 23 hits, for instance, would have a -4 penalty.

You can keep track of more important extras just like they were player characters if you want. If the posse gets in a fight with Jesse James, for instance, you can use the more detailed system.

Boot Hill

Another great cheat for the Marshal is the Boot Hill sheet. This will help you keep track of large numbers of thugs and other extras when the posse gets in a big fight.

Before the action starts, you should write up the bad guys' attacks and defenses, the damage they do with their main weapons, and their hits (usually 30 for humans). We call this page "Boot Hill." There's one in the back of most anything we publish, and there's a blank Boot Hill sheet near the back of the book you can photocopy and use whenever you need it.

Here's an example of how to write up a character or creature destined for a fight with the posse:

Bloody Ones

Attack:
  Claws 4d8/1d8+1d6
  Bite 12/4d8/1d8 + 1d6
Defense:
  Brawlin' 4
Hits: 30
Terror: 9
Special Abilities:
  Piercing weapons and bullets do half damage.

Attack lists the extra's primary weapons. The first number is its Aptitude dice for the attack, and the last is its damage.

Defense is the bad guy's *dodge* and *brawlin'* Aptitude, if any, and his defensive skill with any primary hand-to-hand weapons.

Hits is for using the "quick hits" system. The number here is 5 times the extra's Size.

Terror is listed only if the extra is an abomination. This is the TN of the *guts* check a character must make when he first sees the creature.

Special Abilities lists any special notes or weird attacks an abomination might have.

Use the Posse

The last bit of advice we can offer you is to use the posse. You have to show everyone how to play the first few times, of course, but afterward, you need to let them figure out whether or not they hit the bad guys, how many actions they get, and how to subtract their wound modifiers from their rolls. This leaves you free to better describe the action and keep the game moving.

We've tried to make it easy for you to run *Deadlands*. The first game or two could possibly be a little rough, but we think you're sharp enough to get into the swing of things quick. And when you do, you can really cut loose and spin yarns your posse will talk about for years to come.

Chapter Fifteen: Abominations

Some abominations have survived on the earth for hundreds or even thousands of years. New ones were originally "seeds" of fear given life by the Reckoners. These new abominations might be the subjects of legends suddenly made real and twisted into even more macabre and powerful creatures. They could believe they have lived since the beginning of time, a thousand years ago, or last Tuesday.

With the exception of los diablos, no abominations, whether created recently by the Reckoners or having already existed for thousands of years, know they serve a higher master.

A few very clever abominations, usually former humans that were here before the Reckoning, are beginning to suspect their actions serve a greater power, but none have yet formed any sort of link with the faceless Reckoners.

What follows are some of the most horrid creatures found in the Weird West. Most of them are dangerous enemies and require a little thought on the posse's part to defeat. During play, make sure you provide some clues or drop a few hints as to how to defeat these creatures if you don't want them to wipe out your entire group.

Animal Intelligence

Critters are things with near-animal intelligence. Their *Knowledge* and *Smarts* Traits are relative to the animal kingdom. A gunslinger with a *Knowledge* of 1d4 is still smarter than a wall crawler with the same score.

Animals can be *overawed* normally. They can't be *ridiculed* by verbal attacks, but they can be poked with a stick and annoyed all to hell. *Bluff* works the same way. An animal can't be told its shoelace is untied, but it might be distracted by a rock thrown behind it.

Bitin' and Clawin'

Creatures with biting and clawing attacks may usually use both in one action. If the thing has a third or special attack, it must normally use it in place of another attack.

Abominations

Badlands Devil Bat

These critters live in the Badlands of the Union's Dakota Territory. The Sioux call them "kinyan tiwicakte," or "flying murderer."

Devil bats are nocturnal predators who hunt in groups of 1-6. They attack by racing from the night and grabbing prey with their taloned feet. This is an opposed *fightin': brawlin'* roll. If the bat thing gets a success, it causes damage normally. With a raise, it drags the prey into the air and rises at its maximum pace for a medium load (12.) If the prey doesn't break free with an opposed *Strength* roll by the time the devil bat is 50 yards above the ground, it lets go or tries to slam the struggling prey into a rocky outcropping. If successful, the bat then lands and feasts on the broken remains.

The best thing for a traveler to do once she's in the grasp of a devil bat is to grab hold of its ankles and hang on for dear life. This is an opposed roll between the creature's *Nimbleness* and the character's *Strength*. If the creature gets a raise, it manages to shake the prey loose. If the prey gets a raise, she manages to force the critter to within 10 yards of the ground or a rocky outcropping where she can jump free.

Deftness 3d10
Nimbleness 3d12
   Dodge 3, fightin': brawlin' 3, sneak 1 (5 from the air)
Quickness 3d10
Strength 1d12+2
Vigor 2d8
Cognition 4d10
Knowledge 1d4
Mien 2d10
   Overawe 2
Smarts 2d8
Spirit 1d8
Size: 6 (8' tall)
Terror: 9
Special Abilities:
   Claws STR+1d6
   Flying pace 24

   Noise sensitivity: The bat thing "sees" by sonar. If its prey has the guts to stand stock still among other obstacles, the bat thing has to make an Onerous (7) *Cognition* roll to pick her out of the clutter. If the prey does this, however, her *fightin': brawlin'* Aptitude is not added to the devil bat's TN.

California Maze Dragon

All kinds of strange creatures emerged when California fell into the sea. One of the biggest is the California Maze dragon. These tremendous critters attack ships hauling ore and prospectors mining the canyon walls of the Maze.

Unlike most abominations, Maze dragons are known and accepted as ordinary creatures. Most folks just figure they somehow came with the Great Quake. The Chinese warlords of the area started calling them dragons and the name has stuck ever since.

Deftness 1d4
Nimbleness 2d10
   Fightin': brawlin' 4, sneak 5, swimmin' 5
Quickness 1d10
Strength 5d12+10
Vigor 2d12+4
Cognition 2d10
Knowledge 1d4
Mien 1d12
Smarts 1d6
Spirit 1d4
Size: 24 (50 yards long)
Terror: 7
Special Abilities:
   Armor 1
   Teeth STR+2d12
   Swallow: The Maze dragon's mouth is so large that it can swallow a person whole. If it ever gets 2 raises on an attack roll, it swallows the victim alive. The victim takes an automatic 4d6 points of damage every round from the creature's crushing gullet and acidic bile. The only way out is to cut a hole by causing 20 points of damage with a shotgun or cutting weapon.

Abominations

Badlands Devil Bat

California Maze Dragon

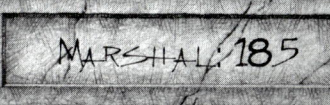

Marshal 185

Abominations

Desert Thing

Dust Devil

Marshal 186

ABOMINATIONS

GREMLINS

HANGIN' JUDGE

MARSHAL 187

Abominations

Jackalope

Los Diablos

Marshal 188

Abominations

Mojave Rattler

Night Haunt

Marshal: 189

Abominations

Prairie Tick

Tumblebleed

Marshal: 190

Abominations

Wall Crawler

Walkin' Dead

Marshal: 191

ABOMINATIONS

WENDIGO

WEREWOLF

Abominations

Desert Thing

What desert would be complete without a tentacled beastie lurking beneath the sands?

Desert things move very slowly beneath the sands, setting up shop along popular trails or in or near a water hole. When a hapless traveler passes by, the thing grabs their legs or hooves with its long tentacles and drag it into its circular maw.

Desert things can sense approaching prey up to 50 yards distant on an opposed *Cognition* versus *sneak* roll. When the prey gets within reach of its 20' long tentacles, the creature attacks.

Each of its 8 tentacles can attempt to pull prey closer to its gaping maw. First a tentacle has to hit the character with a *fightin': brawlin'* roll. If it does, it can entangle the victim instead of causing direct damage. Then it starts to reel the character in. This is an opposed *Strength* roll with every success and raise on the creature's part dragging the prey 1 yard closer to its gnashing teeth. Two raises on a character's *Strength* roll means she's managed to break free.

The only other way to escape the creature is to kill it or mangle a tentacle. The beast lies several inches under the sand, so damage from physical attacks is halved. The tentacles themselves are tough and difficult to cut. They have an armor value of 1 and can each take 20 points of damage before they are effectively destroyed.

Deftness 3d8
Nimbleness 1d8
   Fightin': brawlin' 4, Sneak 4
Quickness 3d10
Strength 1d12+2
Vigor 2d12+2
Cognition 4d10
Knowledge 1d4
Mien 2d10
Smarts 1d4
Spirit 1d4
Size: 12 (8' diameter core)
Terror: 7
Special Abilities:
   Tentacles STR
   Bite STR+1d10

Dust Devil

Dust devils are vicious killers that live in the deserts of the southwest. They lurk about like repulsive spiny serpents until they see prey. Then they use their supernatural power to create a whirlwind about themselves and move in for the kill.

Deftness 1d4
Nimbleness 1d12+2
   Fightin': brawlin' 6
Quickness 1d10
Strength 1d12+4
Vigor 1d8
Cognition 2d8
Knowledge 1d4
Mien 2d10
Smarts 3d6
Spirit 1d8

Abominations

Size: 10 (10' tall)
Terror: 9
Special Abilities:
   Spines STR+d4
   Pace 24

   Whirlwind: Dust devils attack by centering on their prey and whirling around it with their spiny, snake-like bodies. They live at the center of their dirt-filled whirlwinds, making them difficult to see or hit with normal weapons. A character has to take a -8 called shot to hit the creature itself.

   Shots that miss are sucked into the whirlwind and shot out in a random direction. Roll a d12 to determine a clock facing and see if any innocent bystanders are hit by the attack (see Chapter Five).

   Dynamite might affect the creature normally, though sticks thrown inside are normally flung out before they can detonate.

   A character making a *fightin'* attack on the creature must first beat it in an opposed contest of *Strength*. If he wins, he can attack normally. Otherwise he is blown backwards by the force of the whirlwind and can't take a swing this action.

   Blinding: The dust devil kicks up a swirling cloud of sand and stone that blinds everyone within 10 yards of its deadly center unless they make an Incredible (11) *Vigor* roll.

Gremlins

   Gremlins exist solely to cause mischief and disaster via mechanical contraptions.

   Most of the time, gremlins exist in spiritual form only. This allows them to inhabit gizmos and gadgets such as flamethrowers, steam engines, and the like.

   While gremlins can live in any contraption, their location of choice these days is the gizmos of mad scientists. If a mad scientist botches when constructing or repairing a gizmo, he will attract a gremlin. The creature's spirit inhabits the device instantly and begins to make minute arcane alterations to its nature (see the gremlin's "jinx" ability below).

   Worse, every day the gremlin may attract more of its mischievous brothers and sisters. Roll a d6 once per day. On a roll of 1, another gremlin spirit enters the device and causes another jinx.

   The only way to get rid of the gremlins is for someone to make an opposed *Spirit/tinkerin'* roll versus gremlin's *Spirit*. If the tinkerer gets one success, the combined jinx of all the gremlins inside is canceled for 24 hours. On a raise, the gremlins are actually forced out of the item where they involuntarily materialize in the flesh for one hour. If they think they can win, the gremlins will attack. Otherwise they'll make the best of their situation and run around causing as much havoc as possible.

Deftness 3d10
   Filchin' 4, lockpickin' 3
Nimbleness 3d10
   Climbin' 5, dodge 6, fightin': brawlin' 3, sneak 6, swimmin' 3
Quickness 4d10
Strength 1d6
Vigor 1d6
Cognition 2d10
Knowledge 3d8
Mien 3d8
Smarts 2d8
   Ridicule 4
Spirit 2d10
Size: 4
Terror: 7
Special Abilities:
   Jinx: A gremlin causes an item's reliability to drop by -1. Even items without a reliability, such as a wagon or a pistol, is affected by the gremlin's jinx.

Abominations

Hangin' Judges

From 1863-69, five Confederate circuit judges formed a secret alliance to steal land, ruin their rivals, and eliminate anyone who stood in the way of their wealth and fame. Those who opposed them were framed for "hangin' offenses" and hauled to the nearest tree for a lynching.

But after six years of tyranny, the locals, mostly hot-blooded Texans, fought back. They rounded up each of the judges and hung them from trees all along the Chisholm Trail as a warning to other authorities who would abuse their power.

The Reckoners seized the opportunity to infuse their spirits with their unholy energy and send them back to earth as abominations.

Now the hangin' judges stalk the Chisholm by night, terrorizing anyone who happens to cross their path. They might decide blue is illegal one day and whistling Dixie is a hangin' offense the next. Being from Texas is always a heinous crime. Whatever their "charge," the 'judges' sentences are always death.

Hangin' judges are solitary and relentless hunters. Once they're on someone's trail, they stay with him until he's dead or morning comes. If their quarry is killed, they'll string him up along the Chisolm Trail and paint the victim's offense on his forehead in blood.

The judges never speak except to whisper their prey's offense over and over.

Only one wily traveler has thus far survived an encounter with a hangin' judge. A muckraker named Lacy O'Malley escaped their wrath by "self-sentencing" himself to hang. The judge wasn't fooled by Lacy's first false attempts, but once the journalist genuinely hung himself, the judge turned around and never looked back. Fortunately for O'Malley, he was able to wriggle free a few minutes later and lived to tell the tale.

Deftness 2d10
  Shootin': pistol 5
Nimbleness 2d8
  Fightin': scythe 5, horse ridin' 3, sneak 3
Quickness 2d12
Strength 3d12
Vigor 2d8
Cognition 2d10
  Scrutinize 2, search 6, trackin' 5
Knowledge 3d6
  Area knowledge: Colorado to Texas 3
Mien 4d12
  Overawe 5
Smarts 3d6
Spirit 2d8
Size: 6
Terror: 7
Special Abilities:

Single-action Army revolvers: these weapons entirely reload themselves 1 round after they're emptied. The hangin' judges carry two and normally alternate firing one every other action to maintain continuous fire.

Scythes: On the end of each pistol is a scythe-like blade. The judges can use these in hand-to-hand combat to cause STR+2d6 damage.

Immunity: The hangin' judges are immune to normal attacks. The only way to destroy them is to hang 'em high. Bullets fired from a real lawman's gun will "kill" them, but they'll come back the following night hot for vengeance.

Coup: Hangin' judges are fearmongers of the highest order. The Chisolm Trail is Fear level 3 thanks to their efforts.

If destroyed, a Harrowed's coup is the judges twin autoloading Army revolvers. If the Harrowed ever gives the revolvers away or sells them, they'll vanish in a few hours and never return.

Abominations

Jackalope

Jackalopes are omens of bad tidings. They stalk a party and wait for bad luck to strike, then feed off the remains of anyone who's left behind.

When a jackalope stalks a party, it curses them with the *bad luck* Hindrance and waits for disaster to strike. The canny creature never attacks anyone bigger than itself as long as the prey can fight back. A Winded character is in for a surprise, however, for the jackalope instantly rushes to the attack and rips into the victim's throat.

Jackalopes are hard to kill. They have a sixth sense that warns them whenever they are about to meet danger. As long as the creatures make a Foolproof (3) *Smarts* roll, they automatically move out of the way of danger a fraction of a second before they would otherwise be harmed. Jackalopes are also smart enough to hide if someone decides to keep taking shots at them.

The best way to get rid of them is to cross running water. Jackalopes can't swim, so unless they find a bridge or some other way across, they get left behind.

On the plus side, jackalope feet are good luck charms. Anyone wearing one has the *luck o' the Irish* Edge until the charm is removed or it decays after about one month.

Deftness 1d4
Nimbleness 3d8
   Fightin': brawlin' 1, sneak 5
Quickness 2d10
Strength 2d4
Vigor 1d6
Cognition 2d10
Knowledge 2d6
Mien 1d12
Smarts 3d6
   Ridicule 4
Spirit 1d6
Size: 2
Terror: 3
Special Abilities:
   Bad luck
   Sixth sense

Los Diablos

Los diablos have haunted humanity for thousands of years. Other cultures knew them as minotaurs and gorgons. In the Weird West, they have taken the forms of mutated Texas longhorns.

They are harbingers of doom, for they are the only direct servants of the mysterious Reckoners.

Los diablos hunt down heroes who become a thorn in the Reckoners' sides. Fate rules even these mighty beings, however, so los diablos are only allowed to walk the earth on certain occasions. Whenever someone gains their fifth point of Grit, los diablos pays him a visit.

The first night los diablos are on the posse's trail, they hear a distant rumbling, as if a herd of buffalo or steers were stampeding in the distance. At this point, everyone needs to make a Foolproof (3) *guts* check. Anyone who fails loses her highest Fate Chip. The next night the rumbling grows louder, and everyone must make a Fair (5) *guts* check or lose a Fate Chip.

This continues until the TN reaches Incredible (11.) At this point, the rumblings continue, but the Target Number of the *guts* check goes no higher. Los diablos are

Abominations

waiting for the character with the most Grit to miss his check. When she does, the abominations move in for the kill.

The creature appears at the head of a ghostly stampede called the "Devil's Own Herd." These creatures are actually the souls of all those the Herd has slain before.

Even if the posse is indoors, los diablos and the Devil's Own Herd smash through walls, doors, or windows to ride over them.

There is one diablo for every character with a Grit of 5 or better. These heroes are their sworn enemies and the only individuals the forces of Fate allow them to harm directly.

The rest of the posse is "trampled" by the ghostly hooves of the Devil's Own Herd and takes 1d4 Wind per round. As usual, if Wind goes negative and starts causing wounds, the characters can die. Those that do become another soul in the Devil's Own Herd.

Those fighting with los diablos suffer a similar fate. Their souls are taken into the Hunting Grounds where they become the new servants of the malevolent Reckoners.

Deftness 1d4
Nimbleness 2d8
   Fightin': brawlin' 4, sneak 3, swimmin' 2
Quickness 2d10
Strength 3d12+8
Vigor 2d12
Cognition 2d10
   Scrutinize 2
Knowledge 3d4
Mien 4d12
   Overawe 5
Smarts 3d6
Spirit 2d8
Size: 8
Terror: 7
Special Abilities:
   Armor 2
   Horns STR+3d10
Coup: A Harrowed character the absorbs a diablo's essence gains armor 1 and a point of Grit.

Mojave Rattler

They call these great worms "rattlers" because a person's teeth start chattering as the rattler rumbles through the earth beneath him. Though they are most common in the Mojave, rattlers are also found in isolated flatlands in Montana and Utah. The rattlers of each region tend to have their own colors and even personalities.

Mojave rattlers go straight for the kill while the ones in Montana are skulkers. Utah rattlers are smaller but faster and love to chase speed wagons across the great Salt Flats. Like Maze dragons, rattlers are accepted near the regions they terrorize. Other areas still doubt the truth of these tales, but the locals know better.

Rattlers sense their prey by vibrations in the sand. They can detect the movement of a man up to 200 yards distant. This is an opposed *Cognition* versus *sneak* roll if the prey is trying to be stealthy. Horses are detected at double the distance and wagons at triple. Note that if a creature runs, its *sneak* totals suffer the usual -4 penalty.

When a rattler moves in for the kill, it bursts up through the earth and tries to snag its prey with one of its many tentacles. Though rattlers have many tentacles, they never attempt to capture multiple targets unless their prey is very close together, such as a horse and rider.

The tentacles have a *Strength* of 3d12 and are about 1/4 as long as the worm itself. Once they have grappled a target by getting a raise on an opposed *Strength* roll, the worm starts dragging the victim into its crushing maw. Every success on an opposed *Strength* roll drags the rattler's prey 1 yard closer.

The rattler's tentacles can take 30 hits before they're useless and the worm retreats, but bullets and impaling weapons do only a single point each, and shotgun blasts do 2. Cutting weapons do full damage.

Abominations

Deftness 1d4
Nimbleness 3d6
Fightin': brawlin' 3, sneak 2 (when underground)
Quickness 2d6
Strength 6d12+20
Vigor 4d12+24
Cognition 2d10
Knowledge 1d4
Mien 2d10
Overawe 2
Smarts 2d8
Spirit 1d8
Size: 10-20 (10-100 yards long)
Terror: 5
Special Abilities:
  Armor 1
  Bite 2d20
  Underground pace 24
  Surprise: Travelers who don't recognize the rumblings of a rattler beneath them subtract -4 from their surprise checks (see Chapter Five.)

Night Haunt

Night haunts are malevolent creatures of shadow that subsist on human souls. They are lone hunters that appear only at dusk, following settlers and other travelers across the plains, waiting for them to camp for the night.

When a night haunt spots prey, it waits for most of the travelers to sleep before it begins its insidious attack. It then uses mimicry and illusion as a *bluff* test of wills.

The camp's guard, if any, likely sees strange "patches" of darkness, hears a distant baby's cry, or far distant screams—anything the night haunt can do to unnerve its prey. Its goal is to lure the guard out alone, preferably without waking his companions.

If the night haunt is successful, it waits until its prey is isolated before it attacks with its soul-wrenching claws. When it has killed its victim, it sups on the fleeing soul, making it impossible for someone killed by a night haunt to become Harrowed.

Deftness 1d8
Nimbleness 4d10
Fightin': brawlin' 5
Quickness 2d12+2
Strength 2d8
Vigor 1d4
Cognition 4d12
Knowledge 1d4
Mien 1d6
Smarts 2d8
Bluff 6
Spirit 2d10
Size: 6
Terror: 11
Special Abilities:
  Claws STR+1d6 (ignores armor)
  Bite STR+1d4
  Immunity: Normal weapons can't hurt a night haunt. Only light (see below) and magical attacks cause it damage.
  Pace 24; Night haunts hover a few feet off the ground and aren't slowed by material objects.
  Light sensitivity: Night haunts are creatures of shadow. They cannot exist in bright light. Torches, lanterns, and other weapons used against them inflict 2d6 points of damage (ignore the user's *Strength*.)
Coup: A night haunt's essence gives a Harrowed character a dark, shadowy appearance. When he concentrates, the Harrowed may add +6 to his *sneak* rolls.

Prairie Tick

Prairie ticks are the scourge of the High Plains. These horrid bloodsuckers live in underground burrows of 11-20 (1d10+10) creatures each. When they sense prey, the ticks crawl out of their burrow and come bounding through the tall prairie grass at maximum speed. They can sense the vibration of a man walking up to 100 yards away, double that for horses, and quadruple for wagons.

Abominations

Deftness 2d10
Nimbleness 4d12
 Dodge 2, fightin': brawlin' 4, sneak 3
Quickness 3d10
Strength 1d4
Vigor 2d8
Cognition 2d6
Knowledge 1d4
Mien 2d8
 Overawe 2
Smarts 1d4
Spirit 1d4
Size: 2 (18" long from end to end)
Terror: 5
Special Abilities:
 Armor 1

Hooks: Prairie ticks attack by leaping for the mouth and pulling the victim's lips down with their two front hooks. This is an opposed *fightin': brawlin'* roll. If the tick gets a raise, it's in and slides down the victim's throat. Once inside, the thing's hooked legs sink into the innards and it begins to drain blood at the rate of 1d4 Wind per hour. As the host loses wounds to bleeding, the tick gets larger. When the host dies, the tick has grown so large it bursts the ribcage and comes crawling out of the stomach or throat. Anyone who sees this needs to make a Hard (9) *guts* check.

The only known way to remove a prairie tick once it's inside a host is to pour a quart of castor oil down the victim's throat. The host needs to make a Hard (9) *Vigor* roll to get the castor oil down. If he does, the tick comes crawling out in 1d4 rounds, doing its *Strength* in damage each round as it does so.

When prairie ticks can't get at someone's mouth due to a covering of some sort, they swarm over him and try to pick him into unconsciousness with their hooks, then try to crawl inside. Consider this a *fightin': brawlin'* attack that causes the tick's *Strength* in brawling damage.

Tumblebleeds

Tumblebleeds are vicious critters that disguise themselves as tumble weeds. They attack by rolling into a victim and entangling them in their thorny branches. The things' mouths and spiny thorns then penetrate the skin and drain the prey's blood.

A tumblebleed that has just feasted looks like a pile of wet, bloody sea-weed.

Deftness 1d4
Nimbleness 2d10
 Fightin': brawlin' 4
Quickness 2d8
Strength 1d6
Vigor 1d4
Cognition 1d6
Knowledge 1d4
Mien 1d4
Smarts 1d4
Spirit 1d4
Size: 4 (2-3 foot diameter spheroid)
Terror: 7
Special Abilities:
 Thorns STR (brawlin' damage): Lost Wind is actually drained blood and so cannot be healed as easily as normal. Wind lost in this way returns at the rate of 1 per day.
 Mouth STR
 Pace 18
 Sensitivity to fire: The thorny branches of a dry tumble bleed burn easily before it has fed. If hit by a lit torch, a tumble bleed starts burning on a 1-3 on a 1d6. Flamethrowers set the tumble bleed alight immediately. Once on fire, the tumble bleed takes 3d12 damage per round.

Abominations

Walkin' Dead

Pulp novels describe zombies as slow and mindless. Obviously the writers have never truly encountered the walking dead.

These suckers are mean. They're also clever. They know people think they're supposed to be slow and stupid, so sometimes they act that way just to get close. And by the way, they do feed on brains.

Deftness 2d6
Shootin': pistol, rifle, shotgun 2
Nimbleness 2d8
Climbin' 1
Dodge 2
Fightin': brawlin' 3
Sneak 3
Swimmin' 1
Quickness 2d10
Strength 3d8
Vigor 2d8
Cognition 2d10
Search 3
Knowledge 1d6
Mien 1d6
Overawe 5
Smarts 1d6
Ridicule 1
Spirit 1d4
Size: 6
Terror: 7
Special Abilities:
　Bite STR
　Guns: Many walking dead carry weapons they've taken from their victims.
　Immunity to Wind or physical stress. They are affected by other forms of damage just like Harrowed characters.

Wallcrawler

Wall crawlers are predators that hang on the shadowy sides of mesas waiting for unsuspecting travelers to pass below. When they spot prey, they race down the side of their perch and strike with lightning speed.

This is a good time for a surprise check.

Deftness 1d4
Nimbleness 2d10
　Climbin' 8
　Fightin': brawlin' 5
　Sneak 4
Quickness 2d12+2
Strength 3d10
Vigor 2d8
Cognition 2d10
　Scrutinize 2
Knowledge 1d4
Mien 1d10
Smarts 1d4
Spirit 1d6
Size: 14
Terror: 5
Special Abilities:
　Armor 2
　Bite STR+2d8
　Tail strike STR+3d10
　Pace: 20 when racing downhill

Abominations

WENDIGO

Wendigos are twisted spirits of those who resorted to cannibalism to survive a harsh winter.

Wendigos can be found in any cold climate, such as any state along the Canadian border. They might also appear in more southern areas during harsh winters, but return north as it grows warmer.

Deftness 2d6
Nimbleness 2d12
   Dodge 3, fightin': brawlin' 6
Quickness 4d8
Strength 3d12+6
Vigor 3d12
Cognition 2d12
Knowledge 1d6
Mien 4d12
   Overawe 7
Smarts 1d8
Spirit 2d8 
Size: 10 (8' tall)
Terror: 9
Special Abilities:
   Claws STR+2d6
   Bite 1d12+2d6
   Armor 1
   Night vision
   Heat sensitivity: Wendigos take double damage from fire and heat. A burning club (such as a torch) causes the Wendigo an additional 1d6 points of Wind (or damage if using quick hits) per hit.
Coup: A Harrowed who feasts on a wendigo's essence gains complete immunity to cold and cold-based attacks.

WEREWOLF

Lycanthropes come in many forms, such as wolves, jackals, and coyotes. Most of the time lycanthropes are normal people. When a full moon emerges, however, they lose control of themselves and revert to snarling creatures of evil bent on murder.

Many werewolves existed before the Reckoning. They are still supernatural creatures of evil, however, and so can be affected by holy rituals such as *protection*.

Deftness 2d8
Nimbleness 2d12+4
   Fightin': brawlin' 6, dodge 4
Quickness 4d12+4
Strength 2d12
Vigor 2d10
Cognition 2d12
Knowledge 1d4
Mien 3d10
   Overawe 2
Smarts 1d6
Spirit 1d6
Size: 6
Terror: 9
Special Abilities:
   Claws STR+1d6
   Pace 24
   Infectious Bite: A character bitten by a werewolf must make an immediate Hard (9) *Vigor* test. If he fails, he'll become a

Abominations

lycanthrope himself in 1d6 days. From that time on, he'll transform into a werewolf every full moon. The character isn't in charge during these episodes, and he won't remember what he's done the following morning.

Silver sensitivity: Werewolves take half damage from normal attacks. Silver bullets, daggers, canes, and the like cause normal damage.

Varmints

They're not abominations, but they'll still rip your throat out if given half a chance.

Below are a few normal critters. Use these statistics to help you create any other animals you need during the course of the game. We'll give you more in future *Deadlands* books.

Bar

Bears can be found throughout the northern territories. They are not common in the southwest.

The statistics below are for an average grizzly.
Deftness 1d6
Nimbleness 2d8
Fightin': brawlin' 4, sneak 2
Quickness 3d10
Strength 1d12+2
Vigor 2d12+2
Cognition 2d8
Knowledge 2d4
Mien 2d10
Smarts 1d4
Spirit 2d6
Size: 10
Terror: 3
Special Abilities:
  Claw STR+1d4
  Bite STR+1d4

Mountain Lion

You can use these statistics for any of North America's big cats. Most won't attack someone larger than themselves without provocation, but children are frequent targets.
Deftness 1d4
Nimbleness 3d10
Fightin': brawlin' 4, sneak 4
Quickness 2d12
Strength 4d6
Vigor 2d8
Cognition 2d10
Knowledge 1d4
Mien 1d8
Smarts 1d4
Spirit 2d4
Size: 4
Terror: 3

Rattlers

Rattlesnakes are a frequent hazard throughout the West.
Deftness 1d4
Nimbleness 1d6
Fightin': brawlin' 4, sneak 5
Quickness 4d12+2
Strength 1d4
Vigor 2d4
Cognition 2d10
Knowledge 1d4
Mien 1d8
Smarts 1d4
Spirit 1d4
Size: 2
Terror: 3
Special Abilities:
  Bite STR
  Poison: if a rattler causes damage, it injects its victim with a toxic poison. The victim must make a Hard (9) *Vigor* roll immediately. If he is successful, the area of the bite swells painfully and can't be used for 1d6 days. If he fails, the victim dies in 1d6 hours unless someone else sucks out the poison with a sharp knife and a *medicine* roll of Hard (9) or better.

Chapter Sixteen: Fate Awards & Bounty Points

We've told you how to maim, mutilate, and kill your posse. Even the grave might not give them peace. Now it's time to be nice to them.

You can do this by awarding them Fate Chips and bounty points.

Fate Chips

The players in your posse likely put a lot of work into their characters. Aside from their Edges and Hindrances, they've probably put a good amount of thought into their background stories as well.

This is what sets roleplaying games apart from other games: the depth of the characters. They're not just playing pieces on a board. They're fictional characters with hopes, dreams, fears, strengths, weaknesses, and personalities. When a player uses these things to make the game richer, you want to reward him with Fate Chips.

White Fate Chips are awarded whenever a character does something amusing or clever, or whenever her Hindrances make life inconvenient.

Red Fate Chips are given out when the character does something particularly clever, finds important clues, or defeats or outwits some minor opponent. You should also hand out a Red chip whenever a character's Hindrances make life miserable but aren't particularly life-threatening.

Blue Fate Chips are the reward for playing in character even when it might cost the character his life. You should also award a blue chip whenever a hero defeats a major menace or discovers a critical clue.

Rewards

Bounty Points

The other way to reward the posse is with bounty points. These are what let them improve their individual Traits, Aptitudes, Coordinations, hexes, rituals, and other talents.

Bounty points are awarded for finding clues, getting through some sort of event, or defeating bad guys. Individuals may be given Fate Chips for the same reasons, but the entire posse benefits from their actions and gets part of the bounty as well.

At the end of each game session, award the posse its bounty points. They must split the bounty points evenly among all the player characters. Leftover points remain in the pot.

The next chapter shows you how to set up adventures in *Deadlands*, and give guidelines for the number of bounty points you should award along the way.

Coup

There's one last award you can give the characters—at least those that are already dead.

The Harrowed can gain powers from defeating the most powerful abominations. These are usually the fearmongers, the creatures behind the plot of your adventure or maybe even your campaign. These are always individual and very unique. The coup you create should give the character some minor but useful power as well as some small drawbacks.

The fearmongers we feature in other *Deadlands* adventures and products have specific coups. You need to create coups when making your own monstrous abominations.

Here's an example everyone should be familiar with. Let's say Dracula comes down out of his mountains and decides to tour the West. Your posse somehow manages to catch him in Tombstone and put a stake in the Count's heart.

One of the posse is Harrowed, having caught a bullet in the gizzards several weeks prior. He stands over Dracula as the vampire lord starts to disintegrate, and he sucks in his essence.

Now you've got to come up with a coup power. You want to derive the power from Dracula's own abilities. We know the Count sucks blood, he's very fast and strong, he can turn into mist or a bat or a wolf, and he can plant suggestions in people's minds.

Of all those things, you think giving your player character the suggestion ability would work best in your campaign. So how does it work?

You decide the Harrowed can make a very powerful *persuasion* test of wills. If he gets at least a raise, he can implant a powerful suggestion in a character's mind. It's not mind control, but he might talk a guard into looking the other way or getting a shopkeeper to give him some minor item for free.

The downside is that the cowpoke's eyes now hurt whenever he's in direct sunlight. This counts as a 2-point *bad eyes* Hindrance, but only when the character is outside in bright sunshine.

Chapter Seventeen: Adventures

In *Deadlands*, adventures read like dime novels. The format we'll show you will help keep your twisted tales of the Weird West running smoothly.

It also helps you define what you want to take place at a particular location or scene. A few notes describing the action of the game will also help you figure out the names and personalities of any extras in the scene.

The format of a *Deadlands* adventure is very simple. The tale starts with "The Story Thus Far," the introduction to the adventure. The next section is "The Setup" which tells you how to get the posse involved in the adventure. After the Setup, the adventure breaks down into individual "Chapters."

At the end of each Chapter is a section entitled "The Bounty," which tells you how many bounty points you should award the posse for completing the Chapter. At the very end of the adventure is the "Boot Hill" section in which all the bad guys and critters the posse is likely to fight are summed up.

Below is a little more information on each of these sections.

The Story Thus Far

The introduction describes the background that sets everything in motion. You're probably the only one that's going to read it, but establishing a solid background is very important.

Posses being what they are, things will happen that you hadn't counted on during the course of your adventure. If you've got a detailed background, you can figure out the answers to questions you hadn't thought of and determine how the extras react to the posse's schemes.

The Setup

The point at which the posse gets involved is called "The Setup." This is where you figure out how to rope the heroes into the shenanigans that are about to occur.

There are lots of ways to pull the player characters into your adventures. The most common is to have someone hire them to do

Adventures

a job or solve some problem. The difficulty with this is you have to keep the party poor. Wealthy characters aren't likely to go chasing dangerous outlaws, after all.

Another good way to get the group together is to let the players tell *you* why their characters are involved. Even if the characters have been hired by someone, the players should still have a good reason why their character would be interested in the offer.

Chapters

Now you're ready to get into the meat of the adventure. Each chapter describes a location and the events that occur there when the posse shows up. You might occasionally want each chapter to represent certain events if an entire adventure is set to take place in one massive location (such as a haunted mansion), but as a guideline, using one location per chapter works best.

This is where you describe extras' personalities, critter's statistics, the locations of clues, and the events that need to happen before moving on to the next chapter.

The Bounty

At the end of each chapter is the "The Bounty." This tells you how many bounty points you should add to the pot for completing the scene. Here's some guidelines.

Bounty Rewards Table

Bounty	Situation
1-2	A scene in which the posse encounters a minor threat and/or uncovers information and clues.
3-4	A scene in which the posse gathers important clues and/or has to outthink or outgun a significant threat.
5-6	A tough scene filled with tons of minor bad guys, a few big ones, and/or the big payoff.

Chapter Eighteen: A World of Fear

The Reckoners thrive on fear. Some poor soul wets himself and they gobble his terror down like candy.

The unknowing minions of the Reckoners, the abominations, create an "atmosphere of fear" within a certain location when they do their dirty work. The location is usually a town, a hollow, a haunted mansion, a gulch, or the like, but it isn't necessarily restricted to a geographical area.

Sometimes an abomination inhabits arcane artifacts or haunts a particular group of people, such as a family with some ancient curse. In essence, the "Fear Level" of an abomination encompasses everyone who lives in its shadow on a day-to-day basis.

As an abomination's Fear Level rises, it's awarded more power from the Reckoners. The highest level of fear possible (6) makes the area into a "Deadland." If the Reckoners have their way, the entire earth is destined to one day become such a place.

Fearmongers

Chapter Twelve describes the Fear Levels and their effects on the local populace. What we didn't tell the pesky posse is that the goal of the Reckoners is to turn the entire world into a Deadland.

The Reckoners know they cannot simply create thousands of abominations out of the blue to ravage the Earth. Mankind would soon fight bravely back against such an overt attack. Fear and dread of the unknown are far more effective weapons in their mysterious quest for power.

The creature responsible for raising the Fear Level in a particular area is called the "fearmonger." This is the main creature behind the tale of horror the Marshal has spun—the adventure.

Lesser abominations may also exist in the area, perhaps as servants or not, but it is

World of Fear

the fearmonger that best serves the Reckoners' ends and drives up the fear level. A vampire lord reigning over a coven of lesser blood-suckers is a good example of a fearmonger and its servants. If the local terrors are a group of creatures, such as an infestation of tumblebleeds, the group itself is the fearmonger.

When the fearmonger is defeated, the Fear Level begins to drop. Abominations terrorizing their domain can raise a Fear Level by 1 about once every month or so assuming the cause some mischief. When the local fearmonger is inactive or defeated, the Fear Level drops by 1 about every 2 months or so.

Abominations that get too wild can actually stagnate the Fear Level. Remember that the unknown is the greatest horror of all. A rumor of a four-legged wolflike creature on the prowl for young maidens strikes fear into the hearts of everyone. A werewolf that wades into Dodge and starts eating people certainly makes for some wet crotches, but then it becomes just another varmint and a boon to the local silversmith.

The Power of Fear

The power of fear is an incredible tool for the Reckoners and their minions. Only the manitous know they serve a higher master. Most abominations know only that their actions somehow make them more powerful.

In areas with a Fear Level higher than 0, the posse suffers a minus to its *guts* checks. Abominations gain Fate Chips in areas of very high fear whenever the Marshal draws certain cards (see the **Fear Effects Table** below.).

These chips should be set aside from the Marshal's normal pile and discarded at the end of an encounter. Only creatures of supernatural evil can draw upon these extra rewards of fate. Thugs and other bad guys can't use them.

Fear Effects Table

Level	Advantage
0	None
1	-1 guts checks
2	-2 guts checks
3	-3 guts checks
4	-4 guts checks; the Marshal draws a Fate Chip whenever One-Eyed Jacks are dealt from the Fate Deck
5	-5 guts checks; the Marshal draws a Fate Chip whenever One-Eyed Jacks or Suicide Kings are dealt from the Fate Deck
6	-6 guts checks; the Marshal draws a Fate Chip whenever One-Eyed Jacks or Suicide Kings are dealt from the Fate Deck; the fearmonger draws an extra card from the Action Deck every round

WORLD OF FEAR

One-Eyed Jacks are the Jack of spades and the Jack of hearts. The Suicide King is the King of hearts. If you don't understand the names, take a look at the cards. You'll get it.

The Land

In *Deadlands,* even the hills and trees feel the power of the Reckoning. A canyon with a Fear Level of 1, for example, seems a little darker than normal. At level 2, its rocks look more jagged. At level 3, its cliff walls are more foreboding. At levels 4 and 5, the flora and fauna begin to die and wither.

A Deadland (level 6) is a twisted and macabre landscape. Trees look like splintered skeletons or haunted souls, weeds grow impossibly tall, and water turns dark and stagnant.

Tale-Tellin'

Defeating a fearmonger and spreading the tales of the deed has dramatic effects as well as rewarding the heroes of the tale. When the posse defeats a fearmonger, one of them should try and spread the word of their deed. If they can get the word out and inspire others, they can actually reduce the Fear Level and add a Legend Chip to the pot. The details are back in Chapter Eleven if you need a refresher.

Terror

When a Mojave rattler chases you across the desert, most feel something warm and wet running down their breeches. Many men and women still try to deny the existence of haunts, spirits, and things that go bump in the night, even though the *Tombstone Epitaph* tells them differently every day.

The mortal mind just can't seem to handle such a sharp turn in the sanity trail. Even those hardened souls who've been around the Deadlands still can't get used to seeing Aunt Minnie crawl up out of a grave, hungry for brains.

World of Fear

The more startling or frightening an abomination is, the more difficult it is for a character to get over his own terror and get to shooting. Whenever a hero spots a horrible critter for the first time, he needs to make a *guts* check. He also has to make a check when he comes upon a particularly gruesome scene or a frightening piece of information "man was not meant to know."

The TN of the roll depends on the Terror score of the abomination, scene, or event. The creatures listed in this book already have a Terror score assigned to them. You need to assign your own Terror score to any new abominations you create or scenes the posse comes across.

Here's some helpful guidelines along with the number of dice you should roll on the Terror Table below if a character fails his *guts* check. Add an extra 1d6 to the roll if he botches, by the way.

Terror Table

TN	Dice	Description
3	1d6	Someone else's description of a strange event or creature; a nasty wound on a living victim
5	2d6	Something "slightly" out of the ordinary, like a vampire who isn't "vamped out" or a very fresh walking dead with no obvious wounds, such as the Harrowed; a dead body with "normal" wounds
7	3d6	A bizarre but not particularly gruesome creature such as a mad grizzly bear, a jackalope, or a prairie tick; a gruesome corpse with greater than normal damage such as a slit throat or a shot to the head
9	4d6	An undeniably supernatural creature such as a devil bat, a night haunt, or a devil bull, or a gruesome abomination like a walking dead; a sickening scene such as a dismembered or mutilated corpse
11	5d6	A unique and overwhelming horror such as a Maze serpent, a wendigo, or a Mojave rattler; a nauseating scene of mass carnage
13	6d6	A creature that defies imagination; grisly carnage that obviously serves some arcane and evil purpose that "man was not meant to know"

No Guts, No Glory

Failing a *guts* check is a "bad thing." Usually it means that something a character can't defeat anyway just got some extra time to beat on him. Roll the dice listed on the terror table then read the results on the Scart Table on the next page. Like most *Deadlands* rolls, add in any Aces you get.

World of Fear

Scart

Roll Effect

1-3 Uneasy: The character stares for a moment at the scene and loses his next action.

4-6 Queasy: The character stares in horror at the scene. He loses his next action and subtracts -2 from any totals made the rest of the round.

7-9 The Willies: The character staggers back and stares in horror, missing his turn for the round. He takes 1d6 Wind and his actions are at -2 until he makes a *guts* check, which he may attempt once per action.

10-12 The Heebie-Jeebies: The character turns white as a sheet and loses his entire turn and 1d6 Wind. All actions are at -2 for the remainder of the encounter.

13-15 Weak in the Knees: The victim loses 1d6 Wind. If the scene is grotesque, he loses his lunch and staggers away from the scene. If the scene is more frightening in nature, the character puts his tail between his legs and gets the Hell out of Dodge. In either case, the character is completely ineffectual until he makes the *guts* check that caused this result. He remains at -2 for the remainder of the encounter. A white Fate chip will negate this penalty once the *guts* check is successful.

16-18 Dead Faint: The character takes 3d6 Wind. If he's reduced to 0 or less, he faints dead away until he recovers. Chips can be spent to reduce Wind normally. If the character has *faith*, she must make an Ornery (7) *faith* total immediately. If she fails, the horrors of the Deadlands causes her to lose 1 Aptitude level of *faith* permanently.

19-21 Minor Phobia: The character goes *Weak in the Knees* and gains a minor phobia centered around the event. A minor phobia is a 2 point version of the *loco* Hindrance. Whenever the character is around something that reminds him of his phobia, he suffers a -2 penalty to any actions he takes against it or while it is in sight.

22-24 Major Phobia: The character goes *Weak in the Knees* and gains a major phobia focused on the event. A major phobia is a 5 point version of the *loco* Hindrance. This is the same as a minor phobia (see above,) except that the character must make a Hard (9) *guts* check to directly affect the object of his fear.

25-27 Corporeal Alteration: The character gains a *Minor Phobia* and suffers a physical defect of some kind, such as a streak of white hair, his voice box contracts and he can only speak in whispers, etc.

28-30 The "Shakes": The cowpoke gets a *Major Phobia* and must make a Hard (9) *Spirit* roll or reduce *Deftness* by one step permanently. If the roll is made, *Deftness* is reduced only for the next 1d6 days.

31-35 Heart Attack: The character's heart skips a beat. He must make a Hard (9) *Vigor* roll. If the roll is made, the character suffers 3d6 Wind and gains a *Major Phobia*. If the roll is failed, the character suffers 3d6 Wind and his *Vigor* is permanently reduced by one step. Now the character must make a second Hard (9) *Vigor* roll. If this roll is failed, the character has a heart attack and will die unless another character makes an Incredible (11) *medicine* roll within 2d6 rounds. If *Vigor* is ever reduced below 4, the character kicks the bucket.

36+ Corporeal Aging: The character has a *Heart Attack* and ages 1 year.

Chapter Nineteen: The Harrowed

At some point, you're going to end up having to kill some of your player characters. It's okay. *Deadlands* has a high character turnover rate compared to most games. But don't let your players start ripping up their character sheets too fast—their characters just might come back from the dead.

We already told you how to find out who comes back in Chapter Eleven. Now you need to know some of the details.

Nightmares

When a character dies and attracts the attention of the manitous, she wages a spiritual battle for control of her mind and body. The winner comes back in charge. The loser sits in limbo waiting for another chance to strike back and steal Dominion.

There are two ways to resolve the results of this spiritual battle. The first way is faster. If you are playing for only a single night or can't think of a good nightmare scenario for a particular player, use the first method.

After it's determined that a character is on the long road back from the dead, she has to make an opposed *Spirit* plus Grit (add your Grit to your *Spirit* roll) check versus the manitous for each Dominion point. A character has a number of Dominion points equal to her *Spirit*.

The number and type of dice rolled for the manitou is determined by a draw from the Action Deck. Use the card to figure the manitou's *Spirit* just like you would for a character when you create one. Since multiple manitous can vie for control of the Harrowed's corpse, draw a new card for each contest to represent the ill winds blowing through the manitous' world.

The winner of each check gets that Dominion point. When the fight is over, the one with the most Dominion points returns to the physical world in charge of the body. The Harrowed player character wins ties.

Nightmares

The Nightmare Scenario

The second way to determine the result of the nightmare is to actually play it out. This is a lot more fun and creepy, but it takes some work on the part of the Marshal.

The back of each character sheet has an area that describes the character's worst nightmare. The Marshal should use this to construct a nightmare scenario when it's determined a character is coming back from the dead. That's why we put it there, after all.

Running a solo nightmare takes some time. Plan ahead, and do this alone with the character's player before your group's next play session or while everyone else takes a break.

If several characters die and come back at roughly the same time (perhaps they were hanged together), the manitous might absorb several of them into a collective nightmare. If this is the case, you can construct a longer scenario that encompasses all of the characters' nightmares.

Milestones

The goal of the adventure is to overcome several "milestones." These symbolize the hero's mental duel with the manitou. The results determine who has Dominion when the character returns.

You need to set a number of milestones equal to the character's *Spirit* die type. Every milestone he conquers, defeats, or negotiates gives him a Dominion point. Every one that he cannot overcome gives the manitou a Dominion point.

Nightmares

During the nightmare, the hero is in charge regardless of who has Dominion. When his soul returns to earth, he's in charge if he has equal or greater Dominion. The manitou is in charge if it has Dominion.

Losing Dominion

In the physical world, a character with less Dominion than the manitou inside him is trapped in limbo. He has no memory of what happened while he was under (sometimes for years at a time), and he can't affect the manitou's actions in any way.

The only time a character can attempt to recapture Dominion is when the manitou controlling her body is dealt a Red Joker from the Action Deck. If the manitou is given time to roam, the Marshal should give the hero inside a chance to recapture a Dominion point about once per month. Some Harrowed have lost control for years on end.

Any time a manitou gains Dominion points but doesn't control the majority, it controls its host for 10 minutes for every Dominion point stolen. This allows it to sneak around and cause its host considerable grief, even though it can't actually take more or less permanent control.

Whenever the hero loses Dominion, take the player aside and tell him that he has lost control. Ask him to play along and take on the role of the manitou in his character's body. Then give him a goal and let him attempt to accomplish it without alerting the other players. You can also take control of the Harrowed yourself on occasion (like when even the player thinks he's supposed to be sleeping) so that absolutely no one can know what he's been up to while he was under.

Manitous

Manitous are bound by a few limitations while inhabiting physical forms. First, they can only use the powers and abilities of their host. If the host hasn't developed any powers, the manitou can't use them either. Although the reverse isn't true, manitous can see and hear while the Harrowed character is in charge. This makes it nearly impossible to fool a manitou into revealing its true identity unless it wants to.

Second, if a manitou is trapped and somehow forced to speak, it proves a clever but ignorant spirit. They know they serve greater masters, but they do not know what their true name or purpose is.

They also know that while they are in spirit form they gather fear from mortals and take it back to the Hunting Grounds, but again, they don't know what their masters do with it. They aren't usually privy to secret information about abominations or their motives either.

So what exactly does a manitou do when it's in charge? Whatever they can. Their goal is chaos and mischief, not necessarily death. They never make an outright attack—unless they've got one of the Harrowed's companions in an inescapable and precarious position. Say, for example, a mad scientist friend of the Harrowed stands on the edge of deep pit flaming prairie ticks. No manitou could resist giving him a little shove.

Chapter Twenty: Arcane Happenings

The world of *Deadlands* is filled with arcane happenings. Mad scientists fly above the deserts in ornithopters powered by ghost rock. Hucksters blast a man's soul with mystical energies. The undead crawl out of their grave to fight for dominance with evil spirits.

Now it's time to show you how to whack player characters upside their noggins when they deal with the arcane and mess up. This chapter deals with mysterious pasts, huckster backlash, mad scientist dementias, and device malfunctions.

Mysterious Past

Many folks have been affected by the Reckoning. Some don't even know it.

When a player draws a Joker during character creation, draw a card from your own Action Deck. This card determines the character's "mysterious past." If a character draws 2 Jokers, draw two cards.

Compare the card you drew to the table below to get an idea for the character's mysterious past. You should always feel free to substitute your own ideas if you have something more specific to the character in mind.

Draw

Deuce: Curse

The character is cursed in some way. Figure out when and why it happened. The character has the *bad luck* Hindrance until he resolves whatever issue caused the curse. If the character winds up also having *bad luck* in some other way (like by purchasing it during character creation), the curse proves doubly catastrophic.

The Arcane

Three: Sworn Enemy

The character has an enemy in her past that she doesn't know about. Look over the character's background and pick an enemy or a group of enemies that are looking for the hero. The nature of the enemy and the frequency of their occurrence is entirely up to you.

Four: Doppleganger

The hero looks eerily like some other well-known person. A red card means the other person is someone who is generally considered "good," at least in the USA or the CSA, if not both. A black card means the character looks like a wanted bandit, gunman, or someone else with a "bad" reputation.

Five: Kin

A family member or close companion gets involved in the adventure every now and then. The relative tries to help but can't really take care of himself. The hero occasionally benefits from the relative's actions, but usually just winds up rescuing him. Kid brothers and sisters, a previously unknown father, or a trouble-making cousin with the same last name make great personal interests.

Six: Sixth Sense

The character has an uncanny sixth sense that sometimes warns her of danger. Whenever a hidden danger or ambush is about to occur, the hero can make an Onerous (7) *Cognition* check. If she is successful, she knows something's up and can react accordingly.

Seven: Blackouts

The character has "holes" in his past. He can't quite remember certain periods of his life. He probably doesn't even know he can't remember them. What happened to him during these "blackouts" is up to you. The character might occasionally experience glimpses into his mysterious past. These visions eventually make sense, but they just confuse and confound him until the past finally catches up to him.

Eight: Ancient Pact

The character's ancestors made a pact with a manitou some time in the distant past, before the Great Spirit War. The power of that pact still traces through the family's bloodlines.

The character gains a power of the Harrowed at level 1. The level cannot be raised unless the hero someday becomes Harrowed.

The Marshal should decide which power to grant the character. You can base the ability on his personality if you choose, or you can choose an ability at random, since the power was chosen by a distant ancestor.

Nine: Arcane Background

Though the character doesn't know it, she has the ability to cast spells, rituals, or favors. Some strange and obscure event in her past granted her this power, but she has yet to learn of it.

The character has the *arcane background* Edge. If she is an Indian, she is a shaman and can call upon favors with appeasement levels greater than 1. Other characters generally become hucksters or mad scientists.

You might also want to make the character *blessed.* Only "good" heroes are surreptitiously chosen by the divinities to carry out their holy work.

When someone else nearby invokes the type of magic the character can use, she feel a strange understanding of the events she's witnessing. If she makes a Hard (9) *Smarts* roll, the Marshal should tell the player she has an *arcane background* and describe to her the mysterious past that caused it.

The Arcane

Ten: Favor

Someone owes the character a favor of some sort. Perhaps a town Sheriff was saved by the hero's father long ago. Or maybe an infamous outlaw turns out to be the character's father. Whatever the circumstance, the indebted extra can occasionally bail the hero out of some dire situation.

Jack: Haunted

A ghost of some sort haunts the character. No one else can see or hear the being, but it is always lurking nearby.

Red: The ghost is beneficial. Once per session, it warns the character of danger or provides him with information. The phantom shouldn't be too powerful or all-knowing, but it should prove useful.

Black: The character is haunted by a malevolent ghost. It appears at the most inconvenient times to frighten and confuse the hero. At least once per adventure and whenever the character draws a Black Joker from the Action deck, the ghost appears and tries to trick, confuse, or distract him.

In either case, you should put some thought and personality into the ghost's identity. Perhaps a beneficial spook is the ghost of a dead relative. A malevolent specter could be the ghost of someone who died because of the character.

Queen: Animal Hatred/Ken

Animals react strangely in the hero's presence. The hero may have been this way from birth, or perhaps she somehow gained the attention of the nature spirits.

Red: Animals love the hero. They never attack her unless provoked, and she can add +2 to any *animal wranglin'*, *wranglin'*, or *horse ridin'* rolls. If the hero rides a horse, the animal should be especially intelligent and well-trained.

Black: Animals hate the character. Dogs always growl and sometimes bite. Horses complain constantly and buck whenever the character goes bust on a *ridin'* roll. The characters always suffers –2 to any *animal wranglin'*, *teamster*, or *horse ridin'* rolls.

King: Inheritance

The hero has inherited something, such as an old mansion, a thousand dollars, or even a debt. For fun, let the messengers hunt the hero for a while and make him nervous. He won't know if the news is good or bad until they catch up with him.

Red: The inheritance is by and large a good thing. Whether it's money or a son the hero didn't know he had is up to the Marshal.

Black: The inheritance comes with trouble. A ranch sits in the way of a ruthless railroad, or a trunk full of Grandpa's belongings contains a cursed or haunted relic.

The Arcane

Ace: Cursed Relic/Relic

The character has in his possession an artifact once owned by someone else. It is valuable or perhaps even magical in some way.

Red: One of the character's possessions is a valuable or arcane relic of some sort. Perhaps he has the pistol of a famous outlaw, or a blueprint designed by a great mad scientist.

Black: The artifact is cursed or comes with trouble. Perhaps the hero's pistol was once used in a heinous murder. Or the pocket watch he carries was "altered" by a mad scientist. The effects of the curse depend on the item. At the very least, a cursed weapon should secretly fire at –2, while a mundane item quietly causes the hero *bad luck* until he figures it out and rids himself of it.

Joker: Harrowed

The character is dead and just hasn't figured it out yet. Make up some event that took place in the character's past in which he was left for dead but somehow survived. The event should have occurred within the last few months if possible.

Red: The hero has total Dominion.

Black: The hero has only a 1-point advantage in Dominion.

Madness and Malfunctions

Mad scientists flooded into the Weird West after the discovery of ghost rock. The things they can build are incredible, but sometimes the deranged inventors can take out half a town with their weird gizmos.

Madness

A mad scientist has to actually build something before he can start wreaking havoc. Unfortunately, genius is the closest thing to insanity.

Whenever a mad scientist draws a Joker while devising a blueprint, he develops a dementia of some sort. The dementia does not have to manifest itself immediately, nor is it tied to events surrounding the blueprint process.

Create the dementia at this time, but it may be that the inventor's madness doesn't take hold until some later event. A phobia, for instance, might develop as a result of some incident that occurs the first time the mad scientist uses the device.

You can create a condition on your own or roll 1d20 on the chart below. Feel free to change or alter the result you get to fit the character and the situation. The goal here is to provide a Hindrance of some sort that reflects the mad scientist's precarious walk along sanity's edge. As usual, a player who roleplays his character's insanity well receives Fate Chips. She should have fun with it, and so should you.

Roll   Condition

The Arcane

Dementia

1-2 Absent Minded: The scientist begins to forget everything around him but his work. He might forget to wear his pants one day or eat raw coffee the next. Whenever the scientist needs to remember an important detail, he should make a Fair (5) Smarts roll. If he fails, he can't remember it, and the player should roleplay accordingly.

3-4 Delusion: Some part of the inventor's mind snaps, and he suddenly believes something that is patently untrue. Maybe he thinks he's a werewolf and howls at the moon, or that the sky is blue because the "Moon People" paint it that way every morning. Or perhaps he believes he's not a living person, but the subject of some strange, otherworldly roleplaying game.

5-6 Eccentricity: The inventor becomes eccentric in some way. Perhaps he eats everything smothered in vinegar or eats lots of bran to clear the old digestive system (ugh). The condition is basically harmless and amusing, though occasionally annoying.

7-8 Evil Deeds: An insidious manitou consorts with the scientist when he unwittingly taps into the power of the Hunting Grounds. It convinces him that someone or something is evil and must be stopped. Each time the inventor gets this result, his madness is more pronounced. At first he may only talk badly about his "enemies." Later on he might secretly attempt to ruin or even kill them. A fellow by the name of "Jack" over in merry Old England seems to have this problem.

9-10 Manic Depressive: The inventor becomes incredibly depressed about himself, the futility of humanity, or his chances of surviving another adventure. The scientist has to be dragged along on expeditions and always seems entirely too acutely aware of impending doom. His lack of faith in the human condition causes him to lose 1 point of Grit every time he gets this result.

11-12 Minor Phobia: The mad scientist develops a strange and unnatural fear of some common object or condition. The character suffers a -2 penalty to his actions whenever he is around the object of his phobia.

13-14 Major Phobia: The character develops a major phobia centered around an object, person, place, or event. This is the same as a minor phobia except that the inventor is at -4 to his actions and must make a Hard (9) guts check to directly affect or manipulate the object of his fear.

15-16 Mumbler: The inventor talks to himself constantly, and his sentences often taper off into meaningless drivel. While he's working, the mad scientist might occasionally hear "voices" talking back. Whether these are actually the voices of manitous or not is up to you.

17-18 Paranoia: Everyone's out to get the mad scientist or steal his ideas, or so he believes. Or maybe some sinister creatures from "Dimension X" are lurking about the inventor's lab waiting for his amazing technological breakthrough so that they can return to their homeworld.

19-20 Schizophrenia: The mad scientist adopts drastically different attitudes from time to time. At one moment he might be passive and restrained. Later on he's a raving madman looking for trouble. If the inventor gets this result multiple times, he actually develops entirely new personalities. The new personalities probably don't even have the same names, mannerisms, or even Hindrances. In fact, the personalities don't even have to be of the same gender.

The Arcane

Malfunction Results

Weird gizmos are prone to malfunction. Mad scientists are known for creating noxious fumes and spectacular explosions, often at the hazard of their own lives as well as those of the people around them.

Every time a character makes an Aptitude roll to use a weird gizmo, he must also roll 1d20. If the number on the die is greater than the malfunction score of the gizmo, a malfunction of some sort has occurred.

Roll 2d6 on the table below to determine how bad the malfunction is.

Malfunction Table

Roll	Malfunction
2-5	Major Malfunction
6-10	Minor Malfunction
11-12	Catastrophe

The descriptions below should help you figure out what to do whenever a gizmo malfunctions. You need to figure out which of the charts below best fits the device. If none of them fit, come up with an appropriate malfunction on your own, but you should still roll 2d6 to check the severity

Mechanical Gizmos (No Moving Parts)

Armored vests, diving suits

Minor Malfunction: The device fails, falls out of position, or otherwise has no effect until it is repaired with a Hard (9) *tinkerin'* roll.
Major Malfunction: The device falls to pieces and must be reassembled.
Catastrophe: The device proves dangerous somehow. If the gadget is worn, it collapses with the wearer trapped inside.

Muscle or Mechanically Powered Devices

Clocks, Epitaph cameras, Gatling guns and pistols, gliders

Minor Malfunction: The gadget jams and won't operate again until the user makes a Fair (5) *tinkerin'* roll.
Major Malfunction: The gizmo jams. Locomotion devices won't steer or brake and guns misfire, or worse, can't stop firing. A Hard (9) *tinkerin'* roll stops the madness.
Catastrophe: Guns backfire and injure the firer, cameras catch fire, or gears munch on tender fingers. If a gadget is a locomotion device, the gizmo goes wild and crashes into the nearest obstacle.

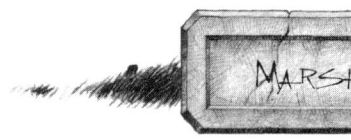

The Arcane

Steam or Ghost-Rock Powered Devices

Flamethrower, rocket pack, steam wagon, train

Minor Malfunction: The engine, stove or boiler conks out. A Fair (5) *tinkerin'* roll gets it moving again.

Major Malfunction: The power source grinds to a halt, goes out, or falls apart. If the gadget is a locomotion device, it continues on its path uncontrolled or comes to a grinding stop. Fixing the situation requires an Incredible (11) *tinkerin'* roll. If the device hits an obstacle, the damage is 1d6 for every 5 points of pace the vehicle was moving at that round.

Catastrophe: The device's engine explodes! The damage depends on the size of the engine. The damage roll loses 1 die every 10 yards, just like dynamite and nitroglycerin.

Catastrophe Damage Table

Size	Damage
Small (flamethrower)	3d10
Medium (steam car)	4d20
Large (train boiler)	8d20

Backlash

Hucksters open themselves to manitous every time they perform a hex. Most of the time, they can control the spirit, and they're perfectly safe. Other times, these malicious spirits are able to cause their hosts pain and suffering or even madness.

Roll on the Backlash Table below whenever a huckster draws a Joker while trying to cast a hex. Unless an entry says otherwise, the hex takes effect normally unless the huckster passes out or dies from the Backlash.

Backlash Table

Roll (1d20)	Effect
1-4	Brain Drain: The manitou fries part of the huckster's mind with energy from the Hunting Grounds. The huckster's hex fails, and his skill with the hex drops a level.
5-8	Backlash: The manitou rebels and overloads the huckster's system with magic from the Hunting Grounds. The huckster takes 3d6 damage to his body.
9-12	Spirit Drain: The manitou tries to take over. The huckster manages to regain control but loses 3d6 Wind in the spiritual struggle. The hex fails only if the huckster goes unconscious.
13-16	Madness: The manitou ruins the spell, and worse, drives the huckster insane. Roll on the mad scientists' Dementia Table on page XXX to determine the nature of his insanity.
17-20	Corruption: The manitou twists the spell's effects; damage-causing hexes hit friendly characters, protection hexes protect the enemy or make the huckster more vulnerable, etc.

BOOT HILL

Goon/Critter #1:
Attacks:

Defense:
Hits:
Special Abilities/Gear:

Goon/Critter #2:
Attacks:

Defense:
Hits:
Special Abilities/Gear:

Goon/Critter #3:
Attacks:

Defense:
Hits:
Special Abilities/Gear:

Goon/Critter #4:
Attacks:

Defense:
Hits:
Special Abilities/Gear:

Goon/Critter#5:
Attacks:

Defense:
Hits:
Special Abilities/Gear:

Goon/Critter#6:
Attacks:

Defense:
Hits:
Special Abilities/Gear:

Goon/Critter#7:
Attacks:

Defense:
Hits:
Special Abilities/Gear:

Goon/Critter#8:
Attacks:

Defense:
Hits:
Special Abilities/Gear:

Monster/Major Villain:
Corporeal:

Mental:

Main Attack:
Fightin' Defense:
Wounds
Right Leg: Left Leg:
Right Arm: Left Arm:
Guts: Noggin:
Wind:

DEADLANDS

Name _____ **Occupation** _____

Ammo 1
Ammo 2
Ammo 3

Mental

○ **Cognition** ___
- Artillery
- Arts:
- Scrutinize
- Search (1)
- Trackin'
- _____
- _____

○ **Knowledge** ___
- Academia:
- Area Knowledge home county (2)
- Demolition
- Disguise
- Native Tongue: (2)
- Language:
- Medicine
- Professional:
- Science:
- Trade:
- _____
- _____

○ **Mien** ___
- Animal Handlin'
- Leadership
- Overawe
- Performin':
- Persuasion
- Tale Tellin'
- _____

○ **Smarts** ___
- Bluff
- Gamblin'
- Ridicule
- Scroungin'
- Streetwise
- Survival:
- Tinkerin'
- _____
- _____

○ **Spirit** ___
- Faith
- Guts

Corporeal

○ **Deftness** ___
- Fannin'
- Filchin'
- Lockpickin'
- Shootin':
- Shootin':
- Sleight O' Hand
- Speed Load:
- Throwin':
- _____
- _____

○ **Nimbleness** ___
- Climbin' (1)
- Dodge
- Drivin'
- Fightin':
- Horse Ridin'
- Sneak (1)
- Swimmin'
- Teamster
- _____
- _____

○ **Strength** ___

○ **Quickness** ___
- Quick Draw

○ **Vigor** ___

Edges N' Hindrances

_____

Grit

Wounds

Light   Green
Heavy   Yeller
Serious Red
Critical Black

Shootin' Irons & Fightin' Weapons

Weapon	Shots	ROF	Range	Damage	Speed

Weapon	Def. Bonus	Damage	Speed
Fist			

Wounds
- Head
- Right Arm
- Left Arm
- Guts
- Right Leg
- Left Leg

Wind (Vigor N' Spirit)

1 2 3 4 5 6 7 8 9 10 11 12 13 14 15 16 17 18 19 20 21 22 23 24 25 26 27 28 29 30 31 32 33 34

Occupation

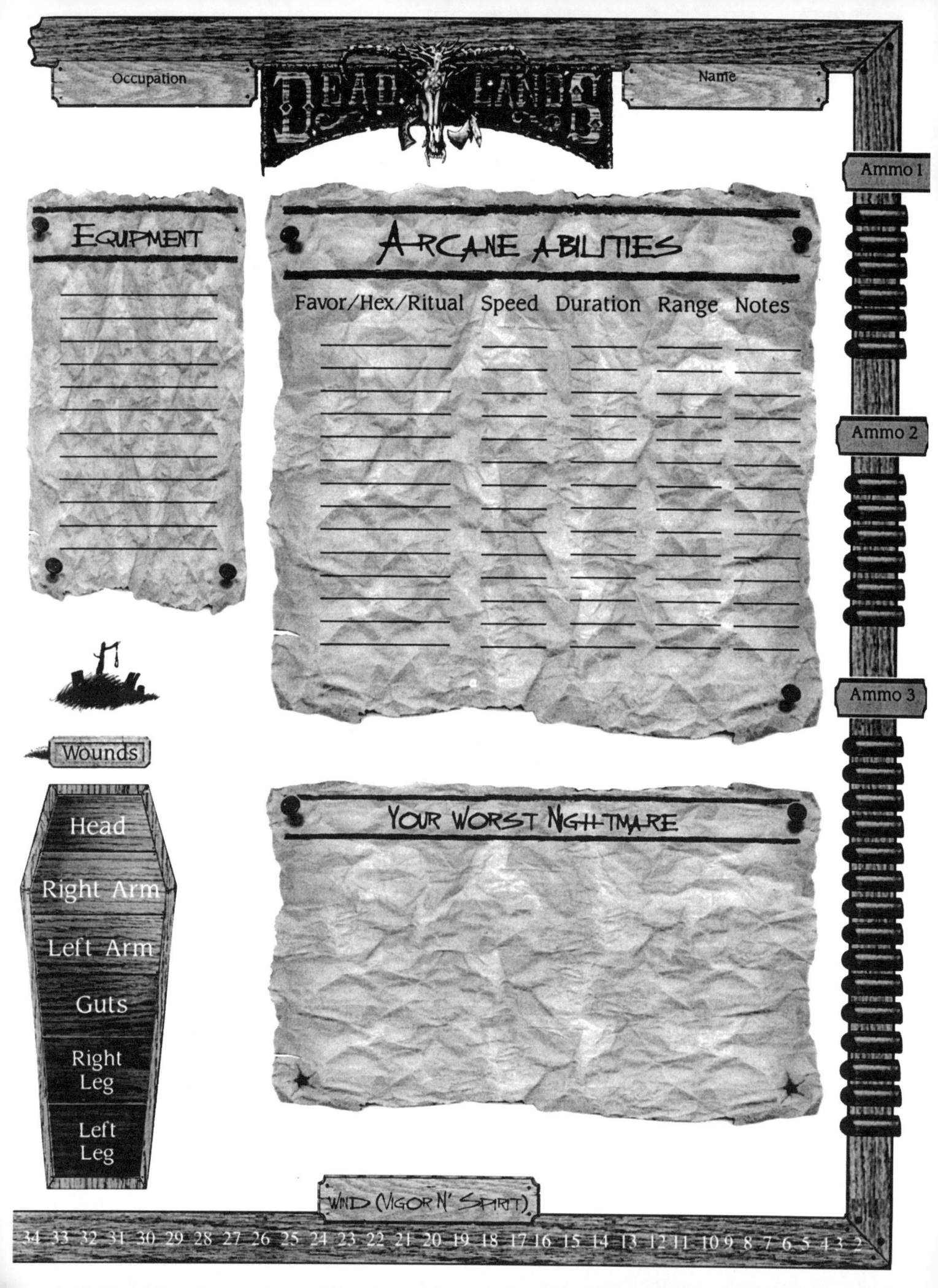

DEADLANDS

Name

Equipment

_____
_____
_____
_____
_____
_____
_____
_____
_____
_____

Arcane Abilities

Favor/Hex/Ritual	Speed	Duration	Range	Notes

Ammo 1

Ammo 2

Ammo 3

Wounds

- Head
- Right Arm
- Left Arm
- Guts
- Right Leg
- Left Leg

Your Worst Nightmare

Wind (Vigor N' Spirit)

34 33 32 31 30 29 28 27 26 25 24 23 22 21 20 19 18 17 16 15 14 13 12 11 10 9 8 7 6 5 4 3 2